THE REDEMPTION DUET

THE FORBIDDEN SERIES

TRACY LORRAINE

Andy and Amelia

A NOTE

The Redemption Duet is written in British English and contains British spelling and grammar. This may appear incorrect to some readers when compared to US English books.

CRAVING REDEMPTION

"You want the usual?" I watch as Joe gestures for the barman. Much to everyone else's annoyance, she takes one look at him and saunters over, ignoring her other customers who have been waiting longer.

"What can I get you, handsome?" She bats her very fake eyelashes at him, and he leans forward on his elbows, eating the attention right up.

Rolling my eyes at them, I glance around the bar. It's not unusual to bump into a couple of the guys from work here. This place might be a little classier than it was back in the day, but it's still our regular. It was called Fire back then and was full of drunken students. Now, it's a fancy bar called The Avenue and has chrome fittings everywhere and chandeliers hanging from the high ceilings. I'd like to think we've also grown and are a little more sophisticated, but I usually end up questioning that once we get a few drinks inside us.

"Here you go," Joe sings, sliding a prosecco towards me. "To your awesome new housemate." He clinks his glass to mine, his face deadly serious.

"You're an idiot." I can't help but laugh at his puppy dog eyes.

I haven't lived with anyone since my ex suddenly vanished on me a little over six months ago. I must admit that I'm looking forward to having someone else to talk to. Joe promised me it would be only a short-term fix for his little homeless problem, but I'm in no rush to get rid of him—well, not yet, anyway. We've only been living together for a few days. I've not had the chance to discover if he has any weird quirks I'm not going to be able to deal with.

If I start finding stray toenails littered over the bathroom floor, there are going to be issues.

"So, anyone catch your attention?" I shake myself from my nightmare and look up into his dark eyes.

"Huh?"

"Anyone catch your eye?"

"Oh no, I'm not really interested." I've been going through somewhat of a dry spell recently. When I admitted how long it had been since I'd had sex, Joe immediately demanded I put on my sluttiest dress and dragged me out of the flat.

I was excited in the taxi on the way here but now, looking around and finding absolutely no one who catches my eye, I kind of want to go home, put my pyjamas on, and snuggle up on the sofa.

Joe's brow rises before he turns to scout the perfect man for me himself. I know it's unlike me. I used to have a reputation for being the party girl, but, after my last two bad experiences with men, I'm more than happy keeping my distance for a while.

Sipping my drink, I keep my focus on the colourful bottles behind the bar. I used to live for this, for a night out and the thrill of meeting someone new, but with everything that's happened over the past few months, I've totally lost the enthusiasm.

"Erica, come on. You need to get yourself back out there. Hiding isn't healthy. It's not *you*."

"Maybe it's the new me," I mutter, sipping my drink. "Anyway, who are you to start dishing out advice? I hate to break it to you, mate, but your life isn't all that great right now."

"What makes you say that?"

"Oh, come on. You can't tell me you don't realise you've been moping around since the day you moved out of yours and Lauren's flat. I know you miss her. I'm trying not to let it affect me, being your new roommate and all." I wink to let him know I'm only winding him up. If he needs time to 'grieve' or whatever the fuck it is he's doing, he's more than welcome to it. I know he appreciates my offer of a place to stay.

"I just—"

"You can say it, you know, that you miss her. I know how tight you two were."

"Yeah, fine. I miss her, okay?" Something passes through his eyes, and it only feeds my earlier suspicion that there might be more to this than he's letting on.

I open my mouth to say more, but I don't get the chance. Joe is too keen to change the subject.

"Do not tell me you passed up the guy at ten o'clock?"

Following his instruction, I look to my left and immediately lock eyes with a handsome older man. A shiver runs down my spine as our eye contact holds. I can't tell from this distance what colour they are, but they're dark. Ripping my gaze away, my mouth waters when I take in his pristine white shirt covered with a sharp black waistcoat. *Fuck.* I'm a sucker for a man in a suit.

"He is *so* your type, and by the way he's staring at you like he wants to devour you, I'd say you're his, too."

"Nope, not interested. I am off men for the foreseeable future."

"Fuck off. You don't really expect me to believe that, do you? You're Erica Wilde, this is what you do: go out, have fun, pick up guys." I wince at his opinion of me.

"Well, if that's how you see me, it's even more reason for me to swear off men."

"I didn't mean it like that, and you know it. I just meant that… fuck, I'm screwing this up. You're not yourself right now, and I hate it. You've lost that sparkle in your eye. Your zest for life. *He* stole that from you."

"No," I spit. "We do not talk about him. *Ever*. You got that?"

"I know. I'm just…I'm worried about you."

"I could say the same thing."

"I'm fine. I just need a good fuck. You've been winding me up all week, walking around in those little fucking shorts and practically see through top—"

"That top is not see through."

"Maybe not, but I sure as shit know you don't wear a bra under it."

"Yeah, you really do need a fuck." I pull my eyes from his and look around, much like he did for me earlier. "Guy or girl?"

"A guy. Definitely a guy. I need him to—"

"Spare me."

Rolling his eyes, he moves to scan the room, looking for his target.

With Joe's attention averted, I risk another look at the suit. My skin's been burning the entire time we were talking, so I know he hasn't got bored and moved on. Our eyes lock once again, and I swear they fucking call to me. They drop to my lips and I watch as his tongue sneaks out and runs along his bottom one. My thighs clench and my fingers curl around the bar stool I'm perched on as my body temperature spikes.

I allow myself a minute to appreciate him.

His eyes are hard, and there are a few lines creasing his forehead. His lips are pressed into a thin line. From anger or desire? Only he knows, but damn if I don't want to go over there and find out. He's got the perfect amount of stubble on his jaw, just enough to enhance what I'm sure his mouth is capable of but not enough to leave a rash.

Biting down on my bottom lip, I try to imagine what it might be like to be with a man who looks as dominant and dangerous as him. I've experienced my fair share of demanding lovers, but he looks like he might be capable of taking it to the next level. Tingles ignite in my core as I think about how capable he probably is.

"I'd put one hundred quid on you leaving with him tonight," Joe says in my ear. I laugh but my eyes don't leave the suit's for even a second.

"You don't have any money, and we both know it, so how about you keep the gambling to a minimum?"

"You just know you'll lose. If you need me, I'll be over there. Good luck."

I expect him to get up and walk off, but to my surprise, Joe grabs my chin, tilts my head back and slams his lips to mine. My eyes widen in shock, as do the suit's. "Knock him dead, sweets." And then he's off into the crowd, as if that just didn't happen.

Downing what's left of my drink, I fight to stop my lips curling up in satisfaction when I watch the suit rise from his seat. I quickly try to decide what I should do. Sadly, any decision I might have been coming to is taken away the moment a man slides onto the vacant stool beside me. The first thing I notice is his scent; it's expensive and sexy as fuck. My mouth waters, wondering how it might make his skin taste. Next is the heat of his breath as it skates over my neck, and then it's the deep timbre to his voice. It's so rough it has a slow throb erupting between my legs.

"See, I had him down as your gay best friend. But that wasn't the kiss of a gay man."

"And you would know that how?" My voice comes out as a breathy whisper, and I immediately chastise myself for being so swept away by him already.

"Because he knows how to kiss a woman."

"Did you come over here to discuss how my friend kisses?"

"No, I came to tell you that it worked."

"Huh?" I ask, turning to him for the first time. It's a stupid mistake, because what I thought was a seriously handsome man from across the bar I soon see is breathtakingly gorgeous—and terrifyingly dangerous close-up.

"You weren't listening to him, so he took matters into his own hands. And here I am."

"Yeah...here you are."

His low chuckle causes my temperature to kick up a few more notches. "We'll have a bottle of whatever she's drinking, and I'll have another." He pushes his tumbler towards the barmaid who's looking at him much like she was Joe earlier. *Hussy.* She takes a few moments to appreciate the masculine beauty in front of her before turning to fulfil his order. When he turns back, his eyes narrow in confusion. "What?"

"Oh nothing, Casanova."

His lips curl in an amused smirk. "Oh, her." Shifting forward on his stool, his legs surround mine and my breath catches the second we connect. "There's only one woman I can see in this bar, sweetheart." His hand reaches out and gently tucks a lock of my curled red hair behind my ear. Naturally I'm a mousey brunette, but after my last disaster I decided a change was needed so I went for the brightest box money could buy.

Our eyes hold, and suddenly everything around me disappears. It's just me and him, the captivating darkness of his eyes, and the sizzle of electricity that sparks between where our legs are touching.

"Thank you." Reaching out for the glass the barmaid pushes my way, I rip my eyes from his and take a very large sip of the small amount she poured. It's not enough, but I fear the bottle might not be, either.

CHAPTER TWO

"Dance with me," he demands after a few seconds of heavy silence between us. His hand reaches out, his fingers twisting with mine. It's the first time I've been able to appreciate his muscular, tattooed forearms that are showcased by his rolled-up sleeves.

"I'm not sure that's a good idea."

"It's not optional."

"But...my drink." It's my last attempt to put off the inevitable. The tension between us crackled while we were just sitting here. I can only imagine what it's going to be like once my body's moving to the music alongside his.

A little of the 'old' me trickles through my veins.

So what I've been screwed over by the previous men I've allowed between my legs? That shouldn't stop me from enjoying myself, especially when it's with someone who looks like the man currently pulling me from my bar stool, offering me a release I so desperately need.

He catches the barmaid's attention, and her eyes light up

when she realises who's calling before he barks, "Put it on ice. We'll be back."

She nods and he takes off across the bar. While this floor might be sophisticated these days, both up and downstairs are still clubs with dancefloors to die for. I usually go up, force of habit from my younger days, but when Suit gets to the stairs, he pulls me down. There's something about heading towards the basement with him that has excitement pulling at my lower stomach.

Maybe he's just what I need to drag me out of my rut and to re-start my life once again. Hell knows I've been spending too much time working—not that I really have a choice after the colossal mistakes I made that nearly forced the doors to close on the business for good. I push that thought to the back of my mind. I don't need to be worrying about that right now. I don't need to be worrying about *anything*.

As we descend, the beat of the bass starts to vibrate the floors and rumble through my feet. My heart begins to race and my muscles ache to be dancing, to feel his hot body up against mine and his hands roaming over my skin.

I've no clue what the song is; I'm too lost to the anticipation of what's to come next. In only a couple of minutes, he's shown me that he's a man who likes to be in control. I can't wait to find out how he dances, how he handles my body.

It's only a couple more seconds before I get to find out. His footsteps slow and his arm tugs until I'm forced to come up against his chest. With my favourite heels on, I'm not all that much shorter than him and I'm able to look up into his intense eyes. I'm just about able to see the silver flecks within the dark steel grey that give away his excitement.

The knowledge that he's feeling the same connection between us right now that I am has my stomach clenching in need. Suddenly, I wish we weren't in the middle of the dance floor, surrounded by other people. With his scent filling my nose, his dark stare filling my mind and his body pressed up against mine, the only thing I can think of is getting him out of his fancy suit and finding out exactly what he's hiding beneath.

The arm he's holding around my waist, keeping us locked together, tightens, and his hips roll in time with the music.

Holy shit, he can move.

Sliding my hands up his chest, the softness of the expensive fabric of his waistcoat caressing my palms, I wrap them around his neck and allow my fingers to tease the short hair at the nape.

His eyes drop from mine in favour of my lips, and I'm powerless to stop my tongue darting out in preparation for what I hope is to come.

The hand that isn't holding me threads in my hair. He grips with an almost painful force before his lips find mine.

The moment we connect, my body is on fire. My heart thunders in my chest, ensuring I can feel it in every part of my body. My skin tingles and my core aches. If he can dance and kiss like this, then I really want to find out what else he's capable of.

His tongue forces its way into my mouth and caresses against mine. My knees almost give out as this man takes over my body completely.

Nothing else exists. It's just the two of us, our bodies doing what they were designed to.

Our kiss continues, our tongues duelling as we fight to discover every inch of each other's mouths. Dropping his hand from my hair, he ghosts his fingers down my exposed spine. He swallows my moan, but not before I feel him hardening against my stomach.

Long before I'm ready, he rips his lips from mine and spins me around. My skin burns as he takes in my bare back before his hands land on my hips and my arse is pulled to him. One hand skates up my stomach and comes to rest on my ribs, dangerously close to my breast that's begging for his touch. My nipples are hard as bullets, the fabric of my dress brushing against them only adding to the pleasure building within me.

His lips kiss a trail down my neck. He sucks and bites, making me crazy with desire.

"You'd let me fuck you right here, wouldn't you?" The deep rumble of his voice only makes the answer to his question more obvious.

When my only response is to groan, he continues. "I wouldn't, because I'd have to kill every motherfucker who laid eyes on you."

Jesus.

"But that doesn't mean I don't want to."

Resting my head back against his shoulder, I look up to his hooded eyes. "Take me home."

His eyes get even darker, and the hint of danger in them has heat pooling between my legs. It's been too long, and I need what he's offering more than I need my next breath.

"Let's go." His voice, deep, rough and powerful, vibrates through me. The second his hot palm lands on my lower back, I follow his lead, away from the dance floor and up the stairs.

"I thought we...oh." He pushes me in the direction of the bar. I watch in delight as he leans over and shows off his round arse as he grabs the bottle waiting for me.

"We might need this." His expression is neutral. Anyone around us wouldn't register what I know he's thinking about, but I see it in his eyes. I might have only known him for a few short minutes in reality, but I see it: the desire behind the mask.

With his fingers wrapped around the bottle and his other hand burning the small of my back, he guides me to the exit.

I expect to head towards an awaiting taxi, so I'm surprised when he pushes me a little farther down the street and stops beside a gun metal grey Jaguar.

I miss his contact the moment he pulls his hand away and reaches for the door. Pulling it open, he looks down at me. His face is hard, his lips pressed into a thin line, but his eyes are still burning with fire.

"Thank you."

No sooner has my arse hit the leather seat than he slams the door shut and I watch as he makes his way around the bonnet towards the driver's door.

"Should you be driving?" I ask, realising that I've no idea how much he's had to drink.

"Do you trust me?"

I consider my answer for a moment. His stare turns to me; he's obviously waiting for my answer before committing to this.

I could lie, but that's not really my style, so instead I go with the truth and hope like hell it won't put an end to this. "No. Quite honestly, I don't trust anyone but myself."

"Good answer."

His foot presses down on the accelerator and the roar of the engine vibrates through me. My thighs clench and my nails dig into the leather beneath me.

"Fuck."

I'm jolted back in my seat as the car lurches forward and sets off on a race through the city.

It's only a few short minutes before the car screeches to a halt in a part of town I know well.

"You live here?"

"Yeah, temporarily. Problem?"

"No, not at all. Lead the way."

With his hand possessively placed on the small of my back once again, he guides me through the entrance of the building and towards the lift.

Silently, he presses the button for the top floor and then turns on me. Taking a step back, I bump into the handrail and wobble on my heels a little. I've only had one drink, but I think him on top of that is enough to catch me off-guard.

His steel eyes drop from mine in favour of my body. My temperature rises under his stare and my heart starts to race. Tingles follow his eyes as they travel around my body, and my muscles ache to reach out for him, needing to feel his skin against mine.

The second he does step towards me, it's like the air has been pulled from the enclosed space. His scent gets stronger and my mouth waters to find out how he might taste.

His forearms cage me in as he continues staring down at me. His eyes bounce between mine and I start to wonder if he can read something in them or if he's trying to figure something out. Either way, I'm not sure I like it. I don't need anyone trying to make sense of the shit in my head. What I really need is for someone to take it away, to allow me to forget all my fuck-ups and bad decisions. I'm pretty sure he's very capable of that if he would just step into action.

When the elevator doors open, signalling our arrival, he steps away once again, rests his hand where it seems to be quite at home on my lower back, and guides me towards an oak door.

I expect to find a bachelor pad behind it. This man screams 'minimalistic' with black and chrome everywhere, so I'm a little surprised when the door's pushed open and I discover a very plain, nondescript flat.

Deciding not to focus on how he lives, I run my hand down his arm and turn into his body. "Which way's your bedroom?"

The muscles in his neck ripple as he swallows, making me desperate to run my tongue along them.

"Down the hall, last room on the left. I'll get glasses," he says, holding up the bottle of prosecco that's still in his hand.

Turning so I'm walking backwards, I take in his body: the perfect fit of his white shirt stretching over his strong arms, and the open collar, sans tie, that allows just a hint of the tattoos hiding beneath, the crisp cut of the waistcoat and the slim dark trousers that clearly show off his excitement.

He watches me until I'm forced to turn around and see where I'm actually going. Finding the door, I push it open and slip inside. Like every other room in this flat, it's cream with wooden furniture, not really all that exciting, and nothing like the man himself.

Spotting a door at the other end of the wall, I hope to find an en suite to freshen up in. I make quick work of my business before throwing my hair over my head to give it a little more volume and reapplying my gloss.

I expect him to be waiting for me once I leave the confines of his bathroom, but I'm disappointed to find the bedroom still empty.

The lights of the city beyond call to me, and I walk over to the huge window and stare out at the night sky and the lights in all the buildings beyond. We're just high enough to be able to see over the building opposite and, without it in the way, there's an incredible view.

My heart continues its steady beat as the anticipation grows within me. He's here somewhere—I can hear him, but why is he not in here with me? There's no way he's regretting this. He was as on board as I am when we arrived.

Worrying my necklace, I wonder if maybe he's waiting for me to find him. Deciding to take matters into my own hands, I turn but don't get a chance to take a step, because he's there, standing in the doorway, filling the space with his solid frame. My mouth goes dry and I fight to swallow. His waistcoat is gone and his shirt's unbuttoned, giving me an even better view of the hard lines of his muscles and the intricate patterns of his ink.

He steps into the room and places the bottle and two glasses onto a dresser before returning his attention to me.

"Come here," he demands.

My feet move of their own accord until I'm standing inches from his body. His heat seeps into me and moisture floods my mouth once again. I swallow it and lick my lips as my eyes flit down to his. I need to feel them on me once again.

My nipples pebble against the fabric of my dress, and the lace between my legs gets wetter the longer he stares down at me.

"You get one warning." A shiver runs down my spine at his deep, scratchy voice. "I tell you what to do, you do it. Got that?"

Holy shit. My knees tremble with need for this man to do exactly what he wants to me. I hoped he'd be dominant and demanding, and, so far, he's excelling my expectations.

"I need you to trust me not to take it too far. This is about pleasure, not pain." He winks, and my stomach lurches. "But if you need to stop, say..." He pauses as he thinks of a word.

"Pineapple."

"Pineapple?" His brows pull together in amusement, and I shrug. "What's your name?" I ask, suddenly realising that the only thing I know about this man is where he lives. "I need to know what to scream when you make me come."

"When I *allow* you to come, you can call me anything you like, sweetheart."

"Huh." I would have put money on him requesting me to call him Sir...or even Daddy.

"Anything else?" Something sparkles in his eyes, I'm not sure if it's amusement or frustration that we've barely started and I'm already not doing what I'm told.

"Um...no, I think I'm good."

"You think?"

I take a small step towards him and run my fingertips down the skin his open shirt exposes. He doesn't react apart from the ripple of his abs when I get to them.

I flinch when his warm fingers brush my shoulders, pulling my spaghetti straps down and allowing the fabric of my loose-fitting dress to flutter down my body and pool at my feet. I gasp when the cool air surrounds my breasts and my nipples tighten, begging for attention.

Taking a step back, his eyes drop and he bites down on his bottom lip as he takes his time assessing what I've got to offer. My insecurities threaten to make themselves known, but I fight them down. I desperately want to say something sarcastic, but his earlier dominant tone stops me. I don't think he'd be amused right now.

"Get on your knees."

My eyes fly up to his, shocked by his bluntness but not the least bit turned off. How I'm feeling right now is very much the opposite.

Following his instructions, I drop to the floor and immediately reach for the waistband of his trousers. I can already see his cock straining against the fabric and, in my haste to unveil it, I fumble about with the button.

His eyes burn into the top of my head. I can feel his frustration levels growing the longer this takes me, but at no point does he help me out. I'm not usually this much of a klutz, but there's something about his steel eyes and dominance that has me off-kilter.

Eventually the fabric parts, and I'm able to push both his trousers and boxers down his muscular thighs. His cock springs free and my eyes widen before flying up to his.

Usually I'm irritated by the arrogant smirk that plays on a guy's lips, but team it with his intense eyes and it only makes me want him more.

His eyebrow lifts and I remember that I was doing something before I got lost in his dark stare.

Looking back down to his cock, I lick my lips, take it in my hand and run my tongue around the head. A loud groan filters down from him. It's all the encouragement I need.

Licking down his shaft, I revel in the feeling of it twitching under my touch. Smiling, I pull back and watch as my tiny hand wraps around his width and pumps him a few times before leaning forward once again and taking him in my mouth.

"Fuck," he grunts above me, and I push him deeper until he hits the back of my throat. His fingers twist in my hair, his grip painful but not unwelcome as I continue working him.

Dragging my nails down his stomach and thighs results in his pre-come coating my tongue. Lapping at the head, I take everything he's got.

He's getting close when I'm forcefully pushed back and then pulled to my feet. His lips slam down on mine, one hand gripping the hair at the back of my head and the other on my arse as he walks me backwards. His hard body presses against my curves, making me desperate to feel us skin to skin. Reaching up, I push the cotton from his shoulders so I can run my palms over his bare upper arms.

We must reach the bed, because suddenly I'm released and pushed backwards. My arse bounces on the edge and he reaches for my knickers, ripping them from my body before he finishes the job I started with his clothing and pulls his shirt from his arms and his trousers and boxers from his legs.

My eyes feast on the inches upon inches of toned skin before me. If it wasn't already abundantly clear with his clothes on, then it is now: this man works out, and works out a lot.

I'm in pretty good shape, but I'm by no means a gym bunny,

and I suddenly feel a little less confident about my body. It only lasts a few seconds because he wraps his hands around my thighs, pushing them wide and forcing me to lie back as he drops to his knees. Needing to witness what he's about to do, I prop myself up on my elbows and stare down as he lowers himself to my centre.

He blows out a stream of hot breath that has my hips lifting from the bed and my fingers gripping the sheets beneath me.

His low chuckle has more desire pooling at my entrance. He hovers less than an inch away from me and I can already feel my anticipation building. It's been quite a long time since I saw a man's head between my legs, and even longer since one looked quite as fucking good as he does right now.

I'm just at the point of voicing my frustration when he moves forward, parts me further and sucks my clit into his hot mouth.

"Argh," I cry out as every muscle in my body pulls tight with pleasure. He continues sucking, my back arching off the bed in my need for more, then he presses his tongue down on my clit and it's like my entire body sighs with relief. This has been a long time coming, and it grows faster than I've ever known.

He eats me like no man ever has before. He oozes confidence with his considered movements and teases to the perfect spots. The feeling of him stretching me open with two of his fingers is almost enough to push me over the edge, but just as I think I'm going to fall he stops all movement. My core clenches are nothing as my entire body aches and mourns the pleasure I was right on the brink of.

"Jesus, fuck."

His eyes flit up to mine and I swear they're fucking smiling while my chest heaves and I fight to demand he continue. It would be pointless; it's abundantly clear that only one person's demands are to be heard in this room, and they sure as fuck aren't mine.

Sitting back, a smile tugs at his lips. I don't know what I expected; he's already warned me about *letting* me come.

Starting at my thigh, his lips trail up my body as he crawls on top of me. He licks a line up the centre of my stomach before stopping to suck each of my nipples into his mouth, electric sparks shoot straight to my core, keeping my release just within touching distance. My fingers tangle in his hair in an attempt to keep him there, knowing that if he continues long enough it'll be enough to push me over the edge.

When his fingers find my pussy once again, I start to believe he's going to allow me to come, but, just like before, he has me right on the edge before he pulls his fingers out and his hot mouth away from my body.

"You're a fucking tease," I manage between my laboured breaths.

"Don't pretend you don't fucking love it." Lifting his fingers, I expect him to bring them to his mouth, but instead he runs one along my bottom lip. "Open." I do as I'm told, and he slides the two fingers that were just deep inside me into my mouth.

His eyes flash with desire as I close my lips and wrap my tongue around them. The silver I spotted earlier is almost like diamonds as he stares down at me like he's about to devour me.

"Fuck."

One second I'm sucking on his fingers, and the next his lips are on mine in an all-consuming kiss, his body pressing mine into the mattress. My hands lift from the bed and I find the hot, smooth skin of his back. Dragging my nails down, a moan rumbles up his throat, but I swallow any noise that might have erupted.

He moves so he's back between my legs, his cock nudging at my entrance. I push up, trying to find what I so desperately need, but one large hand on my hip stops any further movement.

"When I say," he repeats, his eyes not leaving any room for argument.

He continues rubbing himself against me, driving me fucking crazy with need before folding himself over my body, his breath tickling my ear when he comes to a stop.

"Unless you stop me right now…I'm taking you bare. I'm clean, I swear."

"Oh fuck," I moan, my imagination running wild with how his thick length will feel, stretching me open and filling me completely.

CHAPTER THREE

My back arches, my nails scratching across his shoulders as he thrusts inside me. My muscles clench as my body tries to accept his size after being ignored for so long.

"So fucking good," he groans into my neck.

He thrusts his hips slowly a couple of times, like he knows I need a moment, before he sits up, slides his hands under my arse and lifts me just so. I squeal as he hits me in the perfect position, my nails digging into the skin of his thighs. My breasts bounce, my skin flushing as he slams into me, over and over. His grip on me is bruising, and I know I'll have his fingertips marked on my skin for days, reminding me of this. Coming here with him might be irresponsible, irrational, but right this second it's the best decision I've made in a long fucking time.

"Oh god. Fuck. So good."

"Eyes," he barks when mine flicker closed. They immediately fly open at his demand and lock onto his. "You going to come around my cock?"

"Yes, yes," I chant as he continues to pound into me. "Please." My voice is almost begging. It's so close I can almost taste it, but I fear I might not be allowed it yet—and I'm right, because just as the beginning of my release tingles in my lower stomach, he pulls out of me and flips me over.

With my arse in the air and my face smashed against his pillow, he lines up and thrusts back into me. I cry out, this angle and his length almost too much to bear, but he doesn't let up as he fucks me into next week.

"You on birth control?" His voice is low and deep, and I barely hear it.

"Yes."

One of his hands fists my hair, keeping my head low, and the other continues to grip my hip painfully hard, my arse slapping against him with every thrust until he releases my hip right before I'm about to crash over the edge. My orgasm hits at the exact same time his palm slaps down on my arse cheek. The sound of the slap can only just be heard over my cry as my release completely takes over my body. I swear I black out for a few seconds, and when I come back around it's just in time to hear his growl of pleasure fill the room and feel his cock swelling inside me as he fills my pussy with everything he has.

"Fuck," he heaves, pulling out of me and falling to my side.

Sitting myself on the edge of the bed, I slip my shoes off and prepare to stand and find my discarded clothing. Once I'm confident my knees will hold me, I begin to wobble my way towards the bathroom, the semen he filled me with starting to run down my thighs.

"Grab the bottle on your way back."

Looking over my shoulder, I watch as he rolls onto his back and throws one arm over his eyes, his entire body on full display without a care in the world—but to be fair, if I were sculpted like that, I'd probably be more than willing to show it off as well.

I run my eyes down his chest and come to a stop on his cock. Even half-mast it's impressive. A deep ache inside me makes itself known, but we've had our fun. It's time for me to get the hell out and get home before Joe sends out a search party.

I do the best job I can of making myself look slightly respectable, but my cheeks are still flushed, and my green eyes are bright with desire.

I can still feel him inside me as I reach for the door handle and go to step out. The second I cross the threshold, his eyes are on me. I scoop up my ruined knickers when I find them, followed by my dress.

"What the hell are you doing?" he barks when I go to pull my dress up my legs.

"Getting dressed?" It's not meant to come out as a question, but my voice rises when I get a look at his hard expression.

"I don't fucking think so. Get the bottle and get over here." I look between him and where I've got my dress halfway up as I try to decide what to do. Go home alone or get a little more of what he's got to offer? I'm not sure there's really anything to consider.

Dropping the fabric, I step out, grab the bottle and the glasses from the side as requested, and make my way back to the bed.

"Good girl."

"I'm not a fucking girl."

"Oh, sweetheart. I'm well aware."

I'm lifted and positioned across his waist, his now fully hard cock teasingly lining up with my pussy. Taking the glasses from my hand, he holds them out so I can fill them up.

25

CRACKING MY EYES OPEN, I try to remember where I am. When the weight of an arm resting over my waist takes my attention, things start falling into place.

The suit with the intense steel eyes.

My thighs clench as I remember all the things that happened in this room last night. Without even moving, I can tell that my insides are tender after weeks of neglect.

Managing to slide to the edge of the bed, I blink a couple of times at the bright light of the alarm clock. Five am. Fuck.

Gently lifting his arm, I slip out of bed, praying that he won't wake up. The last thing I need is the awkward morning after the night before. It's best I just get the hell out of here.

I rush to pull my dress on before swiping my bag and shoes from the floor and tiptoeing from his bedroom. His door squeaks a little as I pull it open, but when I look back, he's still out like a light. I desperately want to stand for a minute or two and appreciate the beauty of the sleeping man before me, but my fear of him waking up is enough to have me running.

In no time, I'm sliding the key into the lock of my own front door. My brain is still sleep and sex fogged, and the last thing I'm expecting is to find Joe racing towards the door looking panicked as I step inside.

"Jesus, Erica," he says, pulling me into his body.

"What's wrong?"

"You disappeared. I had no idea where you were, and you weren't answering your phone." His concern isn't something I'm used to, and I'm not sure how I feel about it.

"Sorry, I guess I'm just used to living alone and not answering to anyone."

He pulls back, his brows pinched together. "You don't have to answer to me. I just wanted to know you were safe. But now I know you are, I'm expecting to hear all the details. Please tell me you've been with the man with the waistcoat." His hand slips into mine and pulls me towards the kitchen. Depositing me on a stool, he turns and kickstarts the coffee machine. I desperately want to fall face-first into my bed and get some more sleep, but coffee is a strong second.

"Yeah, I left with him."

"And?" Joe turns and pins with hard a stare.

"And it was a great night."

"Do you want to tell your face?"

"I'm serious, it was a great night. He was...full on." Joe's eyes light up and his eyebrows wiggle.

"Keep going."

"He was just...I don't know. Intense."

"Intense is good. Memorable."

"Yeah, I guess."

Silence descends around us. Joe brings over two mugs and pours some milk into mine. He waits for me to take a sip before asking his next question. "You didn't want to leave him, did you?" My eyes fly to his, and I try to figure out how to best answer, but it seems I don't need to. "Oh my god. You like him."

"I've not had enough sleep for this," I moan.

"Are you going to see him again?"

"I doubt it. I just left him asleep in his bed. I don't even know his name."

"Fuck, that's hot. I need to find me one of those. It's been way too long."

"You didn't get lucky last night?"

"Nah, the best I got was a hand job while listening to our new neighbours going at it like fucking animals."

"TMI, Joe. TMI." He chuckles, leaning back against the counter.

"Just be glad you weren't here. You'd have been begging for it."

"Been there, done that, got the t-shirt." I run my eyes up and down his body, trying to look disgusted, but he just laughs at me.

"Shut the fuck up, you loved it."

I shrug, because there's no point denying it. The few times we've fooled around have been pretty great, especially for a guy who thinks he'll end up spending his life with a man. Who am I to argue? We were both single, and an orgasm is an orgasm at the end of the day.

"I'm going back to bed," I say, tipping away the dregs of my coffee and placing my mug in the sink.

"Right behind you, sweets."

I turn left into my room while Joe goes right. Shutting the door behind me, I lean back on it and a smile twitches at my lips. It's been quite a long time since someone stayed up worrying about me. It might make me feel a little weird, but at the same time it's nice knowing that someone cares enough.

Stripping out of my dress once again, I stand in front of the mirror in my en suite and assess the damage. It looks like a bird's nesting in my hair, my face is covered in smeared black make up, and my lips are swollen from the suit's kiss. Fuck only knows how Joe could take looking at me seriously. I look like a hot mess, but memories of how I ended up this way has desire tugging at my lower stomach. Did I do the right thing, leaving like that?

That single thought haunts me as I wash his scent from my body and lie in bed, waiting for sleep to claim me. I fear that the answer might be that it wasn't.

CHAPTER FOUR

Before I know it, the weekend's over and I'm making my way down the street toward the tube station for my morning commute to work.

I've worked the same job since I dropped out of university when I was twenty. I never intended to stay, but I soon found myself at home in the small, family-run building company, and the time never really came that I wanted something else.

Lauren, the boss' daughter and our in-house accountant, soon became one of my best friends, and I loved spending my days sitting beside her as we worked. The younger guys on the firm were pretty awesome too, especially the one I now live with.

The fact that I still have the job is nothing short of a miracle after the monumental fuck-up I made. Everyone can tell me that it wasn't my fault, that I was manipulated, but that doesn't help me see it any better. As far as I'm concerned, I allowed it to happen. I allowed the boss, my best friend's dad, to manipulate his way into my bed and blackmail me into keeping his dirty, money laundering secrets. The way I see it, I'm just as guilty as he was. I may not have had a hand in any of the dodgy deals going on, but I sure helped keep his tracks hidden, and at the first threat to my job and my home I opened my legs for him almost willingly.

My cheeks heat as I remember those few months of my life. I'm pretty sure I'll forever be ashamed of myself, but I was at my wits' end, up to my eyeballs in debt thanks to my ex, and I needed help. I just didn't expect it to come with so many strings and so much betrayal.

"Morning," I sing, walking into the office, dropping my bag on my desk and heading straight for the coffee machine and kettle. I'm used to being the first in, but since the boss' heart attack and death a few weeks ago, his stepson and the rightful boss of this place returned and kicked everything into touch.

"Good weekend?" Ben asks, leaning his hip against the doorframe, watching me make both of us our first caffeine hit of the day.

"Yeah, not bad."

"The rings around your eyes tell a different story, E."

"How about yours? Things still good with Lauren?" I wave him off, not wanting to talk about what—or who—has kept my sleep at bay the last few nights. His whole face lights up at the mere mention of her name, and my stomach clenches. How hard is it to find someone who'll look like that when they hear my name?

"She's good. We spent the weekend redecorating Mum's bedroom so we could move into it."

Ben and Lauren have one hell of a story attached to their relationship, but after being apart for six years, they eventually managed to stop arguing for long enough to figure their shit out and embark on their second chance. I'm happy for them...as well as jealous as fuck.

"I can't believe your mum moved out just like that."

"You and me both. But hey, we've got the whole house to

ourselves now." He winks at me, his eyes darkening, probably with some filthy memory I don't need the details of.

"I know I've said it before but I'm so glad you two sorted your shit out."

"Me too. Now it's your turn to find yourself a decent bloke."

"Ha, no. I don't think I'm destined for that."

"You never know. The man of your dreams might just walk through that door at any moment."

We both turn to look at the entrance to the office as the door opens right on cue. Unfortunately for me, it's just Lauren who walks in.

"Everything okay?" she asks when she realises we're both staring right at her.

I hate that I can see disappointment in her eyes every time she looks at me now. She says she understands everything that happened with her dad, and that she doesn't blame me for any of it, but it still hurts. I'll do anything to get our friendship back where it was.

"Just talking about Erica having a man."

"Erica's got a man?" Lauren asks, rushing over to get the gossip.

"Erica is standing right here. And no, I don't have a man nor do I need one. I've got Joe to babysit, that's enough for me right now."

"Babysit?" booms through the office, seconds before he also appears. "Since when did I need babysitting?"

"You've no idea," Lauren mutters, and the two of us laugh, both knowing what it's like to live with him.

"Did Erica tell you about the hot man she spent Saturday night with?"

"No, she was actually saying exactly the opposite."

"Just because I don't *have* a man doesn't mean I don't *make use* of one."

"Christ. I don't need to hear this on a Monday morning," Ben moans, grabbing his now full mug and walking away. "Feel free to do some work when you've all finished gossiping."

"Sure thing, boss," Lauren says with a laugh, saluting him, but he's already rounded the corner into his office. "So..." Her eyes turn back to me. "Tell me all about this man."

"Nothing to tell. Met him at The Avenue, he took me home, we fucked all night, I left."

"Wow, how romantic."

"Who said anything about romance?" She shrugs and I use her moment of silence to run to the safety of my desk. That doesn't mean I don't hear Joe filling her in with all the details of my conquest.

Shaking my head at the two of them, I turn my computer on and get ready to start a new week.

We've got a long few days ahead of us as we continue to fight to keep the business from going under after all of Lauren's dad's questionable investments and embezzlements, but it's also our last week in this building. This has been the home of Johnson & Sons for years, and I know Ben's feeling a little emotional about his decision to move the office to the garages at his family home. It's the right decision. It'll free up some much needed money, but we've got a lot of stuff to pack up and move. On top of that, we've got employees leaving who are concerned about the company's future, along with a new contracts manager starting.

"Erica, make sure you've got everything ready, Trey said he'd be here at ten. I want to at least try to look like we know what we're doing," Ben shouts from his office.

"We do know what we're doing."

"Speak for yourself." He's right. He's been gone for the last six years, so he's not exactly up to scratch with how things work around here these days. I've got every confidence in him fixing all the mistakes I allowed to happen and keeping the company going.

I'm bent over, stacking some of our files into a box ready to move, when a silence falls over the office. I dust my hands off on my skirt and turn around to see what's distracted everyone.

My chin drops and my hands start to tremble when I stare at the man standing in the doorway, waiting for someone to greet him. But it's not just any man. It's him, *the suit*. Only he's dressed more casually in a pair of dark jeans and a perfectly pressed white shirt. It's unbuttoned enough to remind me of how his skin tasted on my tongue, and his sleeves are rolled up to reveal the ink wrapping around them.

His steel eyes hold mine as tension crackles between us.

My heart races as I try to get my brain and body on the same page. Why's he here? I didn't even give him my name let alone my...fuck. Please tell me he's not—

"Trey, good to see you again," Ben booms from behind me, breaking the spell he'd cast over the office. I know that Lauren and Betty are staring at me; their eyes are burning into my skin.

My body is frozen as Ben walks over and the two men shake hands. He turns back, his eyes first finding Lauren's, but he soon notices that something's not right. His eyes narrow on me before Lauren attempts to help me out.

"Trey, it's so good to meet you at last." She marches over and accepts his hand when he holds it out for her. "We're excited to have you on board."

"Thank you. I'm looking forward to getting my feet under the table." My stomach twists and I almost double over when his eyes meet mine over her shoulder.

"Would you like a drink before we get started?"

"Black coffee would be great."

"Fantastic." Turning, Lauren pins me with a stare and starts walking towards me. When she's in reaching distance, she grabs my forearm and pulls me along with her.

"You fucked him, didn't you?"

"Wow, you don't beat around the bush."

"No time for bush beating. Is this going to be a problem because—" Terrified of what her next words could be, I cut her off.

"No, no problem. I just didn't think I'd ever see him again."

"Jesus, Erica. Is there anyone in this office you haven't slept with?" Her face twists, and I know she regrets the words the second they fall from her lips. "Shit, I didn't mean—"

"It's fine. And for the record, I've never slept with Ben."

"You'll never know how grateful I am for that." She tries to say it light-heartedly, but I hear the pain in her voice. I hurt her more than she'll admit by getting involved with her dad.

"I can't believe this is happening." Covering my face with my hands, I will the images that are on repeat in my head from Saturday night away. The last thing I need to picture when I go out there and look in his eyes is him thrusting into me from behind.

Fuck. My. Life.

I'm meant to be trying to redeem myself after everything, not just bouncing from one disastrous office hook-up to another.

"What am I meant to do?" I don't mean for the question to be out loud, but when Lauren turns to me, I realise it was.

"You square your shoulders, hold your head up high and walk out there like you own the place. Forget about where his fingers have been and what he looks like without his clothes on—"

"Not that easy," I mutter, making her chuckle.

"You're going to have to. He's here to help sort this place out, not spend his days trying to figure out the best way to get you to spread your legs again." I hear her warning loud and clear. *Do not sleep with another employee and fuck this up for all of us.*

Nodding at her, accepting that my mistake with her dad is going to haunt me for the rest of my life, I quickly head towards the toilets to freshen up before walking out there like she just suggested.

Blowing out a breath, I grab the mug of coffee Lauren made for him. It sloshes about a little as my hand trembles. I pick up the documents from my desk that I'd prepared for him and take everything into the office where he's chatting with Ben.

"Here you go," I say, handing over the mug, hoping that my voice comes out as strong as I intend.

His eyes meet mine and it's like someone knocks the wind out of me. Swallowing my desire, I place my folder on the table and consider how the hell I'm meant to have a serious conversation with him.

"I've got a few documents for you to fill in and sign, then I need to take copies of your ID and your qualifications."

"I'll leave you two to it. If you need anything before you start next week, just pick up the phone, yeah?" Ben says to Trey before nodding his head at both of us and leaving the room, taking all the air with him.

"I shouldn't keep you long."

"That's a shame, because I've got all day." The deepness of his voice has goosebumps pricking my skin.

"Well, I'm kind of busy, so if we could just focus on the task in hand that would be awesome."

"Sure thing, *sweetheart.*"

"No," I snap. His body stills in surprise. "I'm not having any of..." I wave my hand in front of him. "That. We're colleagues now, apparently, so it's best we both forget everything that happened and move on. This job is important to me, and I won't have another mistake ruin it."

"Mistake, huh?" His eyes darken, as if he's remembering every second of our time together.

"Yes. *Mistake.* Can you fill this in, please?" I shove the personal details form at him and blow out a frustrated breath.

"Careful, I'll start to think you want to get rid of me."

I purse my lips and bite my tongue to stop me from saying that that's exactly what I'm doing.

Trey stays at the office for a little over thirty minutes as I get everything I need to set him up, ready to start on Monday. The moment the door closes behind him, I think I release the largest breath I've ever held.

How can this be fucking happening?

I know it's karma for everything that happened with Nick, I know it is, but it doesn't mean any of it is fair. I'm trying to prove to both Ben and Lauren that they were right in not firing me when the truth came out, but it's just got a load fucking harder if I'm going to have to spend my days being tortured by him.

"You due on your period or something? You've been a right moody bitch the past few days." I cut Joe a seething look, but it doesn't faze him at all.

"No. I'm not."

"So, what the fuck's wrong then. You haven't been yourself since last weekend. Oooh, is it the suit? Having withdrawal symptoms?"

"What? No. It was a one-night-stand. I got what I needed, and if he was lucky then so did he."

His eyes assess me, I guess to try to work out of I'm lying or not. "With the way you looked when you got in, I think it's safe to say he got what he needed."

I fight to keep the blush from my cheeks, it's not like me to get embarrassed so easily, but there was something about that guy. He's still under my skin, no matter how much I may protest to Joe that he's not. Joe is also totally oblivious that he's our new colleague. I made Lauren promise to keep it to herself, seeing as I have no intention of screwing anyone else who works for Johnson & Sons ever again.

"So what gives?"

"Nothing. I'm fine."

"Is your mum okay? Sam?" he asks, referring to my older sister.

"Yeah, everyone's good. Can you just leave it?"

He gives me a look that expresses how unhappy he is, but right now I don't really have the energy to give a fuck. My focus needs to be on work, one-hundred percent. I need to put all my energy into getting the new office set up and then into proving to both Ben and Lauren that I can fix the mess I helped make. I'm a huge part of the reason why we're moving offices and digging the company out of the hole. If I just had a little more integrity and was able to say no when Nick started helping me out, none of this would have happened.

"You need to get laid," Joe states, getting up and putting his empty plate into the dishwasher and heading towards his room. "And don't even think about asking me. I'm not sure I could live up to the suit." His shoulders shake with his laughter as he disappears. *Dickhead.*

Letting out a sigh, I drop my knife and fork and fall back into my chair. I hate feeling like this. I'm on edge all the time, worrying that something else I allowed to fall through the net at work is going to come back and bite me on the arse. It helps now that Joe's living here and helping me with the mortgage, but I can't lose my job and then ultimately my home. I've worked too hard, saved every penny I had spare to own my own place.

Scraping what's left on my plate into the bin, I throw it down on the counter and march towards my bedroom. Joe's right: getting laid would probably help lose some of my tension. It's just a shame that the only man I can picture fucking right now is one I really need to stay away from.

STARING INTO MY WARDROBE, I spend much longer than usual trying to decide what to wear to work. I usually put zero thought into it and drag out the first clean outfit I have, but it's a very different story this morning and I'm already irritated with myself that I care.

In the end, I settle on a pair of cut-off black trousers and a white shirt with a frill down the front. I ignore the little voice in my head that tells me my choice is solely based on the fact that the shirt gives me killer cleavage and instead focus on the fact that I think it makes me look slimmer.

My hair and make-up is done to perfection, and, as the seconds tick on the clock my nerves of what today is going to hold start to multiply.

It'll be fine. He'll just turn up, sit at his desk and get to work, I tell myself. He probably won't even look at me, let alone notice what I'm wearing.

"Whoa. You got a hot date after work or something?" Joe asks after doing a double take when he finds me in the kitchen a few minutes later.

"No, just trying to cheer myself up."

"So you admit something's wrong, then?" His eyebrow pops and I frown at him. "Fine, fine." With his hands up in defeat, he backs away, quickly snatching the travel mug I filled for him a few seconds ago. "I'll cook tonight, and I'll pick up your favourite pudding. Peace offering, yeah?"

"Whatever," I say nonchalantly, but the thought of digging into a New York cheesecake right now makes my mouth water. That should definitely help squash some of my cravings...*if I could eat it off his abs.*

Dragging my mind from the gutter, I grab a cereal bar from the cupboard and head out the way Joe went a few minutes ago. Unlike him, who's just jumped in a Johnson & Sons van to drive to site, I head down the road to the tube station to sit with hundreds of other Londoners on their commute into the city. My journey has more than doubled now I've got to get to Ben's house. It might be closer in distance, but on public transport it's a bitch and makes me mourn the loss of my car that little bit more.

By the time I push through the door of Ben's newly converted double garage, I'm a hot mess. Everyone's already here and all sets of eyes turn towards me as I stumble over the threshold.

"If that was meant to be a glamorous entrance, you failed," Ben says with a laugh, but he's the only one who's amused.

Lauren looks at me with concern laced through her features; no doubt Joe's told her what kind of mood I've been in all weekend. Then there's Trey. He stares at me like he's about to march over and fuck me against the wall. That image entering my head makes my temperature spike even more.

"Getting this side of town is a fucking nightmare," I mutter, eventually managing to break my stare with Trey and walk over to my new desk, which I now realise faces his. *Fuck my life.*

I keep my head down, not wanting to look into my colleagues' eyes. We all know it's partly my fault we're here right now. I don't need reminding of it once again.

"Get a coffee, Erica. We're meeting in ten."

"Sure thing, boss." I give him a quick salute and race towards the kitchenette. There isn't enough coffee in the world to help me get through today.

Ben, Lauren, Trey, and Jenny, Ben's mum, are already sitting around the giant table in the main office when I enter. "You're late. Take a seat," Ben barks, playing the part of being the boss perfectly. I manage to contain my proud smile and rush towards the closest empty seat. Unfortunately, the second I look up from said seat I realise my mistake. It's next to him.

I stop breathing the second his scent fills my nose and his eyes burn into my skin. I fight to ignore him and focus on opening my notebook, ready to take minutes.

Ben starts talking, but I've no fucking clue what about; I'm too lost to the feeling of Trey's body only inches away from mine.

My skin tingles and I watch out of the corner of my eyes as he leans towards me. Sucking in a lungful of air, I wait for what he's about to say.

"Nice shirt."

When I glance over, he's staring right at my tits, and I feel stupid for looking so obvious.

Shifting in my seat, I twist away from him and towards Ben, who's still chatting away, hopefully not about something I need to know.

The whole meeting, almost all my focus is on the man beside me. Thankfully, once I do manage to latch onto what Ben's talking about, I realise most of the information is about our current jobs and getting Trey up to date. I just hope he's able to pay more attention than I am.

"I think that's it. Trey, if you're okay, I'll take you out to a few of our sites now. Erica's got your phone and log on details on her desk. Grab all of that, then we'll head out, yeah?"

"You got it."

I'm out of that chair and then the office like the place is on fire. I continue past my desk and head for the toilet so I can have a minute or two to breathe.

I feel ridiculous for allowing him to affect me this much. He's just a guy. I've slept with plenty over the years; it's not like what I did last weekend was unusual.

What *is* unusual is how badly I want to be back in his bedroom again.

Resting my hands on the sink, I stare at myself in the mirror. I really need to get a grip.

He's sitting on the edge of my desk waiting for me when I eventually emerge. His dark grey trousers are stretched tight over his muscular thighs, giving me just a hint of what I know is hiding beneath. My mouth goes dry as desire ripples through me at the memory of just how tightly he filled me.

Lifting my eyes, I take in his black fitted shirt. It may as well be made to measure, the way it hugs his chest and strong arms. It's not until I get to his face that I realise I've been standing here checking him out for way too long. The smirk playing on his lips tells me that he knows exactly where my thoughts are.

His eyes dance over my body as I force thoughts of him naked from my head and make my way over to my desk.

Rolling my chair forward, I grab his phone and documents from my drawer. When I look again, he's leaning forward on my desk with his palms on the wood and his intense eyes on me.

Clearing my throat, I suck in a breath and attempt to do my job. "Here's your phone. I've already programmed in a lot of the numbers you'll need, and your email is already set up. Here are your computer log on details; the system will prompt you to change your password the first time you log on. You've also got a laptop on your desk." I nod my head towards where he's meant to sit, but he doesn't follow. Instead, his eyes stay locked on my tits. "Did you hear any of that?"

"Phone, password, laptop. Yeah, I think I got it. I think you've missed something, though."

"Oh?"

His eyes drop from mine once again. "I think I need a proper welcome to the office. You know, break in my desk and all that."

"I don't think that's necessary. The boss is waiting for you." Thankfully, at that moment Ben appears from his office and looks over at us. "Best you run along now."

"Fine. But I'll be back, and just so you know, that wasn't a suggestion. We *will* be christening my desk. Yours, too, if you're lucky."

My thighs clench at his words, but thankfully he turns and walks towards Ben and misses my reaction. He, on the other hand, looks totally unaffected about the prospect of fucking me a mere few feet from where the boss lives.

"What are the plans for tonight, then?" Lauren asks after we've finished eating our lunch.

"Uh..."

"You *have* planned a night out, right? It's what you do when a new member of staff starts."

I had a feeling this was going to bite me in the arse. Lauren knows me too well, but luckily for me, I have the perfect excuse to ensure I don't have to end up on another night out with Trey.

"Nope. There are age restrictions, remember?"

"Seriously? You're not organising drinks tonight because Trey is over your thirty-five age limit." Her eyebrows rise, and I think she's expecting me to tell her she's joking any minute.

"Seriously. He's too old."

"Didn't stop you fucking him though, did it?" Her voice is full of amusement as she reminds me once again of my mistake.

"Touché."

"I guess I'll have to take matters into my own hands."

"W-what does that mean?"

"He's here to help save this place." I wince, knowing what she means although her voice holds no accusation. "So the least we owe him is a night out." Rolling my eyes, I go to argue. "Don't even think about finding an excuse to get out of it."

CHAPTER SIX

The more the week goes on, the worse my mood gets. It's all my own fault and my inability to get my head out of the gutter whenever I'm forced to look at Trey.

Thankfully, Ben's kept him pretty busy with site visits, but he's been in the office almost all day today and I'm practically vibrating with the need for release. He hasn't even really done anything to wind me up, just walking past my desk and filling the air around me with his scent is enough. I feel like a horny fucking teenager and I don't like it. I should be able to control my desire, but, at this point, I fear the only thing that's going to dampen it is him.

It's Thursday afternoon and Trey's in Ben's office. They've got the door shut, but the rumble of his deep, gravelly voice still filters through to me, leaving me sitting here squirming.

The main door opens, catching my attention, and when I turn to look I find a very dirty Joe walking in.

"Had a good day?" I ask with a laugh.

"Yeah, great. Will pulled a ceiling down on my head."

"Shouldn't you be at home showering? Ahh, get the fuck away from me," I squeal when he comes over like he's about to hug me."

"Glad to see you're in a better mood," he says with a laugh as he rounds my desk and drops into the seat at the other side. "Apparently we're all going out Friday night. If you're lucky, your suit might be at the bar. Hopefully another round or two with him will—"

I stop listening when I spot the office door opening behind Joe's shoulder. I pray that it's going to be Ben who steps out, but because this is me and my luck is so shitty, of course it's Trey who emerges, a shit-eating grin on his face.

His eyes land on mine, amusement making them look more silver than their usual dark steel.

Joe's still talking, but my panic as well as the effect Trey's stare has on my body means I don't hear a word of it. When Trey's smile only gets wider, I know it can't be anything good.

"Is that right?" Trey's gruff voice fills the room, and it brings me back from my daze.

I break my stare on him just in time to see Joe turn to see who's behind him.

His chin drops before he exclaims, "Holy shit." He turns back to me before looking back to Trey again. "Now it's all starting to make sense," he chuckles. "So you didn't fancy telling me that the 'best shag of your life' now works in this exact office?"

"I...uh...fuck." Joe narrows his eyes. Disappointment oozes from him that I've kept this to myself. All the while, Trey's eyes continue to lighten with amusement.

"Joe, can you...What's going on?" Ben asks when he sticks his head out of his office and looks between the three of us.

"Probably best you don't know. You ready?"

"Yeah." He doesn't sound very positive as he pulls the office door closed, still looking between us like we're a puzzle he needs to work out.

After a couple of seconds, both Ben and Joe leave the office. Glancing around, I realise for the first time that everyone else has left for the day. My heart thunders and my palms start to sweat. Being alone in a room with this man is not a good idea, especially with the way he's staring down at me right now.

"I-I need…I need to leave."

"Why? You got somewhere better to be?"

"Uh…" I rack my brain for a smart answer, the kind that would usually fall from my mouth right about now, but while I'm captive in his grey eyes, my brain refuses to work. "Home," I squeak when his lips curl into a smirk and I'm forced to say something.

"How about I join you."

"What? No, that wasn't an invitation."

"No? Your little friend seems to think it'll be a good idea." He rounds the desk and I roll my chair back in my pathetic attempt to keep some distance between us.

"He…he doesn't know what he's talking about."

"Really? He sounded like he knew *exactly* what would fix your current mood. And I must say, I agree with him."

My chair hits the wall and I scramble out of it. My body screams "Yes!" as I do anything I can to stay far enough away from him, but thankfully my head's winning the fight right now. I can't let him touch me again. Just the memory of it has been haunting me. I can only imagine how bad it'll become if I allow myself to experience him again.

"Trey, we can't do this." My sensible side shows herself, and I continue backing away. We're at work, the place where I should be proving myself, not allowing the new guy to put his hands on me. We can't do this.

I can't do this.

"It's only you fighting it, sweetheart."

The disappointment that haunts Lauren's eyes every time she looks at me pops into my head. I can't let her down again. *I can't.*

"Trey, please." His eyes flash with desire. "No, I wasn't. Please." *Fuck,* even to my own ears it sounds like I'm begging him.

My back hits the wall, and I panic when I drag my eyes from his and realise that he's backed me into a corner.

My chest heaves, desire sitting heavy in my lower stomach, and my clit starts to pound from the memories of his touch alone.

"It's funny, because every time you say that it sounds like you want it more."

"Trey." It's no more than a moan as he takes one last step towards me. His scent fills my nose and my mouth waters for a taste of him, to feel his tongue dancing with mine, to feel the heat of his hands on my skin.

"You need to stop denying yourself what you want, because we both know exactly what that is."

His heat burns my front as he closes the space between us. Ripping my eyes away from him, I stare down at the floor, hoping it'll be enough to convince us both that this isn't about to happen. He's silent for a beat before a low and deep chuckle rumbles up his throat. His fingers find my chin and my head is moved so I have no choice but to look at him.

"You've been thinking about kissing me again since the moment you walked out, haven't you?"

"No." My voice doesn't sound as strong as I was hoping. His eyebrow lifts in amusement.

"So your temperature doesn't spike every time you look at me? Your clit doesn't throb for my touch every time I'm close?"

"Nope, neither."

His eyes shine with delight as they flit between mine and my lips.

"Just as I thought."

I don't get a chance to say any more before his lips are on mine and his tongue is in my mouth. My breath catches and I sag back against the wall. *Jesus,* no man has ever managed to consume me quite like him before.

His hips pin me to the wall, his solid length pressing into my stomach, and my need for more starts to get the better of me. Lifting my hand, I grip onto his muscular upper arms as his hands skim down my body.

A little squeal passes my lips when he bites down on my bottom one before moving across my jaw and down my neck, allowing me a few minutes to drag in some much needed air.

He sucks on the sensitive skin beneath my ear as his fingers find the bottom of my skirt.

My surroundings vanish as his fingertips tickle their way up my bare thighs. The only thing I can focus on is where they're heading.

"Fuck," he grunts when he slips my soaked knickers aside and runs his fingers through my folds.

"Holy shit," falls from my lips as he slides two inside me.

"Are you ready to admit you were lying yet?"

"Fuck, Trey." My chest heaves as my release starts to grow closer.

"I won't let you come until you tell me that you want me, that you fall asleep at night wishing I'd been inside you."

"No, no," I chant, although I've no idea what I'm really saying. All I know is that his fingers and deep voice are exactly what I need right now.

"Erica," he warns seconds before pulling his fingers from me.

"I-I...*fuck.*" The office door flies open and Lauren walks in, totally unaware of what's going on only feet away from her.

"Shit. I...oh..." She quickly looks to the other side of the room, and Trey takes a step back. Coldness engulfs me, but it soon vanishes when I look back to Lauren.

I've let her down again. My stomach twists in frustration with myself for not being able to do the right thing.

"I'm so sorry," I whisper before rushing towards my desk, grabbing my bag and running from the office. I can't hang around and see that look in her eye. I already hate myself for everything I've done to her; I don't need to make it any worse.

Finding a taxi idling down the street, I jump in and give the driver my address, forgetting about the cost. Money isn't my biggest concern right now.

My body's still wound tight as I make my way up the stairs to my flat. Pushing the door open, I head straight for my room and slam it behind me. My chest heaves from running up the stairs, but it's still mostly from the desire still coursing through my body as I remember the feeling of Trey's fingers stretching me open.

"Fuck." Dropping my head into my hands, I scream out my frustration. Why can't I just find a decent bloke to settle down with? I've always known my addiction to bad boys with bad attitudes was going to get me hurt, but I never could have predicted the mess my life has become.

I thought I'd found the one with my ex. He seemed like the perfect mix of bad boy on the outside and kind on the in. Until it turned out it was all an act, and he was just an arsehole through and through who was up to his eyeballs in debt. I was distraught the day he left, but bad soon turned to worse when the final demands and bailiffs started turning up at my door. It turned out it wasn't only him who was drowning, because he'd put my name and address on a load of his debts. I'd worked my arse off saving for this place over the years, and because of him I was on the verge of losing it. That was when the other arsehole stepped in to help ruin my life just a little bit more.

Not wanting to think about Nick and how he manipulated me so easily into doing whatever he wanted, I push myself from the door and walk towards my en suite. I need to wash today off me.

Sadly, no length of shower is going to allow me to forget him. He's well and truly under my skin, and the fucker knows it.

I stand under the spray of the water long after I've used all the hot.

Pulling on a pair of old leggings and an oversized jumper, I head out into the kitchen to make myself some comfort food.

I'm just digging into my macaroni cheese when the front door opens and Joe appears. His face is still minging when he looks up at me, although slightly less so than earlier.

"I can't believe you didn't tell me the suit is our new contracts manager. When were you planning on fessing up, exactly?" His disappointment is obvious in his voice, and it only makes me feel worse than I already do. I'm fed up of disappointing people, but it seems to be all I'm capable of these days.

"I don't know," I whisper. "I didn't exactly expect this to happen. I had no idea until he turned up the following Monday with his ID and shit."

"You've known that long and didn't tell me?"

"I didn't know what to say. My main focus has been not fucking up again, but how long did that last? A few weeks at best?"

"You weren't to know."

"But I know now."

"So? It's not like he's Lauren's dad." My chin drops and my eyes harden. "Too soon for jokes?"

"It'll forever be too soon to joke about that."

"Seriously, Erica. This isn't a big deal. So what, you spend your nights fantasising about the new guy. There's no reason why you can't."

"I just want to show Ben and Lauren that I'm serious, and this isn't the way to go about it."

Reaching over he takes my hand in his dirty one. "They know, Erica. If they had any concerns, they would have let you go, but they haven't. You still have a job, and they're still your friends. Trust them. Trust *yourself*."

Blowing out a breath, I try to force the words he's just said to settle inside me. I'm still on edge after the encounter earlier, and anything short of having his hands on me to finish the job—which isn't happening—isn't going to relax me.

"I need to go and shower, but do you want to go for drinks after?"

I stare at him, weighing up my options. Sit in here and replay everything with Trey over and over, or go and attempt to forget about it.

"We're going. Get your arse up and put something sexy on." Joe's authoritative tone leaves no room for argument, and I follow his instruction.

CHAPTER SEVEN

Going out with Joe didn't really help. He tried his best to keep me entertained and to stop my mind from wandering, but no matter how hard I tried, Trey was still there in my head and under my skin. It's going to take a lot more than a couple of glasses of alcohol to get rid of him, that's for sure.

Much to my relief, Trey's hardly in the office on Friday. He's either out on site or locked in the office with Ben going over stuff that doesn't involve me, thank fuck. The least amount of time I can spend in an enclosed space with him the better.

"I've got a table booked at Blueprint for seven-thirty. Do not be late," Lauren warns, perching herself on the edge of my desk sometime late that afternoon once everyone else has left.

"I...uh..."

"Don't even think about it, Erica. We're all going out together. It'll be good for everyone."

Rolling my eyes, I rest back in my chair and cross my arms over my chest. "Are we just going to pretend last night didn't happen?"

"If you want to. You didn't look like you wanted to talk about it."

Dropping my head back on a sigh, I try to find the words. "I really don't want to talk about it, but I'm...I'm sorry. I just keep fucking up, and I don't—"

"It's okay." Dragging my head forward, I find her soft blue eyes and my own fill with tears that I refuse to cry.

"It's not, though. I need to be working, righting my wrongs, trying to make shit up to you...and here I am getting caught with the new guy's fingers inside me."

"Okay, so that wasn't ideal, but you're not fucking up, E. Trey's hot; anyone with eyes can see that, and he seems to have a bit of a fascination with you. I would never blame you for testing that out. Who knows where it could lead."

"Probably with me fucking another member of staff and getting what I deserve."

"And what is it you think you deserve?"

"For you to hate me." Reaching out, she grasps my shoulders in a show of support.

"Out of everyone, I'm the one who understands what you went through the most. Of course I don't like it, but I also get that what happened with my dad was not your fault. He was a master manipulator, and I should be apologising to you for not seeing what was going on. He was cooking my books right under my nose and disrespecting my best friend at the same time. I hate myself for not seeing any of that. I knew *exactly* how much you were struggling after Matt left, and I should have been a better friend. I should have been the one to help dig you out, not him. I just—"

I don't allow her to say any more. Standing, I throw my arms around her shoulders and hold her tight. We've spoken about this before, but today I think I'm finally starting to accept that what she's saying is true. I'll forever blame myself for allowing that situation to happen in the first place, and for hurting Lauren when she was already going through so much shit, but I think I'm getting somewhere.

"Thank you," I say when I pull back from her.

She grabs my hands to stop me walking away—not that I was going to. "You are coming tonight, aren't you? Please don't think that I'll stop you doing anything with Trey. You never know, he might be *the one*." I can't help but laugh at her. "What? He's totally your type. Brooding, hot, a bit of an arsehole on the surface but a total teddy bear beneath."

"How do you know what's beneath?" My brows draw together, making Lauren laugh.

"I can just tell. He's a good guy, Erica. Give it a chance."

"And what if it doesn't work? What if I fuck it up again and one of us has to leave?"

"Stop worrying about the what ifs. For once, just enjoy it without worrying about the consequences."

That's easier said than done. I've experienced the fallout more than once for acting without considering what might happen when it all goes wrong. I've also been fooled by the ones I thought were hard on the outside and soft in the middle. Those arseholes are good at getting what they want and then showing their full colours when it's too late.

"Stop worrying."

The main office door opens and Ben and Trey walk in, both immediately looking our way where we're still standing with our hands together.

"Looks like we turned up at just the right time," Ben says with a wink. "Please continue." His eyes flick between us as he leans back against the wall as if he's waiting for a show.

"You're a pig," Lauren says, trying to sound as serious as possible, but amusement fills her voice as she steps away from me.

I don't see her go. I only know she's reached Ben when he complains about her hitting him; I'm too lost in the steel eyes that haven't left me since they entered.

"Seven-thirty, Erica." She goes to leave but stops in the doorway. "And you should totally wear that little red dress you've got. It'll work like a charm." She's gone before I can respond. Trey has no idea what my red dress might look like, but already his eyes are darkening and the muscles in his neck are tensing.

Nope, I will not allow him to consume me, I tell myself as I turn back to my computer. *Tonight, I will stay out of his way. And I will go home alone.*

BY THE TIME I'm standing at the entrance to Blueprint in my little red dress, my stomach is full of butterflies and my hands are trembling.

"Will you chill out? I can't cope with you like this, it's weird," Joe complains, threading his arm through mine and all but dragging me inside. "Have I mentioned how hot you look? I'm kinda jealous it's all for him."

"Shut up, you idiot." Shaking my head at him, a little laugh falls from my lips.

"What? It's been a while since I've had any action."

"Enough."

Joe and I have had a fumble about a time or two when we were in need of a little tension release, and while I like to not dwell on getting freaky with one of my best friends and flatmate, he likes to bring it up as often as possible just to make me squirm. I was confused as fuck the first time he leaned in a kissed me after a night out, because I was convinced he was gay. I'd only ever seen him with men up until that point, but shit, he kissed me like he knew exactly what to do with a woman. He also wasn't shy when we got down to it and he got me off in record time. I always thought a body like that was a waste, but knowing a woman could put it to good use did make me feel a little better. If he wasn't one of my closest friends, I might have wanted more, but as much as I love him, romance is most definitely not in our future. I've heard and witnessed him with too many others to even consider it.

I'm practically vibrating with nervous energy by the time we're pointed towards the table. I tell myself that he won't be here yet and that I'll have a few minutes to get settled, but the second we round the corner, I see that none of that will be happening because we're last.

The second Lauren spots us approaching, she calls Joe over and he happily takes the seat next to her leaving only one free.

Rolling my eyes at her antics, I take a step towards the vacant chair but my shoe catches on a bump on the floor and I stumble. Thankfully, Trey sees what's about to happen, and moments before I'm expecting to get extra friendly with the floor tiles, his giant hands land on my waist. Electric sparks shoot around my body and my skin burns where we're touching.

Keeping my eyes on the floor, I mumble a thank you, aware that everyone's silent around us.

"Erica?" he breathes moments before his finger presses under my chin and forces my head up so I have no choice but to look at him. His dark eyes are full of concern, but his lips are pulled up in a sexy smirk.

He feels the connection between us, too.

He leans in and I suck in a breath, thinking he's going to kiss me right here in front of everyone, but at the last minute he moves to the side so he can whisper in my ear.

"I'm taking that dress off you tonight...with my teeth."

My thighs clench and my clit throbs at the thought. A flush the colour of my dress heats my cheeks and neck. He pulls back and returns to his chair as if nothing's happened. I glance over at Lauren as I go to take my seat, and her eyes are full of delight and mischief. I narrow mine at her, hoping she realises how much I don't appreciate her meddling, but all she does is laugh.

I sit ramrod straight in my chair, afraid of what I'll do if I allow myself to relax. My entire body is being called to the one next to me.

Everyone goes back to their previous conversations while I stare at the menu, but it's as if it's written in another language because the only things I can focus on are his hands on my body and his hot breath against my ear.

"You can't stop thinking about it, can you?"

"Don't know what you're talking about." I refuse to look at him or let him see that I'm affected by his words in any way, although I fear it may be a little too late for that.

"What do you fancy?" He nods his head towards the menu. I almost think he's asking a serious question until his fingers brush against my bare thigh beneath the table.

Knocking it away, I turn to him. "I don't know. Are you allergic to anything?"

The silver in his eyes immediately becomes obvious and his lips curl into the most incredible smile as he barks out a laugh. "Sorry to disappoint you, but even that wouldn't stop me."

"Shame. What are you having?" I don't particularly care what his dish of choice might be, but I need to get onto safer ground, especially when I can feel multiple sets of eyes burning into me.

"What I'm eating tonight's not on this menu."

Heat fills my belly and descends to my core. *Fucking hell.*

"I-I was thinking lasagne," I stutter, hoping no one else around the table heard him. His laughter once again hits my ears and my stomach does a little flip. My head might be telling me to stay as far away from this man as possible, but it's very obvious that the rest of my body is totally on board with everything he has to offer.

The sexual tension is so thick between us that I can barely breathe. Everyone around us is either oblivious or they're ignoring it. They chat away about work and life like normal while I sit here, trying not to melt into a puddle on the seat at just being able to feel his body heat.

Every few seconds his eyes flick over to me, but I refuse to return his stare, too afraid of what I might do or suggest if I look into them.

He lowers his cutlery to his plate and drops his hands from the table once he's finished eating. I think nothing of it until the continued movement of his arm catches my eye seconds before his fingertips trail up my thigh once again.

I suck in a breath, successfully managing to inhale a bit of my lasagne at the same time. Coughing, I manage to drag the attention of everyone at our table, but at no point does Trey remove his hand from me—in fact, he uses my coughing fit to turn into me so not only can he start touching me up, but he can tap me on the back to look like he's assisting.

"I'm good, thanks," I mutter when he continues hitting my back long after I've finished.

"You sure will be." The promise in his voice makes my thighs clench. His lips curl the moment he feels it, and it gives him the encouragement he needs.

Thinking the show's over, everyone turns away from us, giving Trey the opportunity he needs to slide his hand higher.

I once again suck in a breath when his fingers brush against the lace of my underwear.

"Trey," I warn quietly. "Don't."

"Don't pretend you don't need this. You're fucking soaked." I can't deny what he's saying is true, but we can't do this in the middle of a busy restaurant with our friends and colleagues sitting only feet away.

"I...shit," I gasp as he slips his finger beneath the lace. "Trey," I whimper.

When I look up, I find Lauren staring right at me, a small smile on her lips telling me she knows exactly what's going on, but all she does is wink at me and turn away to give us some privacy, if that's even possible right now.

Trey presses harder against my clit and I almost jump out of my chair.

"Did you get yourself off when you got home last night?" His low, rumbling voice does little to stop the pressure building between my legs.

"I might have."

He groans in response and my chest puffs out a little, knowing how torturous this is for him. I know that if I were to reach out, I'd find him hard as steel beneath his trousers.

I bite down on my bottom lip as I recall exactly what that looks like.

"You're imagining me naked, aren't you?" My head snaps to him. How does he know that? "I can read every thought in your dirty mind right now, Miss Wilde."

My mouth opens to respond, but his fingers circle my clit, edging me closer towards my release. Pushing lower, he circles my entrance with one finger before sliding it inside me as far as it'll go with me sitting in this position. He ups the ante and pushes a second inside, and the sensation of being filled by him once again causes my orgasm to crash into me. I grip onto the edge of the table, my fingernails digging into the wood as I fight to keep my lips shut and not draw more attention to myself than I'm sure I already have.

The second my release subsides and I can instruct my legs to move, I get up and practically run for the toilets. I don't dare look up for fear of what I'm going to see on everyone's faces.

The door flies open as I slam into it, making it crash back against the wall. I race into one of the cubicles and lock myself inside.

Putting the toilet lid down, I fall onto it and drop my head into my hands.

What the fuck am I doing?

My heart pounds and my chest heaves as I try to get my breathing back under control. I can't believe I just allowed him to do that. I'm such a fucking idiot. I told myself I'd stay away from him yet less than an hour at that table and he's already completely consumed me. I swear there's something seriously fucking wrong with me.

I've no idea how long I sit there chastising myself for my stupid behaviour, but eventually the door squeaks open and footsteps sound out. I expect to hear Lauren's voice, but no one says anything.

Silence fills the air until water runs at the sinks. Footsteps sound out again before the door squeaks and, thinking I'm safe, I unlock my own door and walk out. I only make it two steps before the body leaning back against the sinks like he owns the fucking place makes my legs stop working.

"Thought I was going to have to come in and get you."

"W-what are you doing?"

"Having my dessert."

I don't get the chance to respond, because he's on me. His fingers slide into my hair and move my head to the perfect angle so his lips can crash down on mine and his tongue can plunge into my mouth.

A moan rumbles up my throat at feeling his hard body pressed up against mine. I'm powerless to do anything but submit to his demands and slide my hands around to cup his arse. The move brings us closer still, and his solid length presses into my stomach.

"This fucking dress," he moans, running his finger down the front until he's at my cleavage. Slipping the fabric aside, he pushes my bra down and sucks my puckered nipple into his mouth. A loud moan crawls up my throat and I shamelessly thrust my breasts towards him, needing more of his touch.

"Put your hands on the counter and stick your arse out." Stumbling away from him on shaky legs, I do as instructed with no concern about where we are or who could walk in. The only thing on my mind is him and what he's about to do.

The release he gave me at the table was just a tease of what's to come. I knew that at the time. Men like Trey don't settle for just that; they want it all.

The fabric of my skirt is flipped over my back, exposing my bare arse.

"Fuck," Trey grunts, running his finger along with scrap of lace between my arse cheeks. "Even better than I remember."

"Trey, please," I beg. My pussy clenches around nothing as he rubs me over the fabric of my knickers. "Please." I'm so fucking wet and ready for him that I should be embarrassed, but right now, as long as he slides his length into me, I don't give a fuck. I need this. I've needed this since the moment I walked out of his flat last weekend.

It seems like forever, but eventually the sound of his belt and trousers being undone fills the room. Heat floods my core and I wait impatiently.

His growl of pleasure bounces off the walls around us as he slides into me. My muscles greedily pull him deeper, needing to remember what it felt like when I was full to the hilt with him.

"Yes," he hisses when he's as deep as he can go and nudging at my womb.

He slowly pulls out and it just about gives me the time I need to lock my arms and prepare for the thrust I know is coming. I'm right; he slams back into me, forcing me forward and into the marble surrounding the sink. His fingers dig into my hips as he helps hold me up, obviously aware that he was going to turn me into a rag doll in seconds.

He thrusts into me with punishing blows that hit the exact spot I need over and over. It's only minutes before the tingles of my release start to hit.

"Fuck. Fuck your pussy, fuck," he roars, his length swelling inside me before his hot cum fills me.

"Uh…"

"I really fucking needed that."

Folding his large body over me, he places his lips to my neck and kisses as his breathing begins to slow.

What the actual fuck? My pussy is still convulsing and my clit pounding, waiting to find the release I crave.

His arms wrap around my waist, and I stand so my back is to his front. His cock slips out of me and I immediately feel lost, like I missing a part of who I am.

"Fuck, I don't want to let you go." The honesty in his words has me pulling away from him, even though in reality it's the last thing I want to do. I might be frustrated to hell right now, but still, it would be so easy to fall for him, to grow attached, but that only leads to pain. I need to keep a clear head about this and remember what it is—a quick fling. He'll soon be bored of me and move onto someone more interesting, more successful and with fewer skeletons hiding in her closet.

"That's it?" I ask when he starts doing up his trousers.

"Yep. You got yours at the table. This was for me."

"But—"

"If you're lucky, maybe I'll let you have another."

I splutter in astonishment, but I can't deny that I'm already planning just how to make that happen.

Turning my back to him, right my clothing and then wash my hands in cold water, hoping that it'll help to cool my heated body. It doesn't work; with his eyes burning into my back, there's nothing that could cool me down.

"Erica?" Placing his hand on my forearm, I'm forced to look up at him. Concern flashes in his eyes but it's gone in an instant, the solid and demanding demeanour I'm becoming used to slipping back into place.

"I need to get back."

"That's it? Not even a thank you?" There's amusement in his tone, but I know it's forced.

"Thanks for nothing. It shouldn't have happened, but...it did."

When I get to the door and pull the handle I realise why we weren't interrupted; he must have flicked the lock when he entered.

CHAPTER EIGHT

The second I appear around the corner, Lauren clocks me and elbows Ben in the ribs, who immediately gets up and starts walking my way.

"You okay?" he whispers.

"Of course." His eyes narrow before they quickly scan my face. He doesn't believe a word of it, and I'm sure my appearance right now doesn't really help.

He nods before walking past me and towards the toilets right as Trey exits. I should be embarrassed, but something tells me that Ben already knew exactly what was going on just a few feet down the hall. I continue watching as he stops right in front of Trey, his arm against the wall as if he's caging him in to ensure he listens to every word he's about to say.

Rushing towards Lauren, I sit myself in Ben's vacant seat. "What the hell is he doing?"

"What he's good at."

"And what's that exactly?"

"Well, there are a few things," she admits with a salacious look in her eyes, "but right now he's just being protective."

"He doesn't need to protect me."

"Maybe not, but he wants to. Just let him do his thing."

"Fine," I mumble, although I'm anything but happy about him getting involved.

"Sooo...have fun in the toilets?"

"I don't know what you're talking about."

"Oh, come off it, E. You were totally just fucking him in there." Everyone around the table is suddenly silent, and my cheeks heat as every set of eyes finds me. Most are amused by Lauren's announcement that came at just the perfect moment as the music dropped out, but none more so than Joe's.

"Oh, just fuck off. Don't even pretend you're not all jealous."

"I'm so sorry," Lauren whispers when everyone starts to return to their previous conversations, although some of them seem to be keeping an eye on me.

"It's fine. They all think I'm a slut for sleeping with the boss, so I may as well play up to it."

"They do not think that."

I'm about to argue, but two shadows fall over the table. Looking up, I find Ben with his shoulders pulled tight with tension. He really is in full-on protective mode.

"I'm a big girl, I can look after myself," I whisper in his ear once I'm on my feet.

"I know, but you shouldn't have to."

I give him a quick hug, because although I'm a little pissed that he felt the need to do whatever it was he just did, I do kinda like that he cares enough to look out for me.

He returns my hug, but my grip on him falters when I find Trey's eyes over his shoulder. Ben might be my boss and one of my best and oldest friends, but his normally steel orbs are almost green with jealousy.

Releasing Ben, I head back over to my empty chair and he follows, although no words are exchanged between us.

The tension's thick as we eat our desserts and pay the bill. Everyone keeps a close eye on both of us; I'm not sure what they're expecting, for us to hop up on the table and fuck in the middle of a busy restaurant, or something?

"The Avenue?" Joe asks the group. Most agree, but a couple of the guys who have families decline in favour of heading home.

Standing to leave, Trey's hand lands in the small of my back. His heat radiates through me, and I hate how much I love the feeling. My heart rate increases once again, knowing what those fingers are capable of.

We're only just outside the restaurant when his phone starts ringing. Pulling it out of his pocket, he looks down at the screen and winces. "I'm sorry, I need to take this."

***

"WHERE DID LOVER BOY GO?" Joe asks me when I slide in next to him at the bar.

"He got a phone call and had to leave." My frustration of knowing I'm not getting what I need anytime soon gets the better of me.

"Well, I guess he's already got lucky, no need to hang around until the end of the night," he quips.

"You're a twat."

"You've got it bad for him, haven't you?"

"I don't know what you're talking about. I haven't got anything for him."

He opens his mouth to say more, but the look I pin him with

has his hands rising in surrender. Instead of berating me about my little bathroom session at the restaurant, he slides a shot towards me, encouraging me to down it before taking my hand and leading me to the dancefloor. "Dance so we get some attention. I really need to get lucky tonight." *Yeah, you and me both.*

I slide my hands up his chest and lock them around the back of his neck. Our hips move in time to the music, and it's only a few minutes later when I notice both male and female eyes checking out Joe's arse. He should be in for a good night.

"Toilet break?" Lauren shouts in my ear once Joe's turned and started grinding with someone else, leaving me like a gooseberry with her and Ben.

"Yes."

She gives Ben a kiss on the cheek before taking my hand and dragging me towards the ladies'. We each manage to find an empty cubicle to do our thing before meeting back up at the sinks.

"You okay?" she asks me in the mirror.

"Yeah, why?"

"What happened to Trey?"

"No idea. He had to go deal with something. No biggie."

"Really?" Her eyebrow quirks up and she turns to me.

"Really. It's not like we're a couple or anything."

"Hmm..."

"What?"

"I'm pretty sure he wants you to be."

"No, I'm pretty sure he just wants the excitement of fucking me in the restaurant toilets."

"I can't believe you did that," she giggles, showing that she's had a little too much to drink.

"Like you can say anything. You can't tell me you and Ben haven't done it anywhere you shouldn't." Her face flames bright red. If it weren't for the two of them being my best friends and having to see them every day, I might ask for details, but in reality I really don't need any kind of visual in my head, especially if it involved the office.

Thankfully, my phone buzzes in my bag and I pull it out, hoping to put an end to the conversation.

My brows pinch when I find a message from an unknown number. Curiosity gets the better of me and I swipe the screen to see what it is. Expecting it to be spam, my chin drops when I find an address staring back at me. It's one I know very well, and although my body aches for more of him, I know I won't be following his demands.

"Booty call?" Lauren asks innocently.

"Yeah, actually."

Turning my phone, I allow her to read the address. "Wait. That address is—"

"I know. It's fucking torture." A wide smile splits her face before she starts laughing and drags me from the toilets, exclaiming that we need another drink. It's something I can't argue with.

While she shouts our order at the barman, I pull my phone back out and send a response.

Erica: If you think I take well to orders, you really don't know me at all.

Feeling smug, I slide my phone back into my bag and take the drink Lauren hands me.

"What?" she asks, noticing my expression.

"Nothing, nothing. I just replied to my booty call."

"I don't want to know."

My phone vibrates again. I want to ignore it so he doesn't think I'm waiting for a reply when it comes up that it's been read so quickly, but I'm too damn nosey not to see what he's said.

Swiping the screen, I stare down at his words.

> Trey: You followed orders perfectly well when you were in my bed.

"Fuck," I mutter to myself as heat rushes to my core. Of course, he's right. I fucking *loved* following his orders.

The promise of what I could find at the address sitting on my phone has me ready and raring to go for the rest of our time in the club, but as much as I might want another roll around in his bed, the sensible thing to do is to stay as far away as possible. I've already screwed up twice tonight, I've already had my fill of mistakes, and I know going to him would surely be one.

"Why are you staring at the stairs so longingly?" Joe asks once we've stumbled our way to our floor.

"N-no reason."

"What happened to the woman you were dancing with?"

"She went home with her boyfriend."

"Oh. Ouch."

"I think I'm destined to be celibate forever. Call it karma or some shit for all the lies I've told."

"You think your lack of action is punishment for lying to Lauren?"

"It must be. I'm a total catch and never had any problems before."

"Maybe it's the arrogance that turns people off," I suggest as he steps aside to allow me into the flat. I immediately reach down and pull my heels from my feet, dropping them to the floor, sighing with relief.

"Nah, doubt that. So how about it? You're horny and drunk, and I'm desperate. Little bit of tickling, little bit of sucking, and we can both go to sleep satisfied?"

I stare at him, trying to figure out if he's serious or not, but when all I get is a hopeful expression staring back at me, I bark out a laugh.

"Wow, you sure know how to make a girl feel special, Joe."

"Oh, I can make you feel special all right. You remember how I did that thing—"

"Yeah, I remember, but I'm sorry. I'm not the girl for you tonight." As much as I might need more than I've already had, hooking up with Joe is the last thing I should be doing right now. This is one decision I know I'm not going to screw up. "It's just you and your right hand, big man."

"Cock tease," he jokes as he heads towards his room.

I do the same, and in only minutes I'm sliding between my cold covers. The alcohol flowing through my system mixes with the desire that's been simmering for the past few hours, and before I know what I'm doing my fingers find their way into my knickers to try to relieve the pressure that's built up to an intolerable level.

Not getting the results as quickly as I'd like, I reach over for my top drawer to pull out my little friend, but as I pull the drawer open my phone catches my eye. Feeling brazen, I grab it and hit call on the number that messaged me earlier. I put it on speaker as it rings, place it on my pillow and grab my vibrator. The phone rings loud into the room and my stomach drops with disappointment when it goes to voicemail...until an idea forms in my head.

Flicking the switch on my vibrator, I throw the covers back, shimmy my knickers down and press it to my clit. The new batteries I put in it the other day means it's extra powerful, and my breath catches in surprise. I soon get used to it and my hips start to roll with my need for more. A moan falls from my lips as my long awaited release starts making itself known. Making sure I'm putting on a show, I drop my other hand between my legs and plunge two fingers into my heat.

"Ah fuck," I moan before continuing to fuck myself. "Can you hear that? I'm gonna make myself come so hard. I don't need to cave to your demands to get what I need. I don't need your cock when I can do this myself." My breathy voice continues to explain what I'm doing and nail the point home that I don't need him—or any man, for that matter.

I call out his name as my orgasm rolls through me. It's nowhere near as strong as the one he gave me earlier, but like fuck am I telling him that. My entire body is limp with exhaustion by the time I pull my vibrator away and drop it on my bedside table. I end the call on my phone, roll over, and almost instantly fall into a deep sleep.

My muscles pull and my head pounds when I roll over the next morning. Little flashes of the night before play out in my mind and I groan, knowing that I embarrassed myself once again.

Dragging my body up to sit against the headboard, I look over to my bedside table, hoping that I was sensible enough to at least get a glass of water before passing out, but no such luck.

Something cold hits my leg, and when I reach down my fingers wrap around my phone. The screen lights up and I find a missed call and four messages.

"Oh fuck." Rushing to unlock it, I drop the phone to the duvet and curse myself for drinking so much last night.

Ignoring the missed call, I go straight for the messages. My breath catches the moment I see the dick pic staring back at me. My hand flies to my mouth in shock and my eyes widen in delight. Even with his hand wrapped around it, it's fucking impressive. My core clenches and regret fills me that I didn't follow orders last night. I could have been waking up in his arms right now, not just staring at a picture of his cock.

Underneath the picture are two messages. The first is his address again, the second is one single word...*Waiting.*

Fuck if he doesn't know exactly how to get me going. I'm tempted to have another session with my battery operated friend, but when I see another message sitting on my phone from Lauren asking me to brunch, I push the idea aside and drag my sore body from the bed in favour of getting freshened up to go and gossip with my friend. I need someone to put my head on straight. Getting into something with Trey is a bad idea, and I need someone beside me to nail the point home.

Stripping out of my vest and knickers, I wait for the shower to heat and then step underneath, hoping the hot spray will help wash some of my tension away. That picture sitting on my phone is still front and centre of my mind. I need to do something to get rid of it—something besides following orders and sitting on it.

After getting myself a mug of coffee, I spend a ridiculous amount of time drying and curling my hair in an attempt to pass some time before I need to meet Lauren. I apply my make-up flawlessly, telling myself that it's pointless because under no circumstances am I going to end up at his flat.

After pulling on a black V-neck jumper and my favourite red and black tartan skirt, I dump my mug in the sink and tug my knee-length boots on my feet.

Just as I'm about to pull the front door open, Joe appears looking worse for wear from his bedroom.

"You look too good for this time of the morning," he mutters, running his hand through his messed up hair.

"It's gone ten."

"Yeah, on a Saturday. Too early. I'm surprised you're even here."

"Why? Where else would I be?"

"I had a feeling you were going to sneak out to visit your booty call."

I wasn't intending on making his message common knowledge, but before I could try and hide it, Lauren had dropped me in it to Joe, announcing that I'd been summoned to Trey's bed.

"Nope. I told you, I'm done. I need to focus on my job. Plus, he's not exactly a forever kinda guy, and I think that's what I need. It's time I stopped messing about and thought about my future."

"Whoa, when did you grow up and get all sensible and shit?"

"Since now. I've pretended I'm eighteen for long enough. I want what Ben and Lauren have."

"Don't we all." I narrow my eyes at him, still concerned with how he's taking things after their fall out. I know she says she's forgiven him, but even I can see that she's not as open with him as she once was, and he's taking it harder than he'll ever admit. "Where are you off to?"

"Meeting Lauren for brunch. Wanna join?"

"Nah, I'm gonna have a couple of strong coffees and then hit the gym. If I'm lucky I'll find a gym bunny to spend the afternoon with."

"Do you ever think about anything other than sex?"

"Do you?" My face flames red as what I did last night fills my mind. "Exactly. Wish me luck."

Laughing, I pull the front door open and head out into the hall. I'm still a bit early for meeting Lauren, but seeing as the weather's nice, I figure I'll walk and make the most of trying to clear my head of all things Trey.

I'm walking down the stairs, looking at a message that's just come through from my sister when I bump into a brick wall—or more so a hot and sweaty man chest.

"Shit, I'm so...oh fuck!"

"Erica?" he growls, sending heat racing to my centre.

"Uh..." I'm totally lost for words. He's standing before me with a pair of shorts hanging low on his hips, his sculpted chest and abs on full display and covered in a perfect sheen of sweat. His t-shirt is draped over one shoulder and his hair's wet and all over the place. But it's his eyes that really capture mine. They're dark. Darker than I've seen them before, and they hold a promise that has me squirming.

What was I just saying about forgetting about this man?

"I knew you couldn't fucking resist." In one quick move, he's got me over his shoulder, and together we're running up the stairs. His fingers dig into my arse as he holds me, my hair hanging over my head as I stare at the rippling of his back muscles every time he moves.

It's only minutes later that I hear the unlocking of a door and I'm sliding down his body.

"That sure was something special I had to wake up to this morning, sweetheart. I've been hard ever since. The sounds of you moaning are on constant repeat in my head." He reaches out for my wrist before placing my hand against his length. I can't help myself and I wrap my fingers around the width. "And I jerked off at least three times before going out."

"Trey," I whimper, my own body now trembling with need.

"It seems my reply had a similar effect. Are you ready to give in to me now?" My teeth sink into my bottom lip as I try to make sense of his words. "That's mine." He pops my lip free before slamming his down and sucking it into his mouth. He bites down and I squeal, but the pain only makes the throbbing of my pussy worse.

"You tease me and I'll tease right back, sweetheart. Now, I need what was promised to me."

"I didn't promise anything."

He doesn't respond. Instead he takes a step back, places his hands on my hips and spins me around. My face is pressed against the cushion on his sofa as he presses down on my back to bend me over the arm. With my arse in the air, I'm in the perfect position for him.

He flips my skirt up, the cool air rushing across my heated skin. His fingers grip the sides of my knickers and he tugs until the lace gives and they fall away from my body.

Kicking my feet wider, his fingers find my heated core and I moan like a whore when he presses them down on my clit.

"You really fucking liked that picture, didn't you?" I groan as he starts to circle my swollen clit. "Answer me, or I'll stop." Moisture floods my core at his demanding tone and a growl rumbles up his throat.

"Yes, yes. I loved it."

He rewards me by thrusting two fingers deep inside me. My muscles clamp around him, desperately trying to drag him deeper to hit the magic spot too.

"Greedy little bitch. You're not getting off until my cock's buried deep inside your pussy."

Holy fuck.

"Please," I moan, needing what he's just suggested right fucking now.

The rustle of fabric fills my ears before the heat of his cock presses against my clit and rubs down to my entrance.

"Trey." His name falls from my lips without me realising, a plea for him to stop teasing me and to give in to what we both need.

I don't have the chance to beg any more; his restraint must snap. Finding my entrance, he slides all the way in in one quick thrust of his hips. My feet leave the floor, his fingers bruising my hips to stop me falling completely onto his sofa.

He doesn't give me much time to adjust before he's pulling back out and slamming into me once again. His thrusts come harder and faster, telling me that maybe I made the right decision in ignoring his demands last night if it's made him this desperate for me. His balls slap against my pussy and he circles his hips, ensuring he grazes that perfect spot deep inside me.

I cry out when his palm lands on my arse cheek, pushing me closer to falling over the edge into the mind-numbing pleasure I so desperately need.

My orgasm is about to crash into me when my phone starts ringing.

"Leave it."

I panic and tense. No one ever rings me, which has me on high alert in case there's a problem.

"I need—"

"I said leave it."

Any argument I might have dies on my tongue as he grinds his hips into me. His movement reawakens my orgasm, and with only one more thrust I cry out his name as I fall over the edge. My body shakes, my muscles tensing as he continues to pound into me, desperately trying to find his own release.

I'm just coming down from my high, my body getting heavy and melding itself into the sofa cushions, when his cock swells, filling me even more than before. His roar bounces off the walls around us before his twitches inside me and the feeling of his hot cum filling me has me on the verge of another release.

"Fucking hell," he pants, folding over my back and resting his forehead against my shoulder. He's only there a few seconds before he stands and pulls out of me.

Pushing my exhausted body from his sofa, I turn to look at him. His hair's sticking up in all directions, his cheeks are pink from exertion and his lips swollen. I'm hit with a need so strong to walk into his arms that I reach down for where my bag fell on the floor when we entered and run for his front door.

"Thanks for that. It was...fun."

Throwing the door open, I run for the stairs, hoping like hell that he's not going to chase me because I'm not sure I have it in me to deny him what he so clearly wants right now.

There's a taxi idling across the street. I don't give a fuck if he's waiting for someone; I jump in the back and demand he takes me away right this second. He opens his mouth to argue but takes one look at the state of me and floors it. He probably thinks I'm trying to escape from a mad man or something, although as I sit back and think about it, it's not that far from the truth.

"Just here's fine. Thank you so, so much." I hand over more money than the journey was worth and hop out, knowing I'm a safe distance from our building now.

My shaky legs just about carry me to the wall, where I lean back against it and desperately try to suck in some much needed air.

I can't believe I just did that.

The image of him with his semi-hard dick hanging out as he watched me run for the door fills my mind. I try to fight down the little voice inside my head that's screaming for me to go back.

I did the right thing, I did the right thing, I repeat over and over again.

I probably look like a crazy person on the street right now, but I tell myself that this is London, and there are much odder people around than me.

My phone rings in my bag and it's only then that I remember it going off earlier. I rush to pull it out and breathe a sigh of relief when I see Lauren's name lighting up the screen.

"Hey, I'm sorry. I'm running a little late. I'm just around the corner."

"Okay. I'll wait to order then."

Attempting to smooth down my hair, I rub at my lips, knowing my lipstick is going to be all over my face. Trying to hold my head up high, I walk towards the café my best friend is sitting in. I need her level head right now.

CHAPTER TEN

"What happened to you?" Lauren asks the second I step up to the table.

"Trey happened."

"Couldn't resist then, huh? Temptation just too close to handle?"

Dropping down into the seat opposite her, I grab the menu and quickly make a decision before the waitress comes over. Lauren's stare burns into the top of my head the whole time.

It's not until the waitress has been and gone that she says any more. "So...didn't care to mention that you lived in the same building?"

"I was trying to ignore it. He's been stomping around above my head, taunting me, daring me to go up since the first night I met him. It's been torture."

"So why didn't you just do it?"

"I don't need a man, Lauren."

"I know, you keep saying. But, honestly, none of us *need* a man, E. Life would probably be a hell of a lot easier without one, but sometimes they're impossible to ignore. Especially when they're stomping around above your head."

"This is a fucking nightmare," I moan, dropping my head into my hands.

"Yeah, finding a hot man who's crazy about you...there's nothing worse than that."

"Don't, please. I need you to tell me that this is a bad idea. That he's going to break my heart like all the others and leave me with nothing. I'm already getting too attached, and I haven't allowed him in at all."

"You don't know any of that. Yeah, it could end in disaster but it also could be the best decision you ever make."

"I don't need to hear this," I mutter, making her laugh.

"Oh, come on. Where's the happy-go-lucky Erica who's up for anything? You used to be all about seeing where the ride took you and embracing the bumps along the way."

"She's been burned one too many times."

"You're going to allow Matt and my dad of all people to stop you from taking a chance? They were both arseholes. You can't let what happened with them stop you from living."

"What happened to you? I liked it better when you were heartbroken and hated men with a passion."

"Sorry, my heart was put back together again. Proof that happiness is out there. You just need to put your heart on the line sometimes. I told every single one of you to do anything in your power to keep me away from Ben when he first returned, but look how that turned out. There's no way I'm going to stop you doing something that might turn out to be the epic love story you crave."

"Who says I crave an epic love story?"

Her eyebrow lifts as she sits back in her chair and studies me. "Who doesn't?"

Our conversation slows as our meals arrive, but I can sense Lauren's stare every time she looks up at me.

"So tell me," I say, pushing my plate away and sitting back. "What do you think I should do?"

"I think you need to put the past behind you, forgive yourself for what happened and allow yourself a chance at happiness." Her words sound so simple, so why does even the thought of giving him a chance have my stomach tied up in knots?

"What if it's not that simple?"

"I never said it was going to be simple. You've been let down by men your entire life, I understand that. But he might be the one."

"Or he might be another one to let me down."

"Only one way to find out. Now come on, I want details from this morning. You turned up looking like you'd been fucked six ways from Sunday."

"I literally bumped into him coming back from a run as I headed down the stairs to come and meet you."

"What did he think you were doing there?"

"Following orders." Her brows pinch, so I tell her about the message exchanges we've had.

"Okay, that's kinda hot. But he still has no idea you live only a floor beneath him?"

"Not that I know of. And I'd like to keep it that way, if that's okay with you."

"Don't you think being honest might be the best way to start whatever this thing between you is?"

"And have him turning up whenever he wants, making crazy demands? No."

"Crazy demands...hot and sexy demands..." she trails off with a laugh. "Seriously though, just take it one day at a time. If he deserves your trust, he's going to have to earn it. You've been burned; he'll understand. That could be one of the benefits of an older man. Nothing wrong with a little life experience."

"Why do you have to be so level-headed?"

"Because it's happening to you. You know for a fact that I was nowhere near level-headed while Ben and I were trying to get our shit together."

"True story. More coffee?"

"Yes."

THE REST of my weekend is pretty much as it usually is, aside from the tempting footsteps from the man above my head. Joe tries to convince me to go out with him on Saturday night, but I point blank refuse to change out of my pyjamas and move off the sofa. His face was filled with disappointment, but he didn't push me on it. I think he thought I was lying and had plans with Trey. I feel guilty enough that I haven't told him Trey is actually our neighbour, so if I did have plans with him I would have owned up.

In reality, I haven't heard from Trey since I ran away from him on Saturday morning.

I expected to have had a call or at least a message, but it's been radio silence. It makes me wonder if he's happy now because he got what he needed and he's forgotten about me. I wish I could say that were true for me. Not a second's passed since leaving his flat in which I've managed to get him out of my mind.

As always, I meet my sister for our weekly yoga class on Sunday morning before heading to see Mum. It's been our routine for years now, and it's the one thing I can rely on staying the same as the rest of my life has spiralled out of control. My older sister, Samantha, has the life I crave. She's engaged to a guy who looks at her like she's his entire reason for being. He wasn't her first love, and knowing that does give me a little hope for myself. There was a time when I thought we were both too screwed up from our childhood to find a real, meaningful relationship, but thankfully she's proving me wrong. They're due to get married in a few weeks in an intimate wedding I've helped her plan. I'm looking forward to walking her down the aisle in her gorgeous white dress, but at the same time a part of me feels like she's moving on. She's been such a huge part of my life, especially during my teenage years. I know I'm being selfish, wanting to keep her to myself, but she's been my rock my entire life and I fear what I'll do if she—rightly so—moves on to have her own family.

Having fallen asleep embarrassingly early last night, I'm up at the crack of dawn and, without much else to do, I head for the office early. I expect it to still be in darkness, but, as I approach, the light from Ben's office shines brightly through the window.

A familiar voice fills my ears and a shiver runs down my spine. I don't need to hear the words he's saying; the deep timbre of his voice is enough to affect me.

"Just give her some time and a little space if she needs it. Don't be like all the other men who've been in her life."

"What does that mean?"

"Not my story to tell, man. If Erica wants you to know, she'll have to tell you herself."

My heart pounds as I listen to them talk about me. How fucking dare they? Racing forward, I push on Ben's office door so hard that it swings open and crashes back against the newly plastered wall.

"Have you two just about finished?" I snap, my eyes wide and my brows almost meeting my hairline. "You want to know something about me?" I bark, stepping closer to Trey and poking him in the chest with my index finger. "Fucking ask me. And you," I say turning my heated stare to Ben, "stay out of it. This is my life, and if I don't want to be screwing another member of this firm then I think I have a bloody good enough reason not to, wouldn't you say?" My eyes narrow at Ben and he swallows. I doubt he's scared of me; I think the only person he's scared of is Lauren, but he puts on a good show.

"I was just trying to help," he admits.

"Well, don't. I'm more than capable of looking after myself. I've damn well been doing it long enough."

Tears burn the backs of my eyes. In fear of them spilling over and showing Trey just how much of an emotional mess I really am, I turn my back on them and storm from the office.

No words are said as I make my way to the kitchen and slam the door behind me. Turning the kettle on, I allow the sob I'm fighting to keep down to break free. My eyes pool with water and, before long, tears spill down onto my cheeks.

Fuck them. Fuck all of them, I want to scream as I slam my hand down on the counter, embracing the sting of pain.

I've always been the strong one. I've never allowed anyone on the outside to see what my world was really like, to see the pain that festered inside from all the let downs and betrayals I've endured. What I don't need is for someone else, best friend or not, to be telling Trey what it is I do or do not need.

I am the one in control here. If he has problems, he needs to address me, not go behind my back.

My head's hanging between my shoulders with my palms resting on the counter when the click of the lock drags me from my nightmare. I don't look up. I don't move in the hope that whoever it is will just leave me the hell alone.

Unfortunately, that's not Ben's style. It never has been. Other than my sister, he's the only other person who really gets me, who understands what it's like. I think I knew that from the first day I looked into his eyes. They held the same shadows, the loss, the pain. He knew, and without speaking a word about what either of us had been through, it was like we just gravitated towards each other. Our shared pain was strong enough to bond us together without even understanding it. It's why it hurt so damn much when he joined the other waste-of-space men in my life and upped and left without so much as a fucking warning. Now he's back, and I have first-hand experience of what happened to make him leave. I understand his intentions, but that doesn't mean the bitter sting of being abandoned once again by someone who was meant to love me isn't still buried within me.

His warm hand wraps around my shoulder and I'm twisted around until I'm pressed up against his solid chest. His strong arms wrap around me, and I'm powerless to do anything but soak up his support and cry into his chest.

"I'm sorry, E. I wasn't trying to go behind your back or tell him anything that isn't my place to tell. I was just trying to help. To stop him being quite so full-on. I know that—"

"Enough," I whisper. Even my voice sounds broken. "It's okay. I'm sorry."

I trust Ben one hundred percent with my secrets, but that doesn't mean that what I just overheard doesn't sting, even if I know he has my best interests at heart.

Once my breathing's calmed, Ben pushes on my shoulders and moves me back slightly so he can look into my eyes.

"I know you better than you think I do, and I can tell that you're freaking out right now. You like him, that much is obvious, but you're scared—and I understand why. I can see how intense he is, and I know that's pushing you away. I was just trying to allow you a little breathing space."

Wiping the tears staining my cheeks with the back of my hand, I look up into his blue eyes and can't help but smile. My heart aches with his need to try to protect me, and I love him just that little bit more for it.

"Thank you, I do appreciate it. Things between us are..."

"Explosive?"

"Ha, yeah, you could say that. But I have no intentions on whatever it is continuing. I've screwed up here enough already. You're drowning in debt because of my last mistake. The best thing for me to do is walk away before I screw something else up for you."

"And what if you don't."

"Jesus, you sound just like Lauren," I mutter, going over to the coffee machine. If we're going to have this kind if serious conversation then I need more caffeine.

"I must be rubbing off on her."

I snort, almost dropping coffee everywhere. "I'm sure you are, boss."

"As often as I can," he says with a cheeky wink. "But that's not what I meant. Just trust us, we know what we're talking about."

"Doubtful."

"Careful. I am your boss, you know?"

"Like you're going to let me forget it."

"We good now, yeah?" He glances towards the door, probably ready to escape my emotional breakdown.

"Yeah, we're good."

"All right, well, I don't pay you to make coffee."

"Sure thing, boss." I salute him and he pulls the door open, his shoulders shaking with a laugh.

I sit down at my desk, no less confused about Trey, but after my little chat with Ben I do feel a little lighter.

After taking a cautious sip of coffee, I turn my computer on and drag my diary to the centre of the desk. Flipping it open, I stare down at what's first on my list today, but I don't get that far because written across every single day past the five o'clock line in huge bold Sharpie letters is 'TREY'.

My teeth grind as fire ignites in my veins. See, this is one reason you should never sleep with a colleague: they think it gives them the right to mess with your work day.

"Where is he?" I bark. Seeing as we're still the only two in the office, it should be obvious who I'm talking to and about.

"Gone to site. Why, you need something only he can give?"

"Fuck off." He can't see me, but I flip him off anyway.

CHAPTER ELEVEN

I managed to escape early Monday afternoon, and Tuesday he ended up stuck in a meeting so I was able to sneak off home without being caught, but I know my time avoiding him is coming to an end...and that's not just because every message and email I receive from him tells me so.

Stepping out of the office on Wednesday afternoon ready for a trip to the post office with a load of letters, I sigh in frustration when I discover the rain is harder than I was expecting. Pulling my umbrella from my bag, I'm just about to step out into the torrential downpour when a car pulls into the driveway.

Even from this distance, I see his eyes light up and a smug smile twitch at his lips. I attempt to walk past him with my head held high, but his window is down by the time I get to him.

"Get in," he demands.

"I'm good, thanks."

"Erica." His deep, gravelly voice hits me right between the legs. "You're getting wet."

"It's fine. I quite like it." His eyes glisten in delight, and I chastise myself for egging him on.

"I can put an end to that. Get in."

"I'm sure you've got plenty of work to do." I take another step, but his arm flies out and grabs mine.

"Nothing that's more important than you."

I look back at him. Our eyes meet and my resolve to stay away from him weakens.

"Fine, just drop me at the post office. It's right next to the tube station for me to get home."

"Just get in."

Following orders this time, I quickly make my way around to the passenger door and slide in once I've closed my umbrella.

"See, it wasn't that hard, was it?"

The second I shut the door, the tension between us makes it hard to breathe. The last time I was alone with him, I was bent over the arm of his sofa.

"So..." I say, tapping my hand against my thigh, not really knowing if I should be making small talk or what.

"Why'd you run?"

My head snaps over to his, my eyes wide with shock that he's diving straight into the issue.

"I...uh...got what I came for?" I don't mean it to come out as a question, but the squeak in my voice makes it sound that way.

"You really expect me to believe you made the effort to come to my flat just for that?"

"Of course. That's what a booty call is, right?"

"If you say so."

Silence descends, but it's only a few moments later when he's pulling into a parking spot right out the front of the post office.

"Thank you for the ride."

"You're more than welcome. I'm free for rides any day of the week." I try my best to ignore the innuendo, but it's easier said than done.

"I'll...uh...see you tomorrow. Thanks." Jumping from the car, I slam the door and run before he has the chance to say anything or stop me.

My heart pounds and my chest heaves like I've just run here as I stand in the queue, but that's the effect his mere presence has on me. One look at him and I'm just a ball of need. If it were true that a man could melt a woman's knickers, he'd be able to do it. Mine threaten to drop the second I look at him.

I try to convince myself that that's all it is, just a physical attraction, but as much as I try to ignore it, I know it's more than that. When I'm around him, I have this unnerving need to spill all my dark secrets in the hope that he'll take the weight of them for me. I've never in my life felt like that about another person; even the few who know the truth about my life had to drag it out of me; with him, the words are ready to just fall from my lips.

It's that knowledge that makes me keep him at arm's length. Men before him have managed to break me without the power that comes with sharing my secrets. If I were to open up, when he screws me over it'll be even more earth-shattering.

Thankfully, the rain's slowed by the time I make it back outside. Keeping my head down, I turn towards the tube station—until a very familiar and very solid wall stops me in my tracks.

"Where are you going?" he growls, his hands on my upper arms, causing sparks to shoot around my body.

Dragging my eyes up his shirt-covered chest, I find his intense steel eyes staring down at me. "Home?"

"Let me take you."

"You...you waited so you could take me home?"

"Yeah. Why is that so hard to believe?" Reaching out, he runs a lock of my hair between his fingers. He obviously doesn't expect an answer, but to be fair, if he listened to anything Ben said on Monday morning then he already knows I'm not used to guys being so...nice. I'm used to following demands, taking orders and fending for myself. This...his genuine kindness is a little unnerving. "Wouldn't you rather be in my car than sitting on a sweaty tube?"

"Of course. What are you expecting in return?" My eyes narrow as I try to figure out his angle.

He leans in. I half expect him to kiss me, but at the last minute he turns his head to the side and whispers in my ear, "Have dinner with me?"

"Dinner?"

"Yeah, dinner. You say where and we'll go."

"And then what?"

"Whatever you want."

"You just want to have dinner? No funny business?"

"Like I said, whatever you want."

Standing to his full height, his eyes flit over my face. I've no idea if he finds what he was looking for or not, but he nods his head, runs his hand down my arm and locks his fingers with mine, pulling me back to his car.

Like a real gentleman, he opens the door for me and waits until I'm settled before he closes it and makes his way to the driver's side. I drag as much air into my lungs as possible, knowing that when he joins me and closes his door it's going to suck all the air out.

"So," he asks, turning to me once he's brought the engine to life. "What do you fancy?"

You is right on the end of my tongue, but I manage to bite it back. "A curry."

"Good choice. Any particular restaurant?"

"Nope, I don't have a favourite." The one my sister and I used to order from on a weekly basis closed down a little while after we both moved out of our family home. I've not managed to find one anywhere close to its quality since.

"Lucky for you, I do and it's incredible. It's a little out of the city, though—you okay to drive for a bit?"

I probably shouldn't allow myself to be locked in this enclosed space with him for any length of time, but the promise of an incredible curry is enough to have me agreeing and getting comfortable in his soft leather seat. "As long as it's as good as you say."

"I won't let you down." I know we're talking about a curry here, but something tells me he means more than that. Butterflies dance in my belly no matter how many times I tell myself not to fall for his charm.

He'll only break you, like all the others.

HIS INDIAN OF choice is a little back street restaurant. It doesn't look much from outside, and I probably would never have chosen it if I were walking past, but after descending some stairs the most incredible dining room is revealed. We're shown to our table in a quiet corner, and the waiter leaves us for a few minutes.

"So, tell me..." I look up at Trey curiously and try to ignore the racing of my heart as I wait for the end of his sentence. "Are you the kind of girl who always has the same dish, or do you like to try different things?"

Relieved he didn't demand something more personal, a smile spreads across my face. "You tell me. What do you think?"

"I think you try it all, and the more exotic the better."

"Hmmm..." I run my eyes over the menu in front of me. "I guess you'll never know."

"I don't intend on this being our one and only meal, Erica."

"It takes two to tango, Trey, which means you'd need me to agree to this not being our one and only meal."

"I have ways to convince you."

Heat floods my belly as his eyes darken with desire. "Is that right?" My voice is husky, giving away how he really makes me feel. Lifting the menu slightly, I attempt to hide behind it but all he does is laugh at me. I fear I'm never going to be able hide from him.

The whole evening is incredible...Trey is incredible. He's thoughtful, caring, and a total gentleman. I'm afraid that I'm beginning to like him a little too much. I don't have the strength right now to have my heart smashed to pieces, but I'm having a hard time keeping it out of what's developing between us.

"Thank you so much for the meal," I say as he leads us from the restaurant, his hand tightly wrapped around mine.

"You're welcome."

He holds the car door open for me once again and helps me inside. The second he shuts the door, loneliness settles within me. It's crazy, because he's just walking around the car to get in, but knowing I'm starting to rely on how he makes me feel is unsettling.

After dropping into the driver's seat, he turns to look at me.

"What?" I ask, starting to feel a little self-conscious.

"I've no idea where you live. Point me in the right direction."

The truth is on the tip of my tongue, but a bigger part of me is scared to allow him into my life more than he already is, so, when I open my mouth, another address entirely falls from my lips.

The drive is quiet, and it makes me nervous. He's being so sweet. I know he listened to Ben's warning the other day and is trying to be more than the demanding lover I've known up until this point, but, quite honestly, he was easier to deal with like that.

I knew what he wanted, and I could give him what he needed.

Whatever this is, this getting to know each other...it scares me. If he gets to know me, that means I've allowed him in, and that gives him power.

It gives him the power to break me, and I promised myself I'd never give anyone that kind of power over me again. I can only pick myself up so many times, and I'm not sure I'd survive the level of heartache Trey could cause if I were to give him the chance.

Bringing the car to a stop, he pulls the handbrake and his stare burns into my skin.

"Thank you for a lovely evening."

He's silent for a few seconds. Thinking he's not going to say any more, I undo the seat belt and put my hand on the handle.

"Spend the weekend with me," he blurts out.

"W-what?" I stutter.

His fingers twist with mine and he tugs my arm so I have no choice but to turn back towards him. His face is deadly serious and hope shines from his eyes.

"Spend the weekend with me. Get to know the real me. Let me show you who I am, prove that you can trust me."

"Uh..." My eyes run over every inch of his face, looking for any indication that he's joking, but I find nothing.

My heart hammers against my chest as I fight to drag in the air I need, but it's like someone's suddenly sucked it all out of the car.

"I...uh...I need to go." He allows me to pull my hand from his and, as quickly as I can, I jump from the car and practically run towards the building. His eyes don't leave me the entire way to the front door, but I don't dare turn around. Instead, I pull the keys from the bottom of my bag and let myself into the ground floor flat.

"Hello?" my sister shouts, sounding a little panicked from the living room.

"It's just me."

Samantha pops her head around the doorframe, concern etched into every one of her features. "What's happened?"

"You got any wine?"

"You know it. Come on."

I follow behind her towards her kitchen, stopping on the way to say hello to her fiancé.

I sit at her small dining table as she pulls a bottle from the fridge and fills two glasses.

"So, tell me about him."

"How do you know there's a him?" She lifts a brow but doesn't say anything. "Okay, fine. Yeah, there's a him."

"I'm waiting."

"I hooked up with this guy a couple of weeks ago. Totally my type. He's—"

"An arsehole?"

"What?" My brows pinch together.

"Oh come on, Erica. We both know exactly what your type is. You've got this natural ability to pick out the utter scumbags every single time. How is this guy any different?"

My sudden need to defend Trey to my sister freaks me out. I don't really know him, so he could very well be as bad as all the others, even if deep down I really want to believe he's different.

"Anyway, he turned up at work. He's our new contracts manager."

A laugh falls from her lips. "You're kidding, right?"

"I wish."

"Jesus, Erica. How do you end up in these situations?"

"Fucked if I know."

"So now what? You've been with him again, I assume?"

My face heats. "He just took me out for dinner and asked me to spend the weekend with him."

"Okay. So...why are you here?"

"He wanted to take me home, but I gave him your address instead."

"Why?" she asks, confusion written all over her face.

I pause briefly, wondering if I should tell her the truth. In the end, I do with a half-truth. "I don't want him getting too close."

"So he thinks you live here?"

"I guess so."

"What did you say about the weekend?"

"I didn't. I ran."

"Fucking hell, Erica."

CHAPTER TWELVE

Although Trey hasn't said anything about the weekend, I can see the question written all over his face every time he looks at me. I hate it. I've no idea what I should do. I hate everything right now. I hate that he seems to be giving me the space that I thought I needed, and I hate that he's no longer the demanding lover that he was at the beginning. I fear he's softening, and fuck if it wasn't his demanding attitude that made him so damn irresistible in the first place.

It's just after lunchtime when he disappears out of the office for a site visit, and I pull my phone from my bag. Seeing a missed call from my sister hours ago, I return it straight away.

"I've got something pretty impressive for you."

"Sorry, I'm not into chicks," I say with a laugh. If it were Trey's deep voice saying those words, I'd damn near lose my shit.

"Ha, you're funny. Has lover boy said anything to you?"

"Not really, he's been pretty quiet actually. Why?"

"Because I've got the biggest bunch of flowers I think I've ever seen sitting in my living room, and they've got your name on them."

"Shut the fuck up. You're joking, right?"

"Nope. You need to come and get them before Cliff starts thinking I'm having an affair weeks before our wedding."

"He'd never think that, but I'll stop by after work."

"I'm sending you a picture now. You need to see them."

"Okay, see you later."

I've barely hung up when my phone vibrates with a picture.

"Fucking hell," I mutter to myself, my eyes widening in shock at the sheer number of flowers. Another picture comes through, and it's of the back of the card.

> Trey: 10am Saturday morning. Pack a bag.

Excitement and fear hit my stomach, making it turn over. Spending the weekend with him is dangerous, but can I say no?

Before leaving for the day, I check the calendar. He's booked in for a meeting with Ben after work. Knowing he'll be coming back any minute, I make a rash decision.

Grabbing a Sharpie from the pen pot on his desk, I find tomorrow in his diary and write across it, much like he did in mine last week.

> Erica: See you soon. E x

A bolt of excitement races through me and, before I can change my mind and rip the page from his diary, I run from the office.

"WHOA, WHO'D YOU PISS OFF?" Joe asks once I've fought my way into our flat with the giant arrangement of flowers I picked up from my sister's.

"I love how you think I must have annoyed someone to receive something like this," I sulk, dropping them to the kitchen counter and shaking out my arms.

"Why else would someone...wait? Do not tell me Trey sent them?"

"What do you think?"

"I think he's not the kind of guy to do romantic shit like that." He plucks the card from the middle and flips it over. "Ha, see. It's just a fancy booty call. You really spending the weekend with him?"

"Yes. No. Maybe." The whole way home, I regretted pretty much agreeing to it, although I've no way of knowing if he's seen my note.

"Want to come out for a drink to help you decide?"

"Nah, I think I'll stay in, have a bath or something."

"Erica Wilde refusing a drink on a Friday night. What is happening right now?"

"Oh shut up. It's not that unusual." His raised eyebrow tells me that it really is, but I ignore it. I need to decide what I'm going to do, and going out and getting drunk is not going to help making a rational decision.

"Oh wait...you're going to spend the night pruning, ready for your hot weekend, aren't you?" His eyes drop between my legs inquisitively.

"Nope. That's already been taken care of, thank you very much."

"I'm sure he'll appreciate that. Well, if you're being a boring bitch, I think I'll leave you to it."

"Have fun," I call when he gets to the front door. "And if you bring someone home, make sure they're quiet."

"You'd better hope I bring someone home, otherwise I'll be coming after you, it's been so fucking long."

Laughing at him, I wish him luck and watch him disappear.

I spend the entire night trying to decide if I should pack a bag or not. My body says 'fuck yes'; it's begging for that amount of one-on-one time with Trey, but my head is screaming something very different. I just don't know which one is shouting louder, and I can't deny that what my body wants is so fucking tempting.

***

I WAKE LATER than I was expecting the next morning, after a fitful night's sleep full of indecision and dirty dreams. The second I swing my legs off the side of the bed, I know what I need to do.

Dragging my suitcase from the top of my wardrobe, I make quick work of stuffing everything I might need inside before having a very quick shower, curling my hair, applying my make-up and sliding my favourite dress up my body. I want to look sexy without looking like I've put too much effort into it.

After sending my sister a text so she's expecting me, I make myself a coffee in my travel mug and set off. I'm already running a little late. The last thing I want is for him to think I decided against his offer after all of this.

I'm a nervous wreck by the time the taxi pulls up outside my sister's house. My palms are sweating and I swear a zoo full of fucking butterflies have taken up residence in my stomach. The journey took longer than it usually would, thanks to some festival in the local park.

"You look like you're about to puke," my sister helpfully points out when she lets me in.

"I need to pee."

Her laughter follows me down to her bathroom, where I have another nervous wee before joining her in the living room. I sit on the chair in front of the window so I can see the second he pulls up.

"I'm not sure I've ever seen you so unsure of yourself."

"Not helping," I mutter, my eyes glued to the window.

"I know I've not met this guy, but something tells me he's different."

Now that gets my attention. "Different how?"

"*You're* different. Although you're nervous as shit right now, I can't help feeling like something's settled inside you."

Narrowing my eyes at her cryptic statement, I turn back to the window. "That's all well and good, whatever it's meant to mean, but where the hell is he? It's almost ten past."

"I'm sure he's coming. You said yourself that the traffic was bad."

Blowing out a slow breath, I tell myself that she's right. He'll be here.

By twenty past ten, I'm starting to lose my shit. I spent all night worrying about this and he hasn't even bothered to show his face. *Was it all one big joke?*

"Has he tried ringing? Where's your phone?"

Pulling my bag from the floor, I slide my hand into the pocket where it lives. Empty. *Shit.* Rummaging through each pocket, my heart starts to race.

"I can't find it."

Dropping to my knees, I open my little suitcase and start pulling everything out in case it got tangled in something.

"Shit, shit, shit." Huffing out a frustrated breath, I try to think of when I last had it while surrounded by the contents of my case. "It's next to the fucking coffee machine."

"He's probably rung to say he's running late or something. Just chill, yeah?"

"Yeah," I agree although I feel anything but chilled right now.

I'm just about to start stuffing everything back into my case when the buzzer rings loudly throughout the flat. My eyes widen in panic as I look at Sam, who's moving to look out the window.

"It's him. I'll go—"

"No," I whisper-shout. "Do not open the door."

"Why?"

"He still thinks I live here."

Shaking her head at me, my sister drops to her knees to help me collect up all my stuff and attempt to get it back inside my case. "You do know you're only going for one night, right?" she asks, counting the number of knickers I flung across her living room.

"You never know how many you'll need on a dirty weekend."

"TMI, lil' sis." I can't help but laugh at the horrified look on her face—that is, until the buzzer goes off again.

"Shit."

"Go fucking answer it, then."

"Okay, okay." Smoothing down my hair, I wheel my case out into the hallway. "Hide!" Sam puts her hands up in defeat and backs into the room, out of sight.

I take a second to attempt to compose myself, but after the last ten minutes I think it might be a lost cause.

I flick the lock but don't get a chance to pull the door open because it's done for me. He takes one look at me and steps a little closer, concern filling his steel eyes.

"What's wrong?"

My forehead wrinkles. "Nothing, why?"

"I've been trying to call you, and you look at bit harassed."

"I'm fine. I left my phone at..." I trail off just in time to catch myself before I admit that I don't live here. "At Joe's."

A noise from behind me forces me to look over my shoulder. All I can do is roll my eyes at my sister who's still hidden from Trey, but I can clearly see her alternating between fanning herself and putting her thumbs up.

"As long as you're okay." When I look back, his eyes are following mine.

"I'm really good. Shall we go?" Placing my hand on his chest, his eyes immediately come back to me, darkening as our gaze holds for a few seconds. I'm beginning to get used to the sparks between us, and the butterflies that had settled in my stomach slightly take flight again.

"This bag?" he asks, nodding down to my little case.

"That's the one." Following him out, I stop to pull the door closed and find my sister making very inappropriate gestures at Trey's back. Flipping her off, I close the door and run to catch up with him.

"Where are we going?" I ask once we're settled and he's pulled away from the curb.

"It's a surprise."

"It's a kinky sex den, isn't it?" The deep laugh that fills the car warms me all the way to my toes. It tells me that I made the right decision in agreeing to spend time with him, although it also confirms that if—when—this goes south, it's going to hurt like hell.

***

"I ALWAYS THOUGHT these places would be in a basement or some old warehouse in the middle of no here," I say when he pulls down a long driveway with only grass and fields as far as I can see.

"I'm sure they probably are. I wouldn't know, I've not been."

"I'm not sure if I'm relieved or disappointed," I admit with a laugh. "Holy shit." My breath catches as we hit the top of the small hill we were climbing and the hotel he's brought us to is revealed.

"Stunning, isn't it?"

"It's...it's really something."

"What's wrong? Don't you like it?" He pulls the car to a stop and turns towards me. My eyes stay on the grand building in front of us, afraid to look his way and exposing my anxiety.

"I...uh...I don't fit in in a place like this. I don't have the kind of money these people do or own the kind of clothes they wear. I'm just not—"

"Erica," he interrupts. His warm fingers brush across my cheek, and I'm forced to turn to look at him, although I keep my eyes downcast. "Look at me." I follow his demand like always and meet his hard eyes. "You're already the most beautiful woman staying in this hotel. I don't even need to get out of the car to know that. You don't need money or designer clothes to fit in in a place like this. You just need to have confidence. I know you have plenty —it's one of the things I find so sexy about you. Hold your head up high, because I can guarantee that every man in that place is going to be jealous that you're here with me and sleeping in my bed tonight."

Tears burn, but I refuse to allow them to fill my eyes. I won't allow him to see my vulnerability and insecurities.

"Okay. Lead the way."

With his hand possessively in the small of my back, he walks us towards the entrance. The huge white building is by far the fanciest I've ever been in, let alone stayed in.

"Good morning, how can I help you?" The receptionist gives Trey her megawatt smile, and I can't help but step a little closer to him when her eyes drop to check him out. It's a move that doesn't go unnoticed by him, and he drops a kiss to the top of my head to really nail the point home.

"We have a room booked under Bennett."

She taps away on her keys before producing a key and pointing us in the direction of our room.

"It's on the top floor?" I ask when he presses the button in the lift.

"It is, and it's nothing less than you deserve." My blush heats my cheeks and spreads down my neck. I've never in my life been treated like this, and I've no idea how to take it.

"I've never stayed in a place like this before. No one's ever taken me anywhere, in fact." The words are out of my mouth before I realise I said them aloud.

As he turns to me, the intensity in his eyes forces me to take a step back until I bump into the handrail.

"Then it's time I showed you how you should be treated." His hand wraps around the back of my neck and I'm powerless but to move towards his lips when his head dips. His lips brush mine in the gentlest of kisses, so alien to the harsh and dominant ones I've experienced from him before.

My heart races and my skin tingles with the need for more. Unfortunately, when the lift announces our arrival, all he does is take my hand and lead me out.

The room he takes me to is beyond my wildest dreams. It's got the biggest bed I've ever seen, covered in the most luxurious gold and cream sheets. All the furniture is huge and made of solid wood, but the space is so big that they almost look too small. The best bit is the french doors which lead to a balcony that looks out over the grounds.

"I think I might move in," I say, spinning around, trying to take it all in.

"You might need to win the lottery first." His mention of how much this might have cost has guilt sitting heavy in my stomach. "Don't," he warns, walking over and taking my cheeks in his hands.

"Don't even think about it. Trust me when I say that if I didn't want this, I wouldn't have done it. I only ever do things because *I* want to. So don't be feeling guilty or any of that shit. Just relax and enjoy what I have planned."

"And what do you have planned?" My eyes flick over to the bed behind me and he chuckles.

"You'll have to wait and see, but right now, there should be a chilled bottle of champagne waiting for us on the balcony. Join me?"

He holds his hand out and I've no choice but to slide mine into it and follow him out. He's right, of course. Tucked beside the giant outdoor sofa is a chrome wine cooler with one very expensive bottle of bubbles inside. He lifts the blanket that's waiting for us and gestures for me to sit.

Dropping down, I allow the early winter sun to warm my skin and watch with delight as Trey pulls the bottle from the ice and sets about popping the top. The muscles of his exposed forearms strain, and an ache starts up low in my belly.

"The view's really quite incredible, right?" His eyes are locked on the scenery beyond, but I'm convinced he must be able to feel my hungry stare.

"Sure is." Turning back towards me, his eyes are dark, the muscle in his neck pulsating. Starting at my eyes, he drops his gaze down, taking in every inch of my body and running over the exposed skin of my thighs before finding my boots.

My body heats, my core throbbing to feel his hands on me. But instead of acting out any of the fantasies currently running rampant in my mind, he just hands me a glass of champagne before holding his out.

"To us."

"To us." My voice is barely more than a breathy whisper, and I swear his eyes get even darker. He knows exactly what I want, and it's frustrating the hell out of me that he's not taking what I'm so clearly desperate for.

"Drink up. We've got plans."

TWO HOURS LATER, I find myself in the building's basement wrapped in the thickest, softest white robe I've ever touched, having just had the most relaxing facial. Stepping out from the treatment room, I find Trey dressed exactly the same and resting back in a chaise longue with another glass of bubbles.

"Fancy seeing you here." His eyes snap up to mine before dropping to my exposed legs.

I fall down beside him. He hands me a glass and then takes my hand, tangling his fingers with mine.

"Thank you for all this. It's...incredible."

"It's about to get better."

"Really?" Biting down on my bottom lip, I think about what would make this experience complete, but when my dirty thoughts are interrupted by a therapist, I realise that's not what's happening—not yet, anyway.

"It's time for your couple's massage. If you'd like to follow me."

I glance at Trey as he stands and pulls me up with him. As soon as I'm at full height, his free arm wraps around my waist, pulling me against him. His cheek brushes against mine, his day old stubble sending sparks shooting off around my body. "I promise it'll be so worth it."

I sag against him and he chuckles in my ear before stepping back and finding my hand. I feel lost without his body pressed up against mine, and that little warning about how much I'm enjoying him starts screaming at me once again.

My head spins as I walk towards him. I've only had two half

glasses, but add that to the desire coursing through my body and my lack of breakfast and I guess the bubbles have gone straight to my head.

"You okay?" Trey asks, looking back when I sway slightly on my feet.

"Yeah, I'm good."

"We'll eat after this. Soak up some of that alcohol."

I nod and smile at him, hoping not to give away just how tipsy I'm feeling all of a sudden.

We're directed into a room very much like the one I had my facial in only minutes ago. It's filled with flickering scented candles, and soft, relaxing music filters through the air.

"If you would both like to get yourselves comfortable on the tables, my colleague and I will be back in a few minutes to get started. He smiles at both of us and quietly steps from the room.

"What are we sup—" My words stop as Trey drops his robe to the floor. My teeth sink into my bottom lip as my eyes trail over every inch of his exposed skin. *Do they have to come back in?*

"Yeah they do." His words make my eyes snap up to his. I had no idea I'd asked that question aloud and, from the amusement in his dark eyes, I'd say he's aware of that fact. "Hurry up. I don't want anyone else's eyes on more of you than totally necessary."

His words only touch on how demanding he can be, but they have the same effect. Heat pools between my legs and my breath picks up pace.

"Don't make me lock that door and take matters into my own hands."

Holy shit.

I'm a second away from begging that he does just that when there's a knock at the door.

"Two minutes," Trey calls out before stepping up to me. His

fingers find the knot at my waist and, in one quick movement, it's undone and he's pushing the fabric from my shoulders.

It pools at my feet, leaving me totally naked. His eyes drop to my breasts and my nipples tighten almost painfully.

A low rumble of a moan escapes him, and I instantly get wetter for him. I'm about three seconds from begging him to touch me when he takes a step back and orders for me to lie on the bed as we were instructed.

It takes me a couple of seconds to get my body to function as it should, something I think Trey notices if his smug smirk is anything to go by as he lifts the towel and places it over my bare body, going over to do the same to himself.

My entire body is alive with desire. I tilt my head to the side and find that Trey's doing exactly the same and staring right at me. He might not be voicing his demands today like I've become used to, but his power and dominance ooze from his steel grey eyes and it makes my stomach tighten with anticipation.

Before long, there's another knock at the door, and after Trey calls out to say we're ready we're joined by two masseuses. One look at them and I breathe a sigh of relief when I notice the man walk over to Trey. I'm not sure how I'd have coped seeing another woman with her hands all over him. A wave of jealousy like I've never known washes through me, making my teeth clench and my muscles to lock up tight. The lady standing beside me says a few things and I agree, but I've no idea what she's talking about; I'm too busy watching the guy walking around Trey.

After a few seconds, her warm hands land on my left leg and I just about manage to contain a moan of pleasure as her nimble fingers press into the flesh. I've never had a professional massage before, and I already know from one touch alone that it's going to be incredible.

I intend on watching Trey, but it's not long until my eyes start getting heavy and I'm forced to put my head in the little hole it's intended for.

The masseuse makes her way up to my back and I lose the fight. The soft music and gentle touch are too much on top of last night's sleepless night.

My eyes fly open the moment his fingers touch me. Every single part of my body is aware of the difference, of the electric current that's always sparking between us.

"Relax," he orders. "It's my time to have some fun."

At hearing his demanding voice, my body melts back into the bed I've been sleeping on for the past however long as the wonderful lady behind me worked out all of my kinks.

I smirk.

Trey is one kink she'll have to work a lot harder to get rid of.

Cool air hits my skin as he lifts the towel from me and drops it to the floor.

"Hmmm," he moans before his palm drops to squeeze the fullness of my arse. My core tightens.

I gasp when the warmth of his breath tickles my ear. My entire body is on fire and waiting for him to do something.

"Do you like happy endings, Erica?"

"I...ahhh." He doesn't give me the chance to answer properly because his fingers trail down my arse, he teases the puckered hole before dropping lower until he finds my entrance.

"So wet," he murmurs, his finger circling and driving me crazy for more.

"Please, Trey. Please," I beg, lifting my hips from the bed and trying to force him deeper. "I need...I need..."

"I know exactly what you need. And you'll get it...eventually." His lips start at the base of my neck and trail down my spine, causing goose-bumps in their wake. "I need to taste you," he admits when his lips hit the fullness of my behind.

His hands grip my hips and I squeal as he effortlessly flips me over. Shifting to the end of the bed, his fingers wrap around my ankles and I'm pulled down until I'm hanging over the edge. He drops to his knees and places my feet on his shoulders while pushing his hands on the inside of my thighs and opening me for him.

"Beautiful." My cheeks heat at knowing he's studying my pussy quite so intently. Propping myself up on my elbows, I look down at him. His eyes flick up to mine and the desire in them almost has me crashing back to the bed. I do exactly that the moment he leans forward and licks up the length of me.

"Fuck."

Pressing my legs even wider, he licks at me until my entire body is trembling with the need for him to push me over the edge, but every time I so much as get close he pulls back.

"Yes," I cry. This is exactly what I've needed since the moment he pushed the door open at my sister's. I need him to give me everything he's got. "Trey, please." My heart races and I have to fight to drag in the air I need as my focus is solely on the orgasm that's imminently going to crash through me.

Two thick fingers press into me. It's almost enough to have me flying, but he stills before sliding deeper, stopping me from falling over the edge. Not once does his tongue stop lapping at me—not that he can go far with my fingers twisted in his hair, holding him against me.

The second his fingers are as deep as they'll go, he bends them and hits my G-spot without any effort. It's like he knows my body almost as well as he does his own.

Every muscle in my body tightens, ruining all that woman's work before I snap. Lights flash behind my eyes and my body trembles as an earth-shattering release races through me. Trey's movements don't falter, ensuring I ride out every pleasurable second.

Once it subsides and my pussy stops clenching around him, he pulls back and out, lifting his fingers to his lips and sucking them into his mouth. His eyes roll back as he tastes me on himself. Little after-shocks flutter in my core, just watching him. I'm so ready for more, but unfortunately, once he's done, he stands and grabs his robe. His cock bobs, rock hard in front of him, but he refuses any offer I make to return the favour. It confuses and frustrates me in equal measures because it's obvious he needs it, but he won't allow himself the pleasure. Instead, he takes my hand and takes me back up to our room to get ready for dinner.

CHAPTER THIRTEEN

I shower alone after Trey point-blank refused my offer to him of joining me, even though desire still filled his eyes and his cock was still tenting his robe.

I tried to fight the ball of emotion clogging my throat as I showered, but the more I tried to rid myself of it the stronger it became, until I found myself sobbing, hoping to get it all out while I was alone.

I take a long time getting ready. I fear what I might find on the other side of the door when I eventually pull it open. Has he changed his mind about me? Is he regretting bringing me here?

By the time my hair and make-up are done, I feel a little stronger. I tell myself that he isn't the kind of man to do anything he doesn't want to, so if he no longer wanted me here then I've no doubt he'd tell me and send me on my way. Blowing out a long breath, I wrap my fingers around the handle and pull it open. He's standing by the balcony, already dressed in a pair of black trousers and a perfectly pressed white shirt, despite the fact it's been packed in his bag for most of the day.

He hears me coming and turns to look over his shoulder. His eyes widen before they dilate. He turns his entire body my way as his eyes drop from mine to take in my body. He still wants me, that much is clear, so why won't he give me what I need?

My body heats as he takes in the trusty little black dress I shoved in my case, not knowing where we were going or what I'd need.

"You look beautiful." Walking over, he reaches for my hand and pulls it to his lips so he can kiss my knuckles. The gentlemanly move has my earlier emotion threatening to climb back up my throat.

"You're looking pretty sharp yourself."

"I'm nothing in comparison to you. Everyone is going to wonder why you're here spending time with me."

"Shut up, no they won't. They'll all be aware that you're my sugar daddy." It's meant to be a joke, but the way it comes out makes it sound anything but.

"That is not what this is," Trey says forcefully. His hand wraps around the back of my neck, his fingers twisting in the hair there, and his forehead drops to mine. "I really like you, Erica." His eyes bore into mine as my heart starts to race.

"I—"

"Shhh." His fingers press against my lips. "You don't need to say anything. Just let me prove to you that I'm worthy."

My forehead wrinkles. It's not the first time he's said that, and it makes me wonder what he knows about me—or what he thinks he knows. Neither option makes me happy.

"Are you hungry?"

"Ravenous." I hold back that the thing I'm ravenous for is him, because with my nipples pressing against the fabric of my dress and my increased breaths, I'd like to think he's already aware.

What he gave me earlier in the therapy room only took the edge off. What I really need is him, all of him, and soon.

"Yeah," he chuckles, "I'm starving, too." His eyes drop from mine in favour of my lips, but he doesn't move to kiss them. "Come on." Pulling back, he takes my hand once again and pulls me towards the door. I want to stomp my foot like a child and demand he give me what we both so badly need, but, wanting to look like the mature and in control adult I am, I refrain and instead follow his lead.

We're shown to a secluded table in the back of the restaurant and Trey orders us a fancy bottle of champagne before we silently choose what we'd like to eat. My stomach summersaults with the confusion that's running rampant in my head, and I struggle to find the desire to eat anything, but when the waiter comes back I give him my order, hoping I look excited about it.

Trey eyes me curiously across the table. He sits back and studies me for a few seconds once we're alone again, sipping on his drink, deep in thought.

"Tell me, how'd you end up at Johnson & Sons? You don't seem the kind of girl who's always wanted a career in construction."

Taking a sip at my own drink, I consider how much I want to reveal about my life. "I'd dropped out of uni and needed a job. I sent out about a million CV's and they were the first to come back to me. I started the very next week."

"Why'd you drop out of uni?"

Sighing, I think back to how hard times were back then. "I couldn't afford to stay. It was kind of a pipe dream, really. I'm surprised I even managed the few months I did."

His eyes narrow as if he's trying to read more than the words I'm saying. I try to keep my expression neutral.

"What were you studying?"

"Business management and accounting."

"Do you regret it?"

I consider his question, because I'm not sure I have a simple answer. "Yes and no."

"Oh?"

"Yes because I'd have loved to be the first person in my family to graduate. I wanted to break the mould, smash anyone's preconceptions about my life and capabilities. It might have led me down a different path that would have hopefully meant less pain. No because...I'd never have met Lauren, Ben and the others and—"

"Me?" I can't help but laugh at the hopeful look on his face.

"Verdict's still out on that."

"Ouch." His hand comes up to cover his wounded heart. "I see how it is."

I fight the words that are on the tip of my tongue, but they tumble out, consequences be damned. "Things for me haven't always been easy. I need to know I'm surrounded by people I can trust, but gaining my trust isn't simple. I've been burned too many times by people who should care."

He nods and opens his mouth to say more, but the waiter arrives with our starters.

Thankfully, Trey changes the subject to lighter topics. It's obvious that he just wants to learn more about me as he asks about my favourite films, music and food, but the little voice in the back of my mind still screams *why?* Why does a man like him want anything to do with a girl like me?

Dinner is incredible, just like the rest of today. I hate to think about how much this must be costing him. I still feel like a total fraud, being here surrounded by all these wealthy and put-together people while I feel like my world is once again on rocky ground.

Without wanting to, I've given Trey power.

He might not yet be able to shatter my heart into a million pieces, although I'm sure that won't be long, but if he were to turn around and tell me this was all one big joke then it would seriously hurt.

Worrying my bottom lip, I allow a large sigh to pass my lips, but it doesn't go unnoticed.

"What's wrong?"

"Nothing. This has been incredible, thank you so much."

"You don't look like you're enjoying yourself right now." His brows draw together and I chastise myself for being so transparent. I'm normally good at wearing a mask and hiding everything I'm feeling, but I have an inkling this man sees straight through that.

"No, I really am. I just can't help feeling like I don't fit." I look around at all the couples surrounding us. Most are at least ten years older than me. Trey fits in with his designer shirt and dominant demeanour, but me? Not so much.

"Everything I said earlier still stands. You're the most beautiful woman in this room. You belong here just as much as everyone else. Are you done?" He nods down to my empty coffee cup and I smile.

"Yeah." I'm so ready to have him all to myself and get what I've been waiting for all day.

"Fancy going for a walk?"

"Oh...uh...sure?"

With his hand on the small of my back, he guides me out of the hotel and into the brisk early winter evening.

"Here, it's cold." Shrugging off his jacket, he drapes it over my shoulders and pulls me to him.

Cuddled up against his side, I walk with him, enjoying the fresh air and his company, although it's not quite what I'd hoped we'd be doing by now.

We walk in a comfortable silence with the stars twinkling above us for the longest time. I almost miss the peacefulness of it when we eventually head back inside and up to our room.

"I just need to go and freshen up."

"Sure, take all the time you need."

Grabbing a few things from my suitcase, I lock myself in the bathroom and try to put all my doubts about this and him to the back of my mind. I want a night full of everything he can give me. Just two bodies and as much pleasure as we can manage before we pass out. I want our first night, the intensity that came with not knowing each other and the excitement of knowing it was only for a few hours.

Slipping out of my clothes, I pull my black lace nighty up my legs and rearrange my boobs so they look pert behind the fabric. I quickly reapply my red lipstick and fluff up my hair a little.

Once I'm happy, I pull the door open and wait for his eyes to find me.

I'm not disappointed. When they do, they widen and darken simultaneously.

"Fucking hell, Erica." My skin burns everywhere his eyes touch. All I can do is stand there and allow him to take his fill.

He's sitting on the edge of the bed in only his boxers, so I get to take in the view just as much as he does.

"Come here," he says, flipping the duvet over and patting the mattress. Disappointment floods me. Where is my dominant lover? Why's he not demanding that I get on my knees and suck him until he's dry?

Still, I follow his orders and climb onto the bed as sexily as I can. The second I'm lying down, he's beside me, wrapping his arm around my waist and pulling me back into him.

"Thank you for coming with me," he whispers in my ear as my blood starts to boil.

He just wants to fucking cuddle?

I lie still for a few seconds, hoping that this is a joke. He's acted like a perfect gentleman all day—aside from the incident on the massage table.

What the hell's going on?

This isn't the man I went home with that night or have been working beside the past couple of weeks. What. The. Hell?

When all he does is hold me tighter, I decide I need to take matters into my own hands if I'm going to end this day satisfied. His hard cock presses into my arse cheek so I know he's up for this.

Flipping over, I push my palm against his shoulder. His eyes widen in surprise but I swear his lips twitch up into a small smile. He allows me to move him, and the second I throw my leg over his waist, his hands land on my hips.

"What?" I snap when he looks up at me with amusement filling his eyes.

"Nothing. Have at it." His thumbs stroke across my hip and dip down to where my thighs meet. My core clenches, ready for what's about to come.

I grind down on him and his eyes flutter in pleasure. I knew he was just as on edge as I was.

Lifting up a little, I free him and take him in my hand. I lower myself onto his cock and we both moan as I sink down as far as I can go.

"Yesss," I hiss when he hits me so deep it borders on painful.

Placing my hands on his solid chest, I use him for leverage so I can lift almost all the way off before sinking straight back down.

The longer I look at him, the more I see the tension on his face. His lips press into a thin line, and the muscle in his neck pulses. He might be allowing me to take control right now, but he's not happy about it.

Tingles of my impending orgasm start to build almost

immediately. I don't bother worrying if he's with me; selfishly, I focus solely on what I need. Hopefully it'll help pull him out of the nice act he's been putting on all day. Of course I want a nice guy beneath it all, but on the surface I need a little more rough around the edges. I need the arsehole I know is hiding within those steel eyes.

Grinding my hips, I ensure he hits me exactly where I need it and, after only a few seconds, my pussy pulls him even deeper as my orgasm rocks my body. I throw my head back as I cry out his name, my hips slowing as I lose control of my muscles. Taking matters into his own hands, his fingers dig into my hips and he pistons in and out of me a few more times before his cock swells and his cum fills me.

Falling down onto him, both our chests heave as we try to catch our breaths.

"Fuck, yes," Trey says into the top of my head. If I weren't suddenly so exhausted I might tell him it's exactly what I've needed all day, too, but instead my eyes close and I fall fast asleep, still on top of him.

CHAPTER FOURTEEN

My heart drops when I reach out for him and all I find is an empty bed where he once slept. Propping myself up on my elbows, I cast my eyes around the room but he's not there. It's not until I register the sound of running water coming from the bathroom that my sleep-fogged brain realises where he is.

Slipping from the bed, I untwist my nighty from around my waist and head over, hoping that I'll find him in the waterfall shower.

Pushing the door open, I have to do a double-take at the sight before me. Trey is bent over a bath full of white fluffy bubbles, lighting candles that litter every surface of the room.

"What are you doing?"

"Oh, you're awake. I was coming to get you once I'd finished this."

"And what is this?"

"It's a bath...for you."

My frustration at how he's been acting suddenly gets the better of me. I don't mean to snap, but it's like I've lost control of my mouth. "Yeah, I can see that. But why? Why are you doing this, being all nice all of a sudden, treating me like I'm something special? What's the catch?"

"The catch?" His brows draw together as he looks between the bath and me, confused.

"Yeah. The catch. What do you want from me out of all this?"

"I don't want anything, Erica. I'm just being nice."

"That's bullshit. Every man wants something. It clearly isn't sex, because you were quite happy to go without last night. So what is it?"

"I just wanted to treat you, to make you happy."

"Not possible. I've never met a man who didn't have an ulterior motive, so come on, just admit it. You might as well confess now so I can decide if I want to continue with this charade any longer."

Trey's mouth opens like he has something he wants to say, but he closes it again, changing his mind. He takes a step toward me and I put my hands up to stop him. He pauses immediately, his eyes softening the longer he looks at me.

"Erica," he breathes, "I don't have an ulterior motive. I wanted to spend the weekend with you and get to know each other better. That really is it."

Tears burn the back of my throat and my eyes fill with water. "I don't believe you."

"Tough, because it's the truth." His voice is hard and it gives me a little hint of the man I thought I knew before this weekend. "I was trying to show you that not all men are arseholes. I was trying to be nice."

My emotions get the better of me and a sob bubbles up my

throat. "Get out." My voice is barely above a whisper, but it doesn't need to be any louder. Trey gets the message loud and clear.

His shoulders drop, his eyes roaming over my face, trying to work me out, but thankfully he doesn't question me. He just nods once and walks past me, closing the door behind him.

Falling down on to the edge of the bath, I suck in a few lungfuls of air, hoping my random onslaught of tears subsides.

It's all Trey's fault.

He's playing with my emotions.

It's exactly why I didn't want to allow him to get too close in the first place. Now here I am, freaking out that he isn't what he says he is while desperately wanting to believe him. But trusting a man is dangerous. I've experienced that enough to know that I should never put my heart on the line. It's just not worth it.

I make the most of the bath because, despite what I said, it really was a nice thing to do. I need to thank him properly when I get out.

I take off yesterday's make-up and moisturise my entire body, anything to put off going out there and facing him after my meltdown. I'm stronger than to allow a man to affect me like this.

The room is empty when I cautiously step out. Thinking I've got a little reprieve from whatever he's going to say after showing him that side of me, I walk over to my case and drag out some clothes.

I've just pulled my t-shirt over my head when something out on the balcony catches my eye. Trey's sitting out there wearing a thick jumper and holding a steaming mugful of coffee in his hands, but that's not what really grabs my attention. It's the tableful of food in front of him. My stomach rumbles despite the three-course meal we consumed last night, and I put my concerns about seeing him to the back of my mind in favour of one of the pastries sitting in front of him.

His eyes fly to me the second I step out onto the balcony. He must have heard me moving around in the room, but he allowed me the space I needed, something I'm very grateful for.

"How are you feeling?" Genuine concern fills his voice, and it makes me hate myself a little for accusing him of wanting something more than this from me.

"Better, thank you. This looks delicious."

"I wasn't sure what you'd want, so I asked for a selection of everything."

"It's really incredible." Reaching for a pastry, I waste no time in taking a bite and allowing the buttery goodness to melt on my tongue. I moan in pleasure and watch Trey's eyes darken.

"That good?" he asks, clearing his throat.

"Almost that good. Bite?"

"Sure."

I hold it up to his mouth and I'm fascinated as his full lips wrap around the sweet treat. My thighs clench, thinking back to those lips being on me only yesterday.

"Good, right?" I ask, trying to focus on the here and now.

He nods as he chews.

As we eat our way through about a week's worth of calories, I can see the million and one questions that fill his mind. I'm more grateful than I'd ever admit that he keeps them to himself.

The silence between us isn't awkward, but it's also not as comfortable as it has been in the past. I only have myself to blame.

"What did you want to do today?" he asks when the silence has stretched on a little too long.

"Well...um...I actually need to visit someone. It's something I do every Sunday morning, and she'll be expecting me, so I'm going to have to bail on any plans."

"I didn't have any plans. Can I take you?"

"Um..." The thought of showing him the side of my life that I try to keep buried has my heart racing, but the look of hope on his face stops me from denying him. I already feel bad enough about what happened in the bathroom, and I feel like I somehow need to make up for it.

"Sure. But then you can go and make the most of your day. I don't want to keep you longer than necessary."

His mouth opens to reply, but he must change his mind because in the end, all he does is nod.

It's no time at all before we're checking out and heading towards Trey's car. I hate that I've ruined our last few hours here, but there's not a lot I can do about it now. I've got a date to keep. Searching for the postcode on my phone, I plug it into Trey's Satnav and he's soon pulling out onto the main road and heading towards our destination.

"Who are you going to see?"

I hesitate, not sure if I want to open up about it or not, but seeing as he's going to see where we're headed in less than thirty minutes, I guess there's no point hiding it. "My mum. My sister and I usually do a yoga class together and then go and see her every Sunday."

"That's nice."

Is it? I wonder. Most Sundays are pure hell, but he's yet to understand the reality of the situation.

The second we turn in where the Satnav suggests, Trey's body tenses. I'm sure this place is far from what he was expecting.

The Park View Care Home signs are impossible to miss as we drive up toward the building. Trey looks over at me. From the corner of my eye, I can see his brows are drawn together in... concern or confusion, I'm not really sure.

"Just here's great. Thank you so much," I say when I spot Sam's car in her usual space. On a normal Sunday we'd arrive together, but not knowing what time I'd get here today, I told her to go on in without me. "It's been...really good."

I move to jump from the car, but the panic in his voice stops me. "Erica, wait."

I don't look back at him. I know that, if I do, everything I don't want to say to him will just fall from my mouth.

"I'll see you at work tomorrow. Thank you." With that, I slam his car door behind me and all but run towards the care home.

"Good morning, sweetie. We weren't sure if you were going to make it this morning," Sally, one of Mum's carers sings when I walk towards their desk.

I just about manage to bite back my short response about me being here *every* Sunday without fail. Poor Sally doesn't deserve to be on the wrong end of my mood right now. "Here I am. How is she?"

"Not good. She's sleeping now, was up most of the night apparently. Your sister's with her."

"Thank you."

I don't really even know why I feel so frustrated. After the luxury I've had for the past twenty-four hours, I really should be more relaxed than ever. I'm not sure if it's having to leave Trey or my residual anger from this morning, but the closer I get to Mum's room, the tighter my muscles get.

My steps slow as I approach her open door, just like they do every time. I hate being here. I hate seeing her like this. But I still do it every Sunday without fail like it's expected of me. And I guess in some ways, it is. But if I were to think back to all her failings as a mother, I'm sure no one could criticize if I were to turn my back.

"Hey," I whisper as I round the corner, knowing exactly what seat I'll find my sister sitting in.

The moment she registers it's me, she jumps to the edge of her seat, a smile playing on her lips. "How was it?"

Blowing out a breath, I walk over and gently kiss Mum's forehead before falling down onto my seat and looking toward my overly excited sister.

"It was...over the top, expensive, incredible, scary."

"Scary?"

"I'm just trying to figure out what his angle is, what he wants."

"Does he have to want anything more than you?"

"Always. Men always want more."

"There will be one who doesn't, Erica. You need to give it enough time to figure out if he's that one." She stares at me for a few seconds as her words settle in my head. "Anyway, he is seriously hot for an older man."

A genuine laugh falls from my lips and I immediately feel lighter. Sam has a way of making everything seem that little bit more bearable.

Mum stays asleep the whole time we visit. As usual when this is the case, we leave a little note and a couple of very questionable drawings for her to look at when she's able. It's horrible, sitting there knowing she has no idea we've visited, especially as we're both very aware that no one else will be here until this time next Sunday, but what else can we do? It's not like we can put our lives on hold for however long she's going to be here. Plus, the chances of her knowing who we are or being aware that we're in the room even if she was awake are slim.

We're chatting away as we walk out through the care home entrance when I suddenly stop.

"What's wrong?"

"He's still here." I've no idea why I whisper; it's not like he could hear me from inside his car at the other side of the car park, anyway.

"Did you tell him to go?"

"Uh…" I think back over our awkward conversation before I ran from his car. "Well, no, but I thought I made it quite clear not to stay."

He must feel my stare, because his eyes lift and find mine. A smile curls his lips while my heart starts to race.

"I think you've found yourself a keeper there."

Her words barely register. The only thing I can really hear is my blood whooshing past my ears.

"I don't…I'm not…"

"Pull yourself together, woman," my sister laughs.

We both watch, Sam excited, me in total disbelief, as Trey pushes the car door open so he can greet me.

"Well? What are you waiting for? Go to him. Go and thank him properly for sitting out here all this time."

"I don't know."

"Erica, you've got to trust someone one day."

With those few words ringing in my ears, I make my way towards him. His smile only gets wider the closer I get. Regret twists my stomach for how I treated him this morning. Maybe my sister's right. Maybe I do need to try to trust him.

"Hey, you didn't have to wait."

"I know. I wanted to." His hand finds mine and his fingers squeeze. My heart damn near explodes. No one's ever actually wanted to do something like that for me before. "What? You're looking at me like my skin's suddenly turned purple or something."

"You really sat out here waiting this whole time?"

"I did."

"I'm sorry about this morning. I acted like—"

"It's okay." His spare hand comes up to tuck a lock of hair behind my ear, and his thumb brushes my cheek. It's so gentle that it makes my chin tremble.

"You fancy going for coffee?"

"That sounds perfect."

As I turn back to walk around to the car, I find my sister where I left her, grinning like an idiot.

CHAPTER FIFTEEN

The remainder of the day passes all too fast, and before I know it we're back in Trey's car to head home.

I rest my head back and take a few deep breaths.

"Are you okay?"

"Yeah, I really am. Thank you for today."

"You're more than welcome."

He took me for coffee as he suggested and then we ended up walking around a park I'd never been to before. On the way back, we passed a cute Italian restaurant and Trey insisted on taking me for dinner.

The day was totally unexpected but exactly what I needed. I'd managed to lose the idea that it was any more than two people enjoying each other's company thanks to my sister's words of advice, and I couldn't be more grateful.

"Oh shit," I gasp. At some point, I'd managed to shut my eyes, and now we're a street away from my sister's place.

"What's wrong?"

"Um..." I stall, wondering if I really want to trust him. In the end, it's not really a hard decision to make. "I don't actually live here."

"Okay. So where do you live?" He glances over at me, his eyes wide as he waits for an answer.

"Please don't hate me."

"Why? Where do you live, Erica?"

"Just drive to your place."

"My place?"

His eyes leave the road briefly and he looks at me, his brow creased with confusion, but he puts the indicator on and does as I suggest.

"You live on the same street?"

"Something like that."

"So whose house did I pick you up from yesterday?"

"My sister's."

"Why?"

"Because I was scared."

"Of?"

"You, me...this."

"You're going to need to spell it out for me a little more here, Erica."

"Just go and park, and I'll explain."

In minutes he's pulling into his allocated parking spot outside our building. He cuts the engine and turns to me.

"Go on."

"That first night. It was meant to just be a one-night thing. I didn't want to tell the truth when I discovered where you lived in case you wanted a repeat, or worse—"

"Worse?"

"I'm a mess, Trey. I've been screwed over by more men than I care to admit, and I had—have—no intention of history repeating itself. So one-nighters were all I had to offer. I promised myself that I was keeping my heart out of everything to do with men. No feelings, no attachments, and no repeats. Then I met you and you brought me here. I didn't think it would matter. I'd never see you again, and really the chances of meeting in the stairwell were pretty slim."

"Wait... you live in this building?"

"I do. I actually live below you."

"Below me?" His eyes widen as he processes what I just said. "All this time you've been right here and I had no idea?" I nod, biting down on my bottom lip, concerned about how he's going to take this. "So the night you left me that voicemail, you were mere feet away. The next morning when you ran into me on the stairs, you weren't there because you'd come to see me? Jesus." He scrubs his hand over his face and I panic that I've just ruined everything.

"I was—I am—scared, Trey. I was worried that—"

"It's okay." Reaching over, he takes my cheek in his hand, his thumb pulling my bottom lip from being attacked by my teeth. "I understand. Frustrated as hell that I couldn't come down and take what I needed whenever I wanted, but I get it."

"Really?"

He doesn't answer. Instead, he leans over the centre console and brushes his lips against mine. My entire body relaxes the second we connect. It should scare me but really, it just feels right.

He pulls back all too soon. I'm tempted to wrap my fist in his shirt and pull him back to me until I spot someone out of the corner of my eye and realise we've got an audience.

"Come up, let's get you up to your flat."

With our bags in hand, we make our way up to my floor. I expect him to invite himself in but, to my surprise, after he's dropped my case inside the door he steps back. "So you really live beneath me?"

"I really do. I'm sorry I didn't tell you." The guilt of lying to him, even though I know he understands, still eats at me.

We're locked in our stare when a deep, rumbling voice comes from behind me. "Glad you brought her back in one piece."

"I also should probably have warned you that that idiot is my flatmate."

"Hey," he argues, "you know your life's been better since I moved in. Don't even try to deny it."

"Was it only me who didn't know?" Now Trey looks pissed off. His eyes have hardened and his lips press into a thin line.

"Know what?" Joe asks innocently.

"That I live upstairs."

"You live upstairs?" Joe goes to the effort of pointing above his head just in case the words aren't enough. "Oh my god." Shaking my head at Joe, I try to stop what I know is about to come. "The night you pulled him, I spent the night down here getting myself off to the hot sex going on upstairs. *That was you!*"

I'm not usually one to get embarrassed by my shenanigans, but this has just hit my limit. Stepping forward, I drop my forehead to Trey's shoulder. It vibrates with his laughter and I groan.

"Yeah, man. That night was pretty hot. If I knew she was this close it might have happened a few more times since, too."

"I'm so looking forward to the coming weeks."

"And I'm looking forward to you moving out," I say as seriously as possible, turning to look at him.

"Aw, don't be like that, sweets. You love having me here and you know it."

"Uh huh."

"I'm going to leave you two to argue this out." Trey grabs my hand and pulls me into his chest. His lips drop to my ear and my skin tingles. "I'll see you tomorrow. Fancy a lift to work?"

"That would be awesome, thank you."

"My pleasure. You know where I am if you need me."

"You too."

He leaves me with a toe-curling kiss, making me want to drag him to my bedroom and let him do all kinds of other wicked things to my body. Instead, I allow him to back away and close the door when he hits the stairs.

"He lives up-fucking-stairs. Were you ever going to tell me?" I shrug because telling Joe about it was the least of my worries. "Well, if it helps at all, from listening to the two of you I'd suggest you go up there more often. Hell, move in with him if it means you get that kind of action regularly."

"You're a fucking nightmare. I'm going to unpack."

"You want dinner?"

"No, I ate with Trey."

"Ooh, this really is getting serious."

I don't respond, mainly because I don't have an answer. I'm terrified of it being true and having my heart trampled on once again, but at the same time I also can't stop myself from starting to fall.

<hr>

IF I THOUGHT it was frustrating before listening to him move around upstairs, then it's downright torturous now. Every creak of the floorboards above and my body's on full alert.

"Just go up there already," Joe suggests from the other end of the sofa where we're sitting watching the TV.

"I'm good."

"No, you're not. You're coiled like a bloody spring. Go and surprise him and let him fuck your brains out."

"I'm trying not to get attached," I whisper, not really wanting to admit it out loud.

"How's that working out for you?"

I stay where I am for a few seconds, feeling a little sorry for myself before jumping up.

"That's my girl," Joe calls from behind me.

"I'm going to the kitchen for hot chocolate. Don't get excited, I don't intend on being your personal porn star tonight."

"Shame. I could do with some."

"You never came home Friday night. I'm assuming you hooked up?" I call, hoping for some details on his sex life to get the heat off me.

"Yes, I met this couple who wanted to, uh...spice things up."

"You spent the night with a couple?"

"Sure did, sweets."

"Were you for her or him?"

"Both."

"No way," I say with a laugh. I know Joe's a bit of a player, but that's a bit much, even for him.

"Deadly serious. It was pretty incredible."

"I'll take your word for it!"

"You're seriously planning on spending the night with me and a mug of hot chocolate that doesn't even have marshmallows on?"

"If you keep going on, I'll be spending the evening in my room with my mug of marshmallow-less hot chocolate."

Joe eventually stops giving me grief and we spend the evening enjoying the slightly boring Sunday night TV and putting the world to rights.

When I walk into my room ready to get into bed, my phone lights up on the bedside table. Seeing Trey's name, I immediately swipe the screen and open the message.

Trey: Thank you for an incredible
weekend. Sleep tight x

Butterflies erupt in my belly, knowing that he's right above my head, thinking about me. Feeling cheeky, I send my own message back.

Erica: How's it feel, knowing I'm beneath you yet you can't touch?

I wait for a few seconds, but when his response doesn't come I force myself to go into the bathroom.

Too anxious to find out if he's replied, I rush back to my bed the second I flush the toilet to see if it's there. I squeal in delight when I see his name. My heart thunders in my chest so much that I can feel it in my toes.

Trey: Get up here now.

There's my demanding, dominant Trey, I think as I pull out my bottom drawer to find something suitable for my visit.

"Fucking knew you'd cave," Joe calls out when he spots me running towards the front door.

"Turn the music up, yeah?"

"I will do no such fucking thing. Make sure you're loud," is the last thing I hear before the door slams behind me.

I probably should cover up to make the short journey up the stairs, but it's too late now. With my head held high, I make my way to his door.

Knocking, I lean against the doorframe and plaster what I hope is a seductive look on my face.

It takes a few seconds but, before long, the sound of his footsteps hits my ears. My stomach knots as anticipation for his reaction hits me full force.

"I didn't think you'd ever get...Get the fuck in here." His fingers wrap around my wrist and I'm harshly pulled inside his flat. I stumble on my heels but he keeps me upright before the door's slammed and I'm pushed back against it.

His eyes are dark and wide, his nostrils flare and his lips part, his increased breath tickling my face.

"Don't fucking ever walk up here looking like that again. You hear me?"

"Yes, Sir," I whisper, looking up at him through my lashes, and it only spurs him on. His eyes get impossibly dark, the muscle in his neck pulsating with need.

He takes a step back from me and I panic until his eyes drop to my black satin covered body. The baby doll has a split all the way up the front and is held together with a red bow under my boobs. The G-string that barely covers me is the same fire engine red, and so are my shoes. My skin burns as his eyes trail over me, my core clenching with need for the release I hope he's going to give me.

"You're going to fucking pay for that. No one, other than me, ever gets the chance to see you dressed like this. Understand?"

"Yes."

"Now...what the fuck shall I do to you?"

"Anything," I breathe.

Reaching back, he pulls his t-shirt over his head and drops it to the floor before undoing the tie around his jogging bottoms. He walks over to the sofa, drops them and falls down on the edge, legs spread wide, his hard cock begging for my attention.

"What the fuck are you waiting for? Get over here and suck me."

My body moves before my brain even realises, and I'm lowering myself to my knees in front of him.

I wrap my hand around his length as his fingers find their way into my hair so he can pull me forward and take what he needs.

"Fuck," he barks when he hits the back of my throat. His hips lift from the sofa with his need for more.

Pulling back, I lick around the head of his cock before sinking back down. His length twitches and he growls.

"Not. In. Your. Mouth." His fingers grip painfully in my hair and I'm pulled off of him.

Kicking his joggers off, he stands and lifts me with his hands on my arse. His lips drop to mine and his tongue sweeps into my mouth. I hungrily accept what he gives, tangling my own tongue with his and sucking on it harshly, his moan of pleasure vibrating up his chest.

He starts walking and I expect us to end up in his bedroom, but about halfway there my back is pressed up against the cold wall. His hips pin me in place as he rips the tiny bit of red fabric from around my waist.

"Can't wait," he grunts, lining himself up with my entrance and dropping me onto his cock.

I cry out at the sudden invasion, not giving two shits about our eavesdropper downstairs.

"Fuck, Trey. Fuck."

"So fucking wet."

My walls clamp down around him as he simultaneously thrusts and lowers me to ensure he hits me as deep as possible.

"Fuck, fuck, fuck," I chant as my release gets ever closer. This is what I needed all weekend. Yes, I want a nice guy, I want him to treat me right, do all the sweet things he's done over the past few days, but when we close the door at night, this is exactly what I need. I need demands, and orders, and this sexy dominant lover who's guaranteed to make me scream time after fucking time.

"Trey," I cry, my body tensing and convulsing as my orgasm flows though me.

He continues with his punishing pace as my pleasure starts to fade. He swells within me, his fingers digging tighter into my arse as he approaches the end.

His head drops back and he roars like a wild fucking animal as he fills me.

The moment he can move, he's carrying me down to his bedroom and throwing me down on the bed. I drop my eyes to get a sight of his arse as he walks towards his dresser.

"Tonight, you're mine. You do what I say when I say it. Got it?"

"Got it." There's absolutely no hesitation in my voice, and, when he turns to look at me, I swear I see pride shining in his dark eyes.

Bring it fucking on, big man.

CHAPTER SIXTEEN

"You ready?" Joe calls through my bedroom door.

"Give me a second." I'm ready—I have been for about ten minutes, but I think I spun around too fast because I've gone all light-headed.

I suck in a few more deep breaths, hoping it'll ease it. Ben announced an impromptu night out this afternoon after he signed off on the job Joe had been running. It was a huge warehouse renovation and we were pretty much relying on it paying off to clear a huge chunk of the company's debt. It's been a stressful few weeks as we've waited for something to go wrong or for someone to demand repayment earlier than they'd agreed.

Pushing myself from the bed, I slip my feet into my trainers and join him.

"Are you okay?" *I'm glad I look as good as I feel,* I think as I head toward the front door.

"Yeah, I'm good. Just relieved things are starting to look up."

"I told you it was all going to be fine."

"I know. I just still feel so guilty that this whole disaster wouldn't have happened if it weren't for me and my bad decision making."

"Stop beating yourself up. He manipulated you into doing his dirty work, just like the rest of us."

"How are things with Lauren?" He hasn't been spending nearly as much time with her as he would have in the past, and I know he misses her more than he'll ever admit.

"They're okay. I hate that I can see doubt in her eyes every time she looks at me. It's like she's trying to work out what else I'm lying about. That was the only time I've ever deceived her. I know it doesn't really matter now, but I was just trying to protect her."

"I know. She'll come around. Just give her time. We hurt her pretty badly."

The sound of Trey's hard knock sounds out around the flat.

We're both silent as Joe pulls the door open, and I'm soon distracted when Trey's revealed, wearing a skin-tight polo shirt and a slim pair of jeans.

"Wow," I breathe.

"I was thinking the same." His eyes drop from mine to take in my body. I don't really think the jeans and t-shirt I'm wearing are worthy of that kind of attention, but I won't argue. My body heats up under his scrutiny, making me wish we weren't about to spend the night bowling with our colleagues.

"Let's go before you two start fucking in the hallway."

Trey opens his mouth to respond but, like me, he must decide it's pointless and instead grabs my hand and pulls me from the flat, allowing Joe to lock up.

"Well, this is a little more fancy than I'm used to," Joe says, bouncing up and down on the back seat of Trey's Jaguar like a little kid, making Trey wince.

"Yeah, and I'd appreciate it if you didn't break it."

Laughing at the two of them, I buckle myself in and sit back.

My head's still feeling a little weird, but I'm hopeful some fast food will sort me right out.

We all meet for burgers before heading towards the bowling alley. I've no idea why Ben decided on this. I haven't been since I was a kid, and that was only for friends' birthday parties. Sadly, this kind of thing wasn't an everyday occurrence for my family.

Ben and Lauren bicker as they put everyone's names into the little computer ready for our game to start, while Joe finds all the heavy balls to show off with. Rolling my eyes at him, I allow Trey to pull me down onto the bench beside him.

"I can't remember the last time I did this."

"Me either. It should be fun."

"You don't look like you mean that."

Plastering a smile on my face, I look up at him. His brows are drawn together in concern as his eyes flit all over me, trying to find what might be wrong. "I do. I think I've just eaten too much," I say as my stomach turns over once again. The burger and chips might have been a little too much after only eating a few biscuits all day.

"Okay," he says, although he doesn't look like he means it. "If you need to leave, just say."

"I'm good, I promise."

I manage to do my first couple of throws fine, although I totally miss each time—unlike Trey who, after only the first round, was already topping the leader board. It seems he might have a hidden talent for bowling.

My body temperature suddenly spikes and my mouth waters like I'm going to throw up. I suck in a deep breath and fan my hand in front of me.

"I'm taking you home."

"No, no. I'm having fun." My argument is weak at best. The only thing I want to do right now is curl up in my bed but I don't want to let anyone down.

"It wasn't a question."

Trey stands and says something to Ben and Lauren who both turn to me, concern written all over their faces. They smile, but they're nowhere near genuine. I can only imagine how bad I must be looking.

I'm pulled up against Trey's side and, after saying quick goodbyes to everyone, we change back into our shoes and head out towards his car.

"I'm so sorry," I whisper once he's backing out of the space.

"Don't be silly. You're ill. Everyone can see that."

"Brilliant," I mutter, a humourless laugh falling from my lips.

"That's not what I meant, and you know it. You look as beautiful as ever."

I scoff at his comment but don't respond. Instead, I rest my head back and will my stomach to settle.

"What are you doing?" I ask when Trey pulls the car to a stop out the front of a row of shops.

"Do you need anything?"

"Sleep."

"Okay, wait here."

I don't get a chance to demand that he stays put and just drives me home, because he's out of the car and marching towards the shop doors before I have a chance to think.

He's not gone all that long. I watch his every movement as his long, denim-clad legs carry him back towards me. I run my eyes up the fitted t-shirt that shows off his sculpted muscles beneath and, despite feeling like shit, tingles erupt between my legs at just the sight alone.

"Here," he says, dropping into the driver's seat and passing me a bag.

"What's this?"

"A few things to make you feel better."

Opening the bag, I stare down at the contents. Instantly, my eyes fill with tears and emotion burns my throat.

"You—" I don't manage to get any more words out, the giant lump clogging my throat stopping me.

"I what?" Trey starts the engine before turning to look at me. "Shit, what's wrong?"

Fighting against the emotions warring inside me, I swallow and force out some words. "You bought all this for me?" My voice is barely above a whisper, and it gives away everything I'm feeling.

"Yeah, I wanted to do something to make you feel better. Is that...okay?" He hesitates as my first tears fall. Dragging my eyes from his, I look back down into the bag. There's some medicine to settle my stomach and some painkillers, but it's the giant bar of chocolate, tub of ice cream, bottle of bubble bath and candles that do me in.

A sob rumbles up my throat and I'm powerless to stop the tears that follow.

"Fuck, I was only trying to do something nice. I can take it all back?"

"No, no," I manage through my sobs. "These are happy tears."

"Really?"

"Really. This is just...it's everything."

"It's just a few things from the corner shop. I didn't exactly go to a lot of effort."

"Effort doesn't matter, Trey. It's the thought behind it. That's... well, it's more than I've ever had."

His face hardens and I kick myself for once again revealing a part of my past I'd rather no one knows about.

"Erica," he breathes, reaching over and taking my hand in one of his and wiping my tears away with the other. "You deserve so much more than what you've had in the past. Let me in, let me show you how it should be."

My tears almost immediately dry at his words, at his demand for me to drop the walls I've spent so many years painstakingly constructing.

Shaking my head, I watch as his features darken with disappointment. "I can't," I whisper, ripping my eyes from his and staring at the dark night surrounding us.

My stomach turns over, but this time it's not with whatever bug I've picked up, it's with the regret that floods me the second those two words leave my lips.

Trey deserves more than me. He deserves someone who can allow him into her life, to show him exactly who she is. Tears burn again, but this time I fight like hell to stop them from dropping.

I don't register any of the trip home. The next thing I know, Trey's warm palm lands on my thigh, and when I look up I find that we're parked in front of our building.

"How are you feeling?"

Numb. "A little better, thank you."

The genuine concern on his face has my heart aching. I so badly want this thing between us to be something. I've refused to allow myself to fantasize about it for fear of it not happening, but little thoughts about him being the one for me keep creeping their way in.

"Come on, let's get you inside."

He has my door open and my hand in his before I get a chance to think about it. He leads me up to my flat and takes the keys from my hand once I've dug them out of my bag.

He doesn't once let go of my other hand, and the second we're inside with the door shut he pulls me up against his chest.

His thumb brushes my cheek and he tucks a lock of my hair behind my ear. "What do you need?"

Well, if that isn't a loaded question. I have a million answers on the tip of my tongue.

I swallow them all down and squeak out a safe one. "A bath."

"You go and get sorted and I'll run it for you."

I stop when I get to my room and watch as he continues down the hall to the main bathroom.

Chewing on my bottom lip, I wonder what it would be like to let him in. To tell him all my dark secrets that I keep locked away from everyone.

He must feel my stare because when he gets to the door, he stops and looks over his shoulder. The intensity in his eyes makes my breath catch. Where I'm doing my best to hide what he does to me, how he feels is written all over his face.

Maybe trusting him wouldn't be so bad.

"THAT WAS QUICK," Trey says, poking his head around my bedroom door after I've finished my bath.

"I got a little hot," I lie. In reality, I just hated being in there alone while he was sitting on my sofa, but I daren't tell him that I missed him. That's crazy.

"Feeling any better?"

"I am, actually. I might give that ice cream a try."

"You must be feeling better," he says with a laugh as I follow him out to the living room. "Sit down. I'll get it for you."

Relaxing on the sofa while he crashes around in the kitchen feels surreal. Since the day Sam and I moved out of our family home, I've only ever looked after myself.

"I'm assuming you want the tub?"

"How else would I eat it?"

"Here." He passes the tub and a spoon to me as he falls down beside me with his own.

"Uh…what are you doing?" I ask when he moves to take some ice cream.

"I was going to have some. Am I not allowed?"

"How much do you know about women?"

"Not enough, apparently. So…I can't have any?"

"Just because you were really sweet and got it for me, I'll allow it. But," I say in a rush, "not too much."

A wide smile spreads across his face as he digs in.

"Whoa, whoa, I said not too much." My eyes almost pop out of my head when I take in the giant lump of ice cream on his spoon.

"This is it. The rest is yours."

The second his lips wrap around the spoon, I forget all about sharing ice cream. He knows I'm watching and makes a show of licking the spoon clean and ensuring his moan of pleasure is loud enough to hit exactly where he intends. My thighs clench and suddenly the only thing I'm interested in having in my mouth is him.

"So your sister's getting married." I get whiplash at his sudden change of topic. My brows draw together in confusion until he helps me out. "The invite is on the front of your fridge."

"Oh right, yeah. It feels like she's been planning it forever. I can't believe it's almost here." I shovel a spoonful of ice cream into my mouth, my eyes flutter shut and a moan rumbles up my throat as the sweet creaminess melts on my tongue.

Trey shifts in his seat beside me and I look over, a smug smile on my lips.

"What about your family?" Somehow I've revealed much more than I intended to with his visit to the care home car park and knowing a little about my sister.

"Um…" he mumbles as he continues his attempt to get comfortable, "my parents both retired and moved out to the

Cotswolds a few years ago, and my older brother is an investment banker, total workaholic."

"Is he married?"

"He has been," he says with a chuckle. "She was just after his money. It didn't last long."

The conversation flows easily between us as we both reveal little bits of our lives. Trey seems totally relaxed as he tells me about his childhood and his career, whereas my muscles lock up tight every time he asks me a question.

"What about your dad?"

"He's gone. Walked out years ago." I don't intend on explaining any more, but when he turns his eyes on me the words just keep flowing. "He wasn't a nice man. He controlled every aspect of our lives and kept Mum in line with his harsh, belittling words. Life at home was never great, but when I was nine, it all went downhill.

"I came home from a friend's house earlier than planned and walked in on Dad with another woman. Everything got a whole lot worse after that. He blackmailed me, told me no one would ever believe a child, that they would all think I was a liar because he loved my mother—that's what the outside world thought, anyway. He never physically hurt any of us that I'm aware of, although if he stuck around any longer I'm sure it would have happened. He was a monster, and only the beginning of a long line of them." I regret the final words the second they slip out, but it's too late now. Although he's never said anything about the reason behind the business' failings and how I played a part in it, I'm under no illusion he must know what went on between Nick and me. "I told myself I'd never be that weak again. After being used and abused more times than I can count, I told myself I'd give up on men. And then..."

"Here I am."

"Here you are." I put the empty ice cream tub and spoon down on the coffee table and Trey takes my hand, stopping me from getting up and instead turning me towards him.

I keep my eyes down, too afraid of what he'll see in them after my little trip down memory lane.

"Look at me," he demands, and just like the little girl who followed all her daddy's orders, I look up, immediately finding his eyes.

"I'm not like them." His palm cups my cheek as he stares deep into my eyes, willing me to believe him.

"Everyone wants something," I whisper, hating that I sound so vulnerable.

"I do want something, Erica." My breath catches at his admission. "I want you."

When I wake the next morning it's with Trey's arm laying heavily across my waist and his breath tickling down my neck.

"Morning." His deep, rough voice has tingles erupting in all the right places. I grind my arse back into him and he groans. "As much as I'd love that, I've got an early meeting to get to."

"You should have woken me earlier."

"You're ill. I wanted you to sleep."

I pout as I continue to rub up against him. He soon reacts. I'm flipped onto my back and my bottom lip is sucked into his mouth.

"Ow," I complain when he bites down.

"Punishment for teasing me," he says with a cheeky smile and a wink when he pulls back. "I really need to go."

Standing, I watch as he stretches and turns towards me. My eyes run over his exposed skin and down to the very obvious tent in his boxers.

"I could be real quick."

"I don't want to enjoy you quickly, Erica. I want to savour ever minute." Lust shoots through me but he stands by his words and turns towards his discarded clothes.

I sit myself up against the headboard with the intention of watching his muscles ripple beneath his skin as he dresses, but the moment I move, my stomach turns over.

Holding my breath, I will it to disappear before he turns and notices.

"I'll make it up to you tonight," he promises as he turns back toward me. "On second thoughts, maybe you should call in sick."

"I can't, I've got too much to do."

"You're better off here if you're ill."

I shrug off his concerns and, after a chaste kiss, I send him on his way. It's only once he's gone that I appreciate how terrible I feel. I probably should call in, but I still feel like I've got so much to prove, so instead I shove to my feet and push through the sick feeling turning in my stomach.

"YOU MISSED A FUCKING AWESOME NIGHT, E. You should have—fuck."

I've no idea what comes over me, but the second Ben turns to look at me, I burst into tears. "What's wrong?" He walks over, throws his arms around me and pulls me against him. It only makes me cry harder, but I've no idea why. I'm not a crier. I've perfected the art of putting on a brave face and battling my way through.

This. Is. Not. Me.

He doesn't let up until I've got my breathing under control, but even then he hardly releases his hold as he pulls back to look at me. "What's wrong? Has Trey done something?" Anger twitches at the sides of his lips and the muscle in his neck pulses.

"What? No, no, Trey's not done anything. He's good, really good, actually."

"So what's wrong? The last woman I knew who burst into tears like that was pre—" The look of pure horror on my face is enough to cut off that final word, but I hear it loud and clear. His arms release me and I stumble backwards, my chest heaving.

"Fuck."

"Erica?"

My trembling hand comes up to cover my mouth as I think back over the previous few days. The sick feeling, the light-headedness. *When was my last period exactly?* I rack my brain but come up empty.

"No, no. I can't be. I'm on the pill. It's just a bug."

"Stranger things have happened."

"Fuck." Resting my palms on the counter, I drag in a few deep breaths. *This cannot be happening.*

"Why don't you take the day off? Go figure out what's going on. Get some rest, you look exhausted. I'm sure Lauren would come if you want some company."

"No, it's fine. I think I need to do this alone."

"That's what I was afraid of." Glancing over my shoulder at his concerned face, my heart drops. I hate being a disappointment. "Please don't shut us out, Erica. We're here to help you."

"I know, and I promise I won't. This is just something that I need to get my head around myself first, if it even is a thing." Even as I say the words, I know I'm only lying to myself. How I didn't suspect anything before now is beyond me. All the signs have been there. If I'd just pulled my head out of my arse and used my brain instead of pining after Trey like a love-sick teenager, I might have seen this coming.

"Call us if you need anything," Ben shouts as I get to the door.

Looking back over my shoulder, I manage a weak smile before

turning back the way I came only minutes ago. I grab my bag from where I dropped it on my desk and walk straight out.

Lauren's walking around the side of the house as I leave, but I don't acknowledge her. I don't need to. Ben will tell her everything in about thirty seconds, I'm sure.

I should probably call a taxi—it will get me where I need to be faster—but at no point do I reach into my bag for my phone. Instead, I just keep walking. I walk, feeling totally numb and utterly stupid for being so blindsided by this. I'm an intelligent woman. It should not have taken my male best friend to point this out to me.

By the time I stumble across a chemist, I've convinced myself that this is all one big joke. So what, I'm a little emotional? It doesn't have to mean anything.

I can't look at the cashier as she scans the test and asks me if I want a bag. I decline the offer and shove the box straight into my handbag—out of sight, out of mind. I throw some cash at her and get the hell out before anyone sees me.

I intend on going home to do it in private, but when I spot a Starbucks before I get to the tube station I find myself walking inside and straight towards the toilets.

The last place I want to do this is in a public bathroom, but now the test is in my possession, my need to find out is too strong.

I lock myself in the last cubicle and pull the box from my bag. I read the instructions, trying to register what the words are telling me, but other than the final result everything passes me by. I know the gist of these things; I've heard them spoken about enough. Pee on the stick and wait for your fate to be decided. So that's what I do.

I balance the little bit of plastic upside down on the toilet roll holder as I right my clothing and begin pacing the tiny space.

I'm not. I can't be. Ben's wrong. I'm just putting too much on myself with work and I'm exhausted. No matter how many times I repeat those words in my head, I know they're not true.

Glancing down at my phone, it confirms that enough time has passed. I take a long, slow breath and shake my hands out, hoping they'll stop trembling, and reach out for the test.

Squeezing my eyes shut, I turn it over, count to three and then look.

Pregnant. "Fuck." I stumble back and crash into the cubicle wall.

"Are you okay?" someone calls out.

"Y-yeah, thanks." I've no idea if it comes out loud enough for anyone to hear; I'm too focused on that one little word.

That one little word that has the power to change my life.

I've no idea how I managed it, but somehow I find my way out of Starbucks and onto a tube heading toward home. Everything around me is a blur; all I can see is that one word.

When I eventually make it home, I drop my bag in the hallway, kick off my shoes and curl up on my bed.

I don't cry, I don't scream. I don't do anything. I'm just numb.

I MANAGE to drag my pathetic arse out of bed, ready for Joe to come home. I try to make myself look a little presentable, but when I glance in the mirror in the hallway I realise I've failed miserably.

I kick-start the coffee machine so I can have a mug ready for him. I've noticed over the past couple of weeks that he's started going out on Thursday nights, although I don't think it's the kind of night out he's used to as he's usually home before ten.

He appears right on time and, as he walks towards me, I push his steaming mug of black coffee towards him, trying to ignore the churning of my stomach as the scent fills my nose.

"Are you okay? Ben said he sent you home."

"I'll be fine. You out tonight?"

Something passes across his face but it's gone too quickly for me to be able to read. "Uh...yeah?"

"This is turning into a regular thing. Have you met someone?" I ask, disappointed that he hasn't even mentioned it if he has.

"What? No," he says, a little too defensively. "I've just been meeting a friend." I don't believe a word of it, and the fact that he can't hold my eyes as he says it confirms that he's not telling me the whole story. "Thanks for the coffee. I need to shower." He turns back before he leaves the room and drops a kiss to my cheek. "Thank you," he whispers before disappearing. I've no idea what he's thanking me for. Shrugging at his elusiveness, I take my glass of water over to the sofa to find something to stare at on the TV.

Joe reappears dressed to impress, including his thick-rimmed glasses that make him look like a sexy bad boy nerd, and rushes out of the door. It makes me even more suspicious about what he's up to.

Resting back, my stomach rumbles. I don't really want to eat anything, knowing it'll probably only make me feel sick, but guilt tugs at my insides. I need to start looking after myself.

I just get to the kitchen when there's a knock on the door. Peeking through the peephole, my heart begins to race as I find Trey on the other side. Ben wouldn't have said anything, would he?

I take a couple of deep breaths, hold my head high and pull the door open.

"Hey, are you feeling any better? Ben said you were pretty rough this morning. Did you get worse after I left?"

"Yeah, eating something before leaving the house didn't really help."

"Are you hungry now? I brought soup."

My stomach growls loudly right on cue, distracting Trey from the tears once again filling my eyes at his thoughtfulness.

"Yes, come on in. I'll get bowls."

It turns out that Trey not only bought soup but also a freshly baked loaf of bread and a new tub of ice cream after I polished off the one he got me last night with gusto. Something about the cold sweetness really helped to settle my stomach, and tonight is the same.

"You've got a little colour back in your cheeks. Chicken soup really does fix everything."

I mumble my agreement but, in reality, soup is never going to fix what I'm hiding right now.

I should tell him, I know that, but the idea of allowing the actual words past my lips has the beginnings of a panic attack clawing at my lungs. I need to figure out how I feel about this before I even think about getting Trey's perspective. Our relationship might have been becoming more serious lately, but we're still quite a way from the marriage and kids talk. I'm worried this new development is going to ruin everything we're been building together.

"If you're feeling better tomorrow, will you have dinner with me? I want to take you to my favourite restaurant."

"That sounds good. I told Ben I'd stay off tomorrow as well, so it'll be nice to get out of the house."

He nods, pulls me into his side and kisses the top of my head. I allow myself to relax into his warmth and fight to keep thoughts of our future out of my mind.

I end up falling asleep beside him. I'm vaguely aware of him carrying me to bed and sliding in beside me, but that's it. The next time I wake, I'm once again alone in my bed with only thoughts of my reality to keep me company.

CHAPTER EIGHTEEN

After another day lying on the sofa watching reruns of *Friends* for the millionth time, I'm glad I agreed to go out tonight. I've grazed on beige food all day, and eating little and often has helped keep my sickness at bay.

As much as I've tried to tell myself that I can keep this a secret, I know I'm only lying to myself. Trey deserves to know about what's really wrong with me. After all, it takes two to tango, and although I reassured him that I was on the pill, we're both intelligent adults who know that it's not one hundred percent effective. There's always a risk. The chance might be low but unfortunately we're now some of the unlucky—or lucky, depending on how you look at it—ones.

Standing in the mirror, I stare at myself in one of my favourite fitted dresses and try to imagine what I might look like in a few months' time if I continue with this pregnancy. I always thought that, if I ever got pregnant, it would be when I was in a stable relationship, married even, and that it would be planned. I've always ensured I've stayed on top of my birth control to stop any unwanted surprises, but now it's here I don't really know what to think. Is it an unwanted surprise, or is it just one of those things that's meant to be? Is it a sign that Trey really could be the one and that we're destined for a life together? Is this the universe pushing us closer and making me pull my head out of my arse and ensuring that I accept how I really feel about him?

I rub my hand down over my flat stomach, thinking about how it might feel to have another person growing inside me. A part of me—a part of Trey.

My heart tumbles again. I need to tell him as soon as possible. I consider phoning him and arranging for us to have dinner here so I can do it in private, but I remember the excitement that glittered in his eyes as he told me about his favourite restaurant.

It'll be fine, I tell myself. *He'll totally accept it.*

Grabbing my phone to check the time, I find a voicemail from him. Quickly swiping the screen, I put it on speaker. It doesn't matter how many times I hear his deep voice, it still affects me like it did that first time he whispered in my ear at The Avenue all those weeks ago.

"Hey, sweetheart. I'm so sorry, I'm stuck in traffic. I've organised for a taxi to come and pick you up. I'll meet you at the restaurant. See you soon."

My stomach drops, knowing that I'm going to have to wait even longer to see him. I need to get the words out that have been taunting me since the moment I revealed the result on that little white stick. The more time I have, the more chance there is that I'll manage to talk myself out of telling him, and that can't happen.

Pulling on a pair of court shoes, I head out of the building to find the taxi he promised.

The second I pull the main door open, I spot the black cab idling outside.

"Erica?" he asks as I walk towards him.

"Yes."

I jump in the back and try to prepare for what tonight's going to bring. My stomach churns with nerves and I feel sicker than I have all day.

By the time the taxi pulls up outside the fancy restaurant, I'm a mess. My hands are trembling, my palms are sweating, and I can barely swallow, my mouth is so dry.

It'll be fine. It'll be fine, I chant as I walk inside and speak to the maître de.

He smiles warmly when I say Trey's name, and he tells me to follow to his favourite table.

I lower myself in the seat when he pulls it out and order myself a lime and soda to sip while I wait.

He's back within seconds and leaves me with the menus to browse. I flick it open but I don't see any of the words; they all just blur into a mix of letters and numbers as what I need to say to Trey runs around my head.

I'm totally lost in my own thoughts and it's not until the chair opposite me is pulled out and a body drops down onto it that I realise I have company.

Looking up, my brows draw together, a deep line forming between them as I stare at a woman. She looks kind of average and most definitely isn't dressed for this place, which confuses me even more.

"Hello," she says with the fakest smile I think I've ever seen.

"Uh...hi?"

"I know you're not expecting me." My eyes narrow as I try to figure out what she's saying. "I'm Sarah, Trey's wife. I thought it was time we met."

ACKNOWLEDGMENTS

When I first embarked on this series, I had no idea that Erica was going to appear, but not long after writing her spunky office girl character, I knew that she had a story to tell. It's safe to say that she threw all my plans out of the window and started to tell me her story instead. And I'm so glad she did, because I love her. I love her hard outer shell that gives the impression that no one can touch her but, in reality, she's craving love and a happily ever after like everyone else. Much like Trey, really. How hot is he? I was really worried about the man who was going to follow on from Ben because he owns such a huge part of my heart, but Trey...I'm pretty sure he rose to the challenge with his dominance and sexy demands. Although he's got his work cut out for him after what's just happened. I'm excited to find out how he deals with it and wins his girl back.

A huge thank you once again to Michelle for being there every step of the way with this book. I couldn't do this without our daily chats, whether it be over tea and cake while the monsters play or over the phone. By the time this book releases it will be five years since we met. That day, neither of us knew it but our lives were about to change forever. Because of meeting you, I've done things I never ever thought I would, my life has changed in so many ways, and I know the woman who made it happen would be up there smiling down on us now, knowing she had a hand in it.

Deanna, Susanne and Tracy, thank you so much for picking

up Erica and Trey's story the second it dropped on to your Kindles and your kind—and not so kind—messages about it. I appreciated every bit of your feedback more than you know, so thank you.

My long suffering editor, Evelyn. Thank you once again for taking my mess of words and commas and turning it into something readable! I could not do this without you.

Huge thank you to Paige who agreed to proofread this around her wedding. Massive congratulations and thank you so much for squeezing me in.

Thank you so much Samantha, who made the somewhat silly decision to help PA for me earlier in the summer. I am the world's worst control freak (sorry for not mentioning that sooner) but you've made my life so much easier and I can't thank you enough for all the time you've put into helping me find more time to write.

I've got so much heading your way—get those Kindles charged, you're going to need them!

Until next time,

Tracy xo

DEMANDING REDEMPTION

CHAPTER ONE

I suck in a deep breath, trying to rid myself of the frustration the drive here created. I had planned to give Erica the perfect date night, to show her exactly how it should be done, but I failed at the first hurdle by getting stuck in London rush hour traffic that was only made worse by the roadworks closing two of the lanes.

I grip the wheel until my knuckles turn white as I prepare for the rest of my night and hope it might go a little more smoothly than my day's been. I've had back-to-back meetings in which all I seemed to have done is firefight issues on our jobs.

Pushing that to the back of my mind, I try to focus on Erica. Imagining what she might be wearing and how she might have done her hair makes me forget about work.

I hadn't intended on taking anyone home the night I spotted her in The Avenue, but one look and I was hooked. I'd never experienced anything like it, but my need for her was all-consuming. It had been a while since I'd been with anyone, but there was no way that I was leaving without her.

Life hadn't been great in the lead-up to that night, but the prospect of a new job did have a little hope creeping in that things were about to turn around for me. I'd spent the weeks before that night trying to give my life some kind of purpose. Everything I'd known up until that point had come to a painful end. I'd instigated it all, but that didn't mean the huge upheaval after years of stability wasn't a shock to the system. All of a sudden, I found myself alone with no one caring what I did or where I went. I'd thought it was going to be freeing, but, in reality, after so many years of the exact opposite it was a little unsettling. I imagined I was going to revisit my youth, have the kind of fun I'd missed out on all those years ago, but after only a couple of nights out with a few of my single friends, I knew that kind of life wasn't for me. I needed something different, and it wasn't until her red hair and sinful curves caught my eye that I discovered what it was.

I thought one night without any expectations or promises might break the spell she'd cast over me, but it only cemented my need for something a little more serious. I didn't want to be giving anyone a ring in the near future or anything crazy like that, but the prospect of getting to know someone new, some dates and some fun, excited me.

Then, she turned out to be even more that I could have imagined. The morning I walked into the office of my new job and found her bent over, dropping files into a box, I knew that I'd do whatever it took to make her mine.

"Good evening, Trey. Long time no see," Mark, the maître de, says as I approach his desk.

"Good to see you," I respond with a chuckle, taking his hand when he offers it.

I have a permanent reservation here once a month on a Friday night. It was a tradition that I started many, many years ago, and it just stuck.

"You're a lucky guy tonight. The woman sitting at your table is a beauty." Something bubbles up in my stomach at the knowledge that he's checked Erica out. I know he's no threat, but still, I hate the idea of another man's eyes on what's mine.

He winks at me before ushering me in. "I know the way." Clasping my hand on his shoulder, I nod, smile, then head into the restaurant.

As always, every table is full. The wait list to get a table here is weeks long, if you're lucky. There are only a few people that I know of who have permanent reservations, and that's only because we're friends with a member of staff or have more money than sense. Thankfully, one of my oldest friends just so happens to be the head chef here.

Excitement flutters in my belly as I round the corner. Lifting my eyes, I scan the room, desperate to find her. Sadly, the moment my gaze lands on my usual table, the feelings I was expecting don't happen. My mouth doesn't water, my body doesn't ache with need, and my cock doesn't swell to be inside her. Instead, the only thing I feel is fury.

Red hot fury.

"Where is she?" My voice is low and menacing, but she doesn't so much as flinch.

"Your little *friend* has left. You really are having a mid-life crisis, aren't you? Filing for divorce. Sleeping with a girl young enough to be your daughter. How do you think this looks, Trey?"

"I don't give a shit about how it looks, and I don't owe you an explanation for any of it. We're done, Sarah. Why are you even here?"

"I've waited long enough, but after the stunts you've been playing the past few weeks, I thought it was time I came and rescued you from yourself."

"Rescued me?" I ask, incredulously.

"Credit where credit's due, Trey, she was beautiful. I can understand why you've been pulling out all the stops and ditching your family to impress her. Fancy hotels, giant bouquets of flowers. Dinner at *our* restaurant."

"This isn't *our* restaurant. It might have been where we came to enjoy each other's company a long time ago, but that hasn't been the case for years, Sarah. What I do now has nothing to do with you."

"No? Then why do I still see all your credit card statements when I log onto our joint bank account? Why is that I still have your email account attached to my phone so I know what you're up to?"

Her words make my blood boil.

"I told you to remove all that."

She shrugs, and it's like a red rag to a bull. Reaching out, I grab her arm and pull her from the chair. "What did you say to her?" I'd never hurt a woman, but if I were ever to change my mind then it would be now. My fingers dig into her upper arms and something inside me settles as her eyes widen in fear.

This woman's known me since I was a child, and the fact that she seems scared of me tells me exactly where her head's at right now. She refused to accept my decision to leave all those weeks ago, so I'm not sure what I expected when she discovered I was seeing someone else. It's one of the reasons I hadn't told her about Erica. I had every intention of doing so once I knew things were serious, but I've got bigger things to worry about than what my ex-wife thinks.

"I just introduced myself." A small smile of victory curls her lips. "It seems you've been about as honest with your little friend as you've been with me."

My heart pounds and my head spins as I try to put myself in

Erica's shoes. I promised her I wouldn't let her down, yet the one thing about my past that I've been keeping a secret was just thrust in her face.

"Stop calling her that. She's not just some quick thing. I really li—"

An unamused laugh falls from her lips. "Please don't tell me that you really believe she feels anything for you. Girls that age aren't thinking about forever, about their future. You're just a toy to her, probably to show off to her friends."

Stepping closer, I stare down at her, my eyes boring into hers. "Don't pretend you know anything about her. About us." She wants to laugh again, but she stops herself when my eyes narrow. "We're done, Sarah, so if you would kindly sign the papers I know you've received, we can move on with our lives." Stepping back, I turn to leave. "And remove my email from your phone," I call over my shoulder before walking straight past Mark, who stares at me with his mouth gaping open, clearly wondering what the hell's going on.

"I had no idea she was here," he calls, but his words don't stop my escape. There's only one person I need to speak to right now, and I'm determined to make her hear me out.

My head tells me she won't be there, but my body's on auto-pilot as I drive towards our building.

I don't remember the journey. My head is too focused on how the hell I'm meant to get her to hear me out. I've no idea what Sarah might have said to her or how bad she's made the situation out to be because, in reality, I've done nothing wrong. Sarah and I are over and have been for a long time. I'm not cheating on her, and Erica is most definitely not the other woman.

She's the *only* woman, as far as I'm concerned.

Sarah will always be a part of my life. That's not something that's ever previously concerned me, because I never expected her to act the way she did tonight. I knew she wasn't happy with our separation, but I never expected her to meddle when I tried to move on.

Slamming my foot down on the brake, I pull the car to an abrupt stop, blocking three parking spaces. Ignoring it, I rush from the car and up towards her flat.

"Erica?" I call, slamming my fist down on her door. "Erica, open up."

My voice echoes down the stairwell, but it doesn't stop me continuing. *If* she's inside, she's not going to be able to ignore me.

After a good few minutes, I stop banging and rest my head on my forearm against the door.

"Erica, please. If you're in there, just open up. Let me explain. Please." My voice sounds pathetic even to my own ears. I'm almost embarrassed of the weak mess of a man she's turned me into, but it only serves to prove how much I need her. I don't deserve a woman like her, I know that. She deserves to be a man's first love, to be his first everything. I can't give her that, but that doesn't mean I'm letting her go anytime soon.

Dragging in a few deep breaths, I try to get my head on straight. If she's not here, where would be the first place she'd run to?

Her sister.

Pushing myself from her door, I make my way back downstairs. I fight the disappointment that threatens at not finding her. I knew deep down that she wouldn't come here. It would be too easy. She'd be expecting me.

"What the fuck, man?" some guy who is clearly one of our neighbours shouts, gesturing to my car that's half parked in his space.

"Sorry, emergency."

"Just move it," he barks, clearly having about as good a Friday as I am.

With a curt nod in his direction, I jump in my car and pull out of our small car park. Thankfully, the drive to Erica's sister's is short, the traffic finally starting to let up a little.

The beep of my car locking behind me cuts through the silence on her street. Stopping at her front door, I take a breath and try to compose myself. Once I'm a little calmer, I lift my hand to knock gently.

It's only seconds before a light comes on and a shadow falls under the door. The moment it starts to open, I push my palm against it and shove it wider, stepping into the small hallway at the same time.

"What the hell?" Sam asks, her panicked eyes flying over me. It's the first time I've seen her, and I'm immediately struck with how similar she is to Erica. Her hair's brown opposed to Erica's fiery red, but everything else—their green eyes, build, height—is so familiar yet so different at the same time. There's no denying they're sisters.

"Is she here?" Just like Erica, Sam doesn't back down from my demanding tone.

"No, she's not. What have you done?" I hesitate. Sam puts her hands on her hips and narrows her eyes on me. "If you've hurt her, I'll—"

"Our meal was intercepted and she ran off."

"Intercepted?"

"Not important right now. Where is she? Erica?" I shout into the flat, convinced that her sister is probably covering for her.

"She's really not here. I haven't spoken to her today."

Ignoring her, I step forward into her living room and then each room I find. All the while, Sam stands in the hallway, watching me with a gobsmacked look on her face.

When I come up empty behind the final door I find, I walk back towards her.

"Happy now?"

"Do I look fucking happy?"

"No, you look like a man who's just fucked up big time."

Her small body blocks the front door, stopping my escape. My lips twitch at her attempt to make me explain.

"I need to find her, not be standing here talking to you. Excuse me." My hands land on her tiny waist and I lift her out of my way.

"If you've hurt her, I'll kill you," she calls out as I head back towards my car. I can't help the small amused chuckle that falls from my lips.

"I'd like to see you try." Looking back over my shoulder before I drop into my car, I expect to find a pissed expression on her face, but what I find is one of pride.

"What?" I ask, confused.

"Just go and sort your shit out. I hope she gives you hell."

Rolling my eyes, I drop down and slam the door behind me. Was that some kind of approval? She has no idea what happened tonight, yet she seems to be weirdly happy about it all.

My only other option is Lauren and Ben, so I set off in their direction.

"TREY?" Ben asks, pulling the door open with a beer in hand.

"Have you seen Erica?" I try not to allow concern to filter into my voice, but with the way his eyebrows rise, I'm not sure I'm successful.

"No. Why?" Accusation drips from his words. I don't need to tell him that I've fucked everything up. He knows, and he's already in full-on protective mode. Taking a step forward, his shoulders widen and his chest lifts. It's exactly the way he looked when he caged me in at the restaurant a few weeks ago after I'd fucked her in the bathroom. Back then, I was glad she had someone like Ben looking out for her. Now I've screwed up, I'm not feeling so good about the fact that he could quite easily keep her from me and end my new job in one foul swoop.

"There's been a bit of a misunderstanding." I cringe as the words leave my mouth, but I don't really feel like standing here and explaining everything to my boss, who also just happens to be one of my girl's closest friends.

"Baby, who is it?" Lauren calls seconds before she also appears and tucks herself into Ben's side. The sight of them together makes my heart twist. They have such an easy relationship, like they've literally found the other half of themselves. "Trey? I thought you were taking Erica out for a meal tonight."

"Yeah, things didn't quite go as planned. Have you seen her? Heard from her?"

"Is she okay?" Her sudden over the top concern is enough to make me think they know more than they're letting on.

"Look, if she's here, please just let me talk to her. It's not like it seemed."

"She's not here," Ben says just as Lauren opens her mouth to respond.

"I just need to explain. Please."

Lauren looks over her shoulder at Ben, and I can't help feeling like I'm getting somewhere... until Ben shakes his head at her.

"If we hear from her, we'll pass on that you're looking for her. But if you can't find her, it's probably because she doesn't want to be found."

"But—"

"I told you not to hurt her," he growls. "We'll always be on her side."

"But it's not—"

"I'm sorry, Trey." Lauren's eyes are full of sympathy as Ben pulls her back into the house and swings the door shut on me.

"Fuck," I shout into the silence of their driveway.

Now what?

CHAPTER TWO

Stumbling out of The Avenue, I stare down the street at my car, knowing that I can't get in it. I came here in the hope that it might have been her place to escape to, but the only thing I found was a vintage bottle of whiskey that was sitting on the top shelf behind the bar.

I've never felt so lost. I have zero fucking clue what I'm meant to do now to try to fix things. I can't even fucking find her, let alone make her listen to me.

I somehow manage to find the strength to flag down a taxi, and, after slurring my address at him, I'm thrown back against the seat as he takes off across town.

The world outside passes by as one big blur, but I don't see any of it. All I can see is her. Her green eyes that darken, hungry with need every time she turns them on me. The delicious lines of her body that make my mouth water to even think about. How hot and tight her pussy is every time I slide balls deep inside her.

My cock swells as I rest my head back and replay all our times together. I'd never experienced sex like that until her. It's fucking mind-blowing. Erica is meant to be a part of my life, and I have to figure out a way to prove to her that I'm still worthy.

***

FORGOING THE STAIRS, I head straight for the lift. The temptation to kick her door down is going to be too fucking high if I so much as catch a glance at it.

Attempting to shut down the thoughts of her flat being right beneath my feet, I fumble with my key and eventually fall into my living room. I just about manage to catch myself when the door I was leaning on for support flies open with a quick turn of the key.

Shrugging off my jacket, I allow it to fall to the floor before tugging at the buttons running down the front of my shirt. I manage a couple before my frustration gets too much and I pull until the satisfying sound of them pinging around on the wooden floor fills my ears.

Reaching into one of my kitchen cupboards, I pull out a half-empty bottle of whiskey and twist the cap. Foregoing a glass, I tip the bottle to my lips and swallow a generous measure.

I pull my phone from my pocket and fall down onto the sofa. The phone calls, voicemails and texts I've left for her have all gone unanswered, but that doesn't mean I don't try again.

Putting the phone to my ear, I wait for it to ring, but this time it just goes straight to voicemail.

"Motherfucker," I slur, throwing my phone down onto the other end of the sofa before lifting the bottle back to my lips.

WHEN I WAKE the following day, it's with one serious kink in my neck, a throbbing head, and the rain pounding against the windows.

"Fucking hell," I groan, trying to drag my body from the sofa but only managing to roll off, hitting the wooden floor with a bang.

I must land on the bottle, because the sound of glass echoes through the room as it rolls off somewhere. The memory of how much I must have consumed last night causes my head to drop back against the floor. The room around me spins, telling me that I'm no use to anyone today.

I somehow manage to pull myself to my hands and knees and embark on the seemingly monumental challenge of getting my arse to my bedroom.

I've no clue how long it takes, but I do know that I pathetically stop for a rest a few times along the way, hoping it'll help stop my stomach churning and my head from spinning. I sigh the second my body sinks into the memory foam mattress, and I'm almost instantly out like a light.

SATURDAY IS MOSTLY A BLUR. I stumble from my bed to use the bathroom and grab some food before falling face-first once again into my pillow. I know that self-pity isn't a good look on me, but I'm struggling to pull myself out of it. I feel utterly useless. I've no idea where she is, and my calls still go directly to voicemail, leaving me with no way of explaining.

It's not until the sun starts streaming in on Sunday morning that I begin to feel a little bit like myself once again. With the raging hangover cleared, I jump from the bed and grab my running kit with a new lease for life. I'm going to fix this, and she will listen to me. I won't give her the chance not to.

My feet pound the pavement as sweat starts to cover my brow. My muscles pull in the exact way I need, and it helps relieve some of the tension that's been keeping my body locked up tight.

I'd hoped that inspiration would hit while I was out, but as I push the key into the lock, I've still no fucking idea what I'm going to do. Pulling off my t-shirt, I wipe the sweat from my face and throw it into the wash basket as I start up the coffee machine.

I call her phone again, but I'm greeted by the automated voice on the other end that I'm getting fairly familiar with. Next, I try Ben in the hope that they might have heard something, but his short, sharp answers don't help at all and all but confirm my suspicions that he knows more than he's letting on.

I wonder about going back to her sister's house when another thought hits me. My parents are too far away for a heart-to-heart, but I know someone who'll probably be able to talk some sense into me right now.

I have a quick shower before pulling on a fresh pair of joggers and t-shirt, grab my keys, and head out. Not wanting to turn up empty-handed, I stop at a bakery on the way and pick up some fresh pastries.

"Trey?" Chris asks, his eyes still clouded with sleep when he pulls his front door open. "Do you know what time it is, son?"

"I'm sorry. I didn't know where else to turn."

Chris, or Uncle Chris, as I've always known him, is one of my dad's oldest friends. Even after my parents both moved away, Chris has always kept in touch. I might be a grown-arse man, but he still likes to keep an eye on me, probably to report back to my parents.

"Come on in."

He pulls the door wider and I follow him down towards his kitchen.

"Morning, Trey," Jenny, Ben's mum sings, sounding and looking much more awake than Chris.

"Morning. I bought pastries."

"Oh, you can come again," she laughs, going for plates.

Chris disappears to change while Jenny makes us all coffee. When he reappears, he walks straight over to her, wraps his arm around her waist and drops a kiss to the top of her head. The move makes my heart twist painfully in my chest. They're both proof that second chances are possible, and it gives me a little hope that things will be okay.

"I'll leave you boys to it," Jenny says with a plate and steaming mug in hand. "I'll be in the snug if you need me."

I thank her; she can obviously tell that I'm not just here for an everyday visit.

"What's up then, boy?"

"I screwed up," I admit.

"Go on," he mumbles around a mouthful of pastry.

"I've been seeing Erica." His eyebrows lift for me to continue, so he clearly knows who I'm talking about. "I didn't tell her about Sarah, and she intercepted our date Friday night. Erica's run fuck only knows where, and she won't answer her phone. Ben and Lauren obviously know something but won't tell me. I don't know what to do."

"Why didn't you tell her? It's not like you're still together. I'm sure she would really have appreciated your honesty."

"I just wanted everything to be perfect. I didn't want to bring my past into our possible future, and I had no idea how she'd cope with the knowledge that it's not just me she's going to have to accept into her life."

"And how well did that work out?"

"Fabulous, thanks for asking."

"Trey," he says, placing his mug down, his serious eyes finding mine. "How much do you know about Erica?"

"Uh…" I really want to be able to say a lot—after the time we've spent together, it really should be more than it is. "Not all that much." Almost every time I've asked her a question about herself or her past, I can physically see her shutters coming down. I know she's been hurt so her hesitance to open up is understanding, but how much she's kept from me has frustrated me more than I'm willing to admit. "She told me about her dad and how he treated her like she was nothing. I know a few little things about her ex and that she had something to do with Nick, but everyone's been pretty tight-lipped about the whole thing."

"Her ex upped and left her in a shit ton of debt. She'd saved for years to buy her flat and she was on the verge of losing it." Pride swells in my chest for what she's managed to achieve. Sadly, it's pushed aside as anger that someone she trusted could have taken that away from her. "If you know about her dad, then I'm sure you appreciate that her upbringing and teen years weren't all that great, so a stable home is important to her."

"Makes sense." I nod.

"That girl's been through so much. She's trusted all the wrong people, and they've walked all over her. It's why she's kept you at arm's length. She's afraid it'll happen all over again. She's used to men taking advantage when she's weak; it's exactly what Nick did."

"What did he do?" Leaning forward on my seat, I hope that he's going to shine a little more light on the situation everyone in the office has skirted around for weeks. The company's issues due to the old boss are impossible to miss; it was ultimately the reason for my employment and the very reason our office is crawling with auditors and final demands for payments.

"He blackmailed her into keeping his dirty secrets. And then he made her one of them."

"He slept with her?" I spit, the disgust evident in my voice.

"Nick was...an arsehole. He took exactly what he wanted and manipulated every situation exactly as he wanted it. Erica was drowning, and he knew it. He used that against her."

"Motherfucker." My heart pounds and my teeth grind as I discover what I had somewhat suspected but wished I was wrong to be true.

Erica needs someone who's going to fight like hell to prove they're trustworthy, not someone who's going to have lied from the get-go. That's exactly what she's expecting, and she needs to learn that not every man wants to take something from her.

"What the fuck am I meant to do?"

"Tell her the truth, beg for forgiveness, and spend the rest of your life proving she can trust you."

"What if she won't listen?"

"Make her."

"Fucking hell."

"Nothing worth fighting for is easy, Trey, but thanks to the events of her past, this fight is going to be even harder. Is she worth it?"

***

CHRIS' words ring in my ear the whole drive back home. There was only one answer to that question.

Yes, she's worth it. She's worth it a million times over.

I just need the chance to prove it.

Taking the stairs two at a time, I hesitate at her floor. Something tells me that she still won't be there, but I can't risk not finding out.

Rapping my knuckles against the door, my heart jumps into my chest when I hear movement inside. The sound of a female voice is enough to have me on the verge of breaking the fucking door down to get to her. It's not until the voices are right on the other side that I realise my mistake. Whoever the woman is, she's not Erica.

My shoulders slump just as Joe opens the door, revealing him and the woman, who is Erica's opposite in every way possible. My eyes widen when another guy joins them and he and the woman go to leave. Stepping aside, the woman nods at me, a small smile twitching her lips in greeting before I watch as the pair entwine their hands and descend the stairs.

Turning back to Joe, I raise both my brows at him.

"I know what you're thinking, and yeah, it was a fucking epic night."

Shaking my head, I focus on what I'm really here for. "She's not here, is she?"

"No, she's not. I don't fucking blame her, either. You're married."

"Separated and waiting for her to sign the damn divorce papers."

He lets out a long breath as he studies me. He must be happy with whatever he finds, because he soon steps aside and invites me in.

"Coffee?" he asks over his shoulder as I follow him to the kitchen.

"Black, no sugar."

"Sweet enough, huh?"

"I didn't mean to deceive her."

"I believe you."

"Really?" I wasn't expecting him to invite me in let alone be on my side here.

"Yeah. I genuinely think you care about Erica, and I believe that you wouldn't intentionally hurt her. But—" I groan at the emphasis he puts on that one word, "—you have hurt her. You lied to her after promising that you weren't like all the others. Although she'd never admit it, she trusted you. She was willing to give you the benefit of the doubt after telling herself that she'd never let another man close to her again, and you've just proved her right that men can't be trusted."

"She trusts you."

"She doesn't trust me, and she's right not to. I'm just as big as a fuck-up as the men of her past, but it's different with us. I'm not in love with her, and we have no romantic future together."

His words confuse me. To the outside world and his colleagues, Joe is this muscular, tattooed guy that, although obviously younger than the majority, oozes confidence and demands respect. What he just said is the polar opposite of that, and it makes me wonder who the man standing in front of me really is.

"I have zero advice when it comes to women and relationships, and if I were to give you some, I'd advise you take it with a pinch of salt. But you've gotta fight for her if you want her. Erica is a stubborn, independent bitch at the best of times, but after what you've just done, her walls are going to be higher and stronger than before. She's been hurt too much."

Every time someone tells me how often Erica has been hurt, that someone has broken her trust, my heart aches that little bit more and my anger and need to avenge her grows. She is hands-down the most incredible woman I've ever met, and the fact she's been used time and time again has fury unfurling in my stomach. My need to protect her and keep her safe explodes through my veins.

"Tell me where she is? I can't set about proving anything until I find her."

"Nah, I'm not getting involved. She'd kick my arse if I told you."

I lift a brow, glancing down at his body. The hours he spends at the gym are obvious: he's got the biggest arms I think I've ever seen in real life. There's no way my little redhead could kick his anything. "I think I'd pay to see that."

"She's stronger than you'd believe."

"Oh, I believe that. I just want to see it."

"Erica's..." he pauses, a small smile appearing on his lips. "Incredible. Her strength is amazing, her ability to bounce back is out of this world, but at some point she's going to break, and you'd better make damn fucking sure you're not the cause of it."

I nod, the emotion of how far he'd go to protect her clogging my throat. Erica might have had some bad people in her past, but I really hope she appreciates the incredible people she has around her now. She's created her own little family who will protect her no matter the cost.

"Can I use your bathroom?"

"Knock yourself out."

I do what I need to do and intend on heading straight to Joe for another shot at getting the information I need out of him, but when I step from the small room, her bedroom calls to me. Slipping down the hallway, I push the handle down and step inside. Her scent hits me immediately, like a bat to the chest. Lifting my hand, I rub at the ache and walk over to her bed. Just being here makes me feel closer to her, which is crazy because she could be miles away.

Lying down on her bed, I allow her essence to surround me and think back to how good everything was before I fucked up just like she was expecting me to do. I knew I should have told her about my previous life from the get-go, but I was so swept away by her that I never found the right time.

Pulling my phone from my pocket, my heart drops at seeing no replies to any of my previous messages or calls. Opening the camera, I stretch my arm out as far as it will go and snap a selfie of myself on her bed.

> Trey: I miss having you beside me.
> Please come back and hear me out. It's
> not how it seems. Please?

It's delivered immediately and, to my amazement, those two little ticks turn blue for the first time in days. My heart thunders in my chest and the phone in my hand trembles as I wait to see if she's going to reply.

Nothing happens. The little bouncing dots I was hoping to see never appear.

CHAPTER THREE

Joe never gave up her hiding place. Although it's frustrating as fuck, it fills me with happiness that she can trust him, even if he believes he's totally untrustworthy.

When I wake on Monday morning, excitement and anticipation fill my veins. She can hide all she wants over the weekend, but she's got a job that she loves and people relying on her, so I know I'm going to see her this morning.

I don't get nervous, but when I pull up outside our office I'm pretty sure the sick feeling in the pit of my stomach and the sweating of my palms is exactly that.

Feeling ridiculous that a woman can have this kind of effect on me, I suck in a deep breath and throw my door open.

It might only be Ben in the office when I walk in but already the atmosphere is heavy.

"Trey? Get in here."

His voice is deep with an angry edge, so I don't hesitate to follow orders, which isn't usually something I'm all that happy about—but if this has anything to do with Erica, I'm all ears.

"What's up, boss?" I try to keep my tone light but one look at his face and my shoulders tense. I'm not going to like what he's about to say, that much is obvious.

"Look," he barks, twisting his screen around violently so I can see it.

Dear Ben,
It's with huge regret that I am giving you my resignation, effective immediately. Johnson & Sons hasn't just been a job for me, it's been my family, and I will miss it more than I could possibly explain. I was welcomed with loving arms and, for the most part, it's continued until this day. I've made incredible friends who I hope will still be there as I embark on the next chapter of my life—hell knows I'm going to need you.
I am contactable via email if there is anything that needs my attention. I will help you out in any way I can until you are able to find my replacement, but I will not be visiting the office.
With regret and love,
Erica Wilde

My eyes burn as emotion fills me. Stumbling back from her words that cut right down to my soul, I fall over one of the chairs and only just about catch myself.

"Motherfucker," I roar. My fist finds the freshly plastered stud wall and smashes right through it.

My knuckles burn on contact, but I welcome it. It's better than the pain radiating from my chest right about now. Dragging some much needed air into my lungs, I pull my hand back and assess the damage.

"You've got a meeting in twenty minutes. Get your shit together. You can worry about fixing that when you get back." His words are harsh. He's placing every single bit of blame for this on my shoulders, as he well should, but fuck this hurts. I've never been such a big disappointment to people I cared about. It's a feeling I'd rather not get too used to.

I wince as warm water trickles over my cut and tender knuckles, but it's only small compared to the pain I deserve for what I've caused. The water immediately turns red, and I watch transfixed as it swirls in the bottom of the basin before disappearing down the waste.

The realisation that in Erica's eyes I'm no different to any of the men of her past makes my breathing falter. I knew my omission of the truth had hurt her, but for her to hand her notice in? A familiar ache reappears in my chest. I hurt her more than I even realised.

Lauren's just walking into the office as I leave. Concern fills her eyes as we pass, but she doesn't say anything, just watches me get in my car and drive away.

I can't help feeling like she wants to help me. The look in her eyes is different from everyone else's. They all want to keep me as far away from Erica as possible, which is exactly as she's instructed, I'm sure. But Lauren is different. Maybe it has to do with everything she and Ben went through to get where they are now. I've no idea, but she wants to help, I can feel it. I just need to get her alone.

ON TUESDAY MORNING, I get my first opportunity to talk to Lauren. She's in the kitchen making coffee, Ben's out at a meeting, and everyone else is engrossed in whatever they're doing.

It's now or never.

Pushing the door closed behind me to cut off eavesdroppers, I walk over to where she's looking out of the window, waiting for the kettle to boil.

"I need your help."

Her head snaps around and her eyes widen when she finds me right behind her. "Shit, I didn't even hear you come in."

"Please. I need to know where she is. I need to talk to her."

"I can't, Trey. I won't break her trust."

"I need her. I need her to hear me out. I promise you it's not as bad as it looks."

"Your wife turned up for your date. It looks pretty bad."

"She's not my wife. Well...technically she is until she agrees to sign the papers. We've been over—this isn't important right now. Erica's the only one I need to explain this to. Please, I know you know where she is, just tell me."

I don't mean to, but the more I start begging, the closer I get and the more I cage her in. I'm so desperate to get the answers that I'll do anything—including intimidating the boss, it seems.

"I can't." Emotion starts to swim in Lauren's eyes, and I know she's about to break.

"I can sort all this out, I promise. I just need her to listen."

"Enough." A large hand lands on my shoulder and forcefully pulls me backwards. "Back off."

My back hits the counter as Ben cages me in. We're similar heights, but he's got a fair bit more muscle than I have, so I wouldn't back myself if something were to kick off. Plus he has the obvious age advantage on his side. His eyes bore into mine, his face hard, his muscles pulled tight like he's about to throw a punch any minute.

"Ben, it's fine."

"He had you pinned in the fucking corner," he seethes, his cold eyes never leaving mine.

"I wasn't pinned. It was nothing. Just leave it." Out of the corner of my eye, I see her wrap her small hands around his arm, and he visibly relaxes.

"Go fucking near her again, and you won't be stepping foot back into this office."

"Ben!" Lauren gasps, her eyes wide with shock.

"Just tell me where she is. I know you both know." I make one last attempt to get what I need.

The couple look at each other. Ben's head shakes ever so slightly, and Lauren accepts it.

"Erica trusted us not to tell you, and I'm sorry, but our loyalties lie with her. You're going to have to figure this one out yourself."

Both of them leave the room and, once I'm alone, I spin around, rest my palms on the counter and hang my head in defeat.

I spend the rest of the day silently getting on with work at my desk, desperately trying not to glance up at her empty one. I can't look anywhere in this place without seeing her, and it's driving me to distraction. I've already fucked up one price I had to submit, and I've ordered the wrong kit to one of our jobs. I'm a fucking liability right now, and I can't see it getting better anytime soon.

As the day comes to a close, Lauren appears from her and Ben's office and sits in Erica's chair. I watch as she blows out a breath and looks at the framed picture on Erica's desk of the two of them, Joe, and another girl I don't know.

Sadness radiates from her in waves as she starts collecting up Erica's stuff and placing it into two empty boxes. I note that she's putting work related stuff into one and her personal possessions into the second. The work box is placed on a shelf while she walks out with the other after having a quick chat with Ben.

Without putting too much thought into it, I close my laptop, grab my stuff and follow her out. I have no idea if she spots me. I keep my head down and pretend I'm done for the day as I climb into my car and start the engine. I allow her to go on a little ahead, but I keep a close eye on the direction she takes and trail after her from a distance.

I'm so focused on not losing her that I have no idea where we are when she eventually pulls the car to a stop. Thankfully, I manage to find a space a little down the street, and I prepare to get out to continue following if necessary, but when I watch her walk into a hairdresser's without the box in hand, I sit back and relax. This plan is really going to go to shit if I have to sit here and wait while she has her fucking hair done.

My phone rings, and, after pulling it from my pocket to check that it's not Erica, I throw it into the console and focus on not missing Lauren's departure. Thankfully, after only a few minutes, she's back out. She casts her eyes down the street before stepping from the shop, and I duck in panic. But she returns to her car and her indicator comes on as she goes to pull away. I follow moments later.

I trail her through a residential area, and my hopes start to rise that, at any moment, she could pull over and reveal where Erica's hiding, but other than stopping for a couple of red lights she just continues.

When she does eventually indicate and pull over, I almost miss it because of the distance between us. I end up passing her and parking on the other side of the road as she gets out and goes into an Indian food shop.

Waiting for her to appear again takes longer this time, and when she does, she has a bagful of stuff. My stomach rumbles loudly as I imagine what she might be cooking later with all of that, reminding me that I didn't have any lunch earlier.

She sets off once again, and I fall into place a few cars behind her.

The cat and mouse act soon starts to get old when she stops

two more times, once at a chemist and again at a corner shop not all that far from her home. Every single time, she gets back in the car and heads off again.

The next time she stops and walks into a shop, I pay a little more attention as the mannequins in the windows show off a selection of sexy lingerie and stickers advertising that the latest Rabbit is now in stock. My balls ache as I imagine how Erica would look wearing what's in the window; better than those plastic dolls, that's for sure. It feels like a lifetime ago I was last inside her. My need to plunge my cock deep inside her body is beginning to get the better of me. My cock swells, and I rest my head back, closing my eyes just for a few seconds as I allow myself to revisit my memories of what it's like to be with her. To feel the softness of her curves under my hands, to suck her sweet skin into my mouth and listen to her moan and beg for more.

Banging beside me scares the shit out of me. Jumping a mile out of my seat, I turn to see who's interrupted my little erotic trip down memory lane.

"Fucking hell," I groan when I find a very smug looking Lauren staring back at me. Lowering the window, I swear her smile only gets wider.

"Credit where credit's due, Trey. I really thought you'd get bored before I did, but I've got shit to be doing. This little tour of London has been fun and all, but I kinda need to get home and cook dinner."

My chin drops at her words. She was playing me?

"Oh, don't look so surprised. I saw you pull out from the office after me and then every time I looked in my mirror, there you were. I get that you want to see her, Trey. I really do understand, but she's asked me not to tell you where she is, so I'm not going to lead you right to her door."

I narrow my eyes at her and she laughs.

She lets out a sigh and looks at me, her eyes full of sympathy. "Use your head a little. Think outside the box. You know her better than she thinks you do. Figure it out. Prove to her that, no matter what, you can find her. That you need her just that badly."

CHAPTER FOUR

This week's been hell, but, as I pull up on the driveway of my old home, I know things are about to look up, if only for a few hours.

It still feels alien knocking on my own front door, but I guess that's what happens when you walk away from your own life.

"Wow, I didn't think you'd show your face this morning."

"Are they ready?"

"No. I assumed you'd be too busy chasing skirt."

"Shut the fuck up, Sarah. When have I ever just not turned up?"

"You've not been here the past two weekends."

"Which I told you in advance about." I shake my head as she stands her ground, keeping her foot behind the door so it'll only open a few inches. "Girls," I call loudly enough to fill the house. "You ready?"

"Two minutes, Dad," Ella calls as Sofia's feet start pounding down the stairs.

"Dad," she wails, practically pushing Sarah aside so she can throw her arms around my waist.

"Hey, baby. I missed you."

"Where have you been? You were meant to take us out last weekend."

"I know, I'm just trying to settle into my new place and my new job."

Sarah scoffs but thankfully decides to leave us to it. "Make sure they're back by seven. Ella's got a sleepover at a friend's."

"Sure thing."

Keeping Sofia tucked into my side, we wait as Ella appears from upstairs with her coat on, ready to go.

"Dad, you okay?" she asks the second her eyes land on me.

"Yeah, of course. Ready to have some fun?" In truth, one look at her and I was struck with a wave of emotions so strong I struggled to fight them back down. My babies are growing up too quickly, and now I'm no longer living with them I'm missing out on so much. It was the main reason I stayed here as long as I did. My two girls are my life. I'd do anything for them, but keeping up appearances that we were a happy family could only last so long. At twelve and fourteen, they aren't babies anymore. They're young women, and I couldn't be prouder of the adults they're becoming.

With them either side of me, we walk out to my car.

"What are we doing?"

"Theme park?"

"Yesss," Sofia squeals happily while Ella has a slightly more composed reaction.

"SO, HOW'S SCHOOL?" I ask Ella who called shotgun and took the front seat, much to Sofia's frustration.

"It's good. Same as usual. Not enough PE lessons and way too much math."

I chuckle. It's the same response every time I ask. With Ella staring down at her phone, I look in the mirror at my youngest daughter. "How about you, Sof?"

Sofia's reply is much more animated as she dives into every detail of school life, barely letting up for air before we reach the theme park. I know everything about her classes, friends, and the birthday party she's going to soon. She's practically bouncing with excitement as we queue for tickets, unlike Ella who's much more placid about what the day holds. It's not unusual for her to be the quieter, more thoughtful one of the two of them, but I can't help but wonder if there's more going on in her head.

We both follow Sofia around and go on all the rides she wants to go on. It warms my heart, seeing her so happy, but that doesn't mean I forget about the quieter one of the two who happily follows her around and smiles at all the right times. She's much more focused on whomever she's texting than on what's going on around her.

"Can we go on the log flume?" Sofia squeals when we walk towards it.

"No way. I spent way too long on my make-up this morning to get wet."

"Dad?"

"How about you go, and we'll watch."

She pouts but after a few seconds agrees to the plan and happily bounces off, while Ella and I find a bench to sit and watch.

"What's up, kiddo?"

"Have you got a new girlfriend?"

"Uh…" I wasn't expecting this. "What's your mum said?"

"Nothing. I overheard her on the phone talking to Auntie Sue."

"Oh right. You shouldn't eavesdrop, baby."

"I wasn't, I just walked to the kitchen and she said it. She said she's young enough to be your daughter."

Rubbing my palm down my face, I try to figure out what to say for the best. "She's not young enough to be my daughter, although she is a little younger than me."

She lets out a disappointed sigh. "You're really not coming back home, are you?"

"I'm so sorry, El. Things between me and your mum haven't been right for years. I needed to get out."

"I get it, Dad. I just miss you."

"I miss you too, more than you could ever know." I wrap my arm around her, pull her into my side and kiss the top of her head.

"Sometimes I just need a hug from you."

I hold her a little tighter as a ball of emotion clogs my throat. I know how important it is for teenagers to have both parents around—hell, everyone needs their parents around, no matter how old they are.

Fuck.

"Dad, are you okay?" Ella asks when I noticeably tense against her.

"Yeah, yeah. I'm fine." In reality, I've just realised how to find Erica, and I'm frustrated because I didn't think of it sooner. She told me herself that every Sunday she and her sister visit their mum. Tomorrow morning, I'll know exactly where she'll be.

Feeling my shoulders loosen for the first time in days, a small smile twitches at my lips.

"Oh my god, that was epic!" Sofia screeches as she comes running over, dripping wet from the ride. "Give me a hug, sis."

"Do not touch me," Ella fumes, standing from the bench and backing away.

"That's enough, you two. Shall we get out of here and get dinner?"

"Yes, I'm starving," Sofia complains, wringing out her hair.

"On second thought, we'd better wait until you've dried off a little."

CHAPTER FIVE

Spending the day with my girls was exactly what I needed, and not just because Ella was the inspiration to figure out where I'd find Erica.

I'm up bright and early the next morning, pacing my living room and hoping the minutes will tick around quicker so I can see her. It's been over a week and I'm missing her like crazy. It's enough to tell me that the words I said to Chris last weekend were true and that she is very much worth it.

I don't leave the flat until I know she'll already be there. I might want to surprise her, but I don't want to ruin her visit. When I got back last night, I Googled the care home and discovered it specialises in dementia patients. I've no idea how old Erica's mum might be, but I was surprised to read that, seeing as Erica is only twenty-six.

Gripping the wheel painfully tight once I've pulled the car to a stop outside the home at the opposite end of the car park to what I recognise as Sam's car, I replay everything I need to say to Erica in my head. I already know that she's going to do anything possible not to listen to me. After a week of hiding, she's not likely to hear anything I've got to say willingly, so I need a plan.

Sucking in a deep breath, I throw the door open and step out. My legs feel like jelly as I head towards reception. The place looks exactly as I expected. Neutral, minimalist and quiet. Finding a seat in a dark corner, I sit and wait. I've no idea how long they'll stay—I guess it depends on how their mum is.

My leg bounces and my heart pounds the longer I sit there. Every time I hear female voices, my heart jumps into my throat, but it's never them.

I begin to think that maybe they're not here and the car I assumed was Erica's sister's in the car park was actually someone else's. Just as I'm starting to think about leaving and giving it up as a failed attempt, two soft voices filter down to me.

"So, how are you really doing? The morning sickness getting any better?"

That's not them. It can't be.

Blowing out a frustrated breath, I wait for the women to appear, knowing it's not going to be her. But they don't get that close before my stomach twists to the point I worry I might be about to throw up on my feet.

"No, it's not subsiding at all. I swear I actually feel worse each day."

I don't need to see her to know that is her voice. Erica's...Erica's *pregnant?* My hands tremble as I fight to drag in the air I need.

I should probably stick with my plan to make my presence known, but when Erica and her sister walk around the corner and my eyes land on her for the first time in a week, my body turns to stone.

She looks as beautiful as the last time I saw her, but even I can't miss the slight greyish tone to her skin, making the words I just overheard seem even more real.

She's fucking pregnant?

Those words are still on repeat in my head as I watch them both get into the car I suspected was Sam's, but thankfully they don't pull out straight away. It gives me a chance to bolt from the reception and into my own car so I can follow them. I need to know where she's going so I can talk to her. If what I just overheard is true, then it's more important than ever that she hears me out.

I trail them from a distance, hoping like hell that I'm doing a better job of it than I did with Lauren. When they pull into a car park outside a pub, I follow and hope that I manage to discreetly park a little farther in the shadows.

They both exit the car and walk towards the pub, so I assume I was successful. I'd like to think that, if they suspected something, they'd come over. I'm not sure about Sam, but I know for a fact that Erica wouldn't be able to ignore me if she knew I was watching.

Waiting for them to reappear is the longest hour of my life as I sit there and think about the possibility of being a dad for a third time and going back to having a baby. It was so long ago that my girls depended on me like that that...I think I've forgotten how to do it all.

A year or so after Sofia was born, Sarah started begging me for a third. I always refused. I think I knew back then that something wasn't quite right, although it would be years before I'd come to terms with it. Having another baby was never an option, as far as I was concerned. We had our two perfect girls, and that was more than enough for me. But what about now? Could I have another baby all these years later? What would my girls think of that?

Would they accept it? Hell, I have no idea if they'll even accept Erica, yet let alone a sibling.

Sitting back in my seat, I wait for them to be inside the car once again before starting my engine and attempting to secretly follow them.

When they pull up outside Sam's flat, I breathe a sigh of relief that they're not going to give me the run around like Lauren did. I park a little down the street and allow them to go inside while I try to figure out what the fuck to do.

Needing to hear a rational voice before I decide if I'm going to go storming into Sam's house and confront her, I grab my phone and call Chris.

"Trey, how's everything going?"

"It could be better."

"What's happened now? Have you found Erica yet?"

"Yeah, I've found her. I've also discovered that this thing between us is more complicated than I thought."

"Why?"

"I think she's pregnant." The words feel unnatural falling from my lips, but I don't panic the way I would have expected if someone would have told me this was going to happen.

"Okay. So does that change things?"

"I've no idea," I say, honestly.

"Is she still worth it?"

"Yes." The answer is out of my mouth almost before he asks the question. I don't even need to think about it.

"So what are you waiting for? If you know where she is, go get your girl and stop wasting time talking to me."

"Fuck."

"Just go," he says with a laugh before hanging up on me.

Blowing out a long breath, I push myself from the car and make my way towards the flat.

Waiting for someone to answer the door after ringing the bell are the most nerve-wracking few seconds of my life. I'm not sure whether I'm excited or relieved when it's Sam who pulls the door open. Not wanting to give her a chance to slam it in my face, I put my foot inside.

"I know she's here. I need to talk to her."

"Hi, nice to see you again," she says with a sickly sweet voice. "I wondered how long you were planning on sitting out there. Oh, don't look so shocked. You'll never make a secret agent." My mouth drops open that I've once again been caught. "She has no idea, mind you," she adds.

"Are you going to let me in?"

"I'm gonna let you in, but you should know that if this goes badly, I'm going to claim you forced your way in."

"Whatever," I mutter as she stands aside and lets me past.

"Kitchen," she calls, pointing down the hallway.

"Who is...fuck," Erica says, her eyes widening when she looks up and finds me in the doorway. "What the hell are you doing here?"

"Coming to pick up what's mine."

"I'm not a fucking object, Trey. I've got nothing to say to you, so I suggest you leave the way you came."

"Erica, please. It's not as bad as it seems."

"What, you didn't lie to me about being married?"

"Can we do this in private?"

"No, we're not doing this at all. You ruined whatever we had the moment you lied to me. You're just as bad as all the others. Actually, no...you're worse, because you promised. You promised you were different and that you'd never hurt me like they did." Seeing tears fill her eyes and her chin tremble as she fights to stay strong almost breaks me. I never wanted to hurt her, and I was desperate to keep my promise to her. I know I should have told her long before she was forced to discover the truth, and that's totally my fault, but I refuse to lose her over it.

"Erica, please. There's so much you don't know."

"Exactly, which is why my answer is no. We're done, Trey." Her determined stare meets mine—until I drop the bombshell that she really isn't expecting and they widen in shock.

"We're not. Especially not while you're pregnant." Her face pales, her eyes fill with tears, and her head shakes in disbelief.

"How'd you know?" she whispers.

"Let's get out of here and we can talk." Her shoulders are still tense as she sits and considers my suggestion.

Eventually, she lets out a sigh and says, "Fine," before pushing the chair out behind her and getting up.

I stand and watch as she gives her sister a hug goodbye. "Just hear him out, yeah?" I don't think I'm meant to hear it, but Sam doesn't whisper quietly enough.

"We'll see," Erica says before turning toward me. "Well, come on then." She sounds far from happy about it, but at least she's willing.

Stepping up to her, I place my hand in the small of her back and hate when she flinches away from me.

"I said I'd listen. I didn't agree to anything else," she hisses, and my heart drops. It looks like I've got an even bigger fight on my hands than I expected.

I hold the car door open for her and wait patiently as she gets in, but at no point does she look at me or say anything. The entire journey is the same: she stares out of the window, totally ignoring my existence.

Not wanting to go back to either of our flats, I head towards the park we walked around the other Sunday after our night at the hotel. It feels like a million years ago now. She was overly emotional that weekend; I guess it all makes sense now I know she's pregnant.

Finding a space on the edge of the park, I pull the car to a stop and get out. Thankfully, she gets out and meets me on the pavement. My arm aches to reach for her, to entwine our fingers together, but I know it would be a bad move, so I attempt to ignore it as I take a step forward, hoping that we can find a bench and that she'll hear me out.

The park is pretty quiet for a sunny winter afternoon. There are a few joggers and dog walkers on the paths and just a couple of kids kicking a ball and laughing in the distance. The sight of them sets me off thinking about what the future might hold for Erica and me. Could we be here in a few years kicking a ball around, or am I about to become a dad to another child I won't have full access to?

Blowing out a slow breath, I try not to get ahead of myself. She's yet to say anything, so there's no point in jumping to conclusions.

Erica follows me over to an empty bench and sits down beside me. When she doesn't say anything, I do.

"It was never my intention not to tell you about Sarah, about my past. Things were just a little intense, and my focus was on you and our possible future. I'd spent the past few months, years really, trying to figure out how to best move on with my life, and it was finally happening." She doesn't respond, but I do catch her glancing over at me from the corner of her eye, so I continue. "Things had been over between us long before I moved out. We'd been together since we were fourteen, and I don't think either of us really wanted to admit that we'd grown apart. But we had. We were no longer the people we once were, and we both wanted different things."

"How?" It's the first word she's spoken in a long time, and it starts to give me a little hope that she's really hearing what I'm saying.

"I wanted to get out and try new things before we got too old. I wanted to travel, do all the things the two of us wanted when we were younger and couldn't afford to. But she was happy at home doing her thing. I started to resent her, and I knew it was time to call it quits before we ended up hurting each other. I moved out about three months ago, although our relationship was long over. I quit my job and went travelling. I needed to find myself. Shit, I sound like a teenager or something, but I had no idea who I really was without her. I'd spent all of my adult life with her by my side, but I couldn't do it to myself any longer. I needed more than she could offer me."

"Okay," she breathes, before she falls silent once again. The sound of the cars behind us filters through the trees and mixes with the bird song up above. The cool air gently blows past us, but neither of us seem to notice. We're too lost in our own world that could be about to crash down around our feet. "Do you have anything else to tell me? Because now would be a really good time." Her voice is weak and broken. I hate that I'm the one to have caused that. I promised never to hurt her, but I fear I may have caused more pain than any before me if her dejection right now is anything to go by.

"Sarah and I have two kids." Saying that out loud feels like a huge load lifting from my shoulders.

Her eyes burn into the side of my head and I turn towards her, my breath catching at the exhausted and devastated look on her face.

"Jesus, Trey." She slumps back against the bench, and I panic.

"I'm so sorry. I never meant to lie to you, I was just so swept away by you and starting a new job, and then as the days went on and we became more serious, I just didn't know how to say it."

Placing a protective hand on her belly, I'm reminded of what she's also been hiding.

"I'm not the only one with secrets though, am I?"

"Do not even try to compare the two situations. You actively hid your family, your past, from me for weeks. I'd only just discovered the truth and I had every intention of telling you that night, only your wife interrupted. How did she even know I'd be there?"

"We used to go there regularly," I admit with a wince.

"So I was just stepping into her place in your life?"

"No, no way. It really is my favourite restaurant—that has nothing to do with her. The head chef is an old friend of mine and the food's incredible."

"I wouldn't know, I didn't get the chance to find out," she snaps.

"Where do we go from here?" I ask, beginning to feel like we're just going around in circles.

"I..." she starts but blows out a long breath instead of finishing her sentence. "Do you want more kids, Trey?"

My silence must clue her in as to where my head's at. "Fuck, you don't, do you?"

"I didn't think I did, no."

"Fucking hell." Standing, Erica stares down at me. She wants me to tell her I didn't mean it, but I promised her, and myself, that I would be totally honest.

"I wasn't expecting this. It was the last thing I thought I'd overhear while I was sitting in the care home waiting room for you to appear."

"You were at Park View?"

"Yeah, I figured I'd find you there."

"Huh, smart move," she mutters to herself like she hadn't considered I'd think of it. "It doesn't really matter how long you've known. People's first reaction to things is usually correct, and if you're saying now that you don't want any more kids, that's how you feel." Seeing her hand on her belly once again guts me.

"No, I'm not saying—"

"That's enough." She puts her other hand up to stop me. "I can't listen to any more right now. I need you to take me home."

"Erica, please. I—"

"No, Trey. Take me home, or I'll call a taxi." She starts digging through her bag, and I panic that our time might be over.

"Okay, okay. Let's go."

Tension radiates from her as she turns her back on me slightly and stares out of the window. The drive to our building is the most painful journey of my life. Every inch of my body is begging to reach out and touch her, to do anything to make it all better, but I know I can't. I can't make it better, and I can't touch her.

"Where have you been all week? I've been going crazy."

"At a friend's."

"Are you planning on staying now?" I ask, nodding towards our building as I pull into the car park.

"I've no idea what I'm doing. I'm without a job, and I've no way of paying the mortgage, so..." she trails off, and I feel like the worst human being on the planet.

"Come back to work, Erica. I'll leave if I have to." She shrugs and reaches for the handle. "Wait. What now?"

"I don't know, Trey. I don't know anything right now."

"Can I see you again?"

"I'll call you."

"When?"

"I don't know." Her voice is getting harder and her words more clipped. I know I'm pissing her off, but I can't let her go, knowing I might not get another chance. "You hurt me, Trey. You lied to me about something so huge. I don't know if I'll ever be able to trust you again. I'll call you, but I don't know when, so I suggest you don't wait by the phone." With that, she jumps from the car and slams the door behind her.

"Fuck," I shout, slamming my palms down on the steering wheel. It must be louder than I expected, because just before she enters the building, she turns to look back at me and my heart damn near explodes in my chest.

CHAPTER SIX

There's still no sign of Erica on Monday morning at work, and I hear no mention of her appearing. I meant what I said yesterday: I'd willingly hand my notice in if it meant she'd come back. The last thing I want is her worrying about how she's going to pay her mortgage.

I spend most of the day out of the office, which is a good thing because I'm not taunted by her empty desk all day. I'm not so lucky on Tuesday, as I find my only meeting rescheduled for later in the week. With a huge pile of pricing to get through, I turn myself into the corner of my desk and try to block out my surroundings.

By the time lunch rolls around, I lose my concentration and find myself staring longingly at Erica's side of the room, wishing she'd come bouncing from the kitchen with a mug in her hand at any moment.

Sensing someone beside me, I turn to find Lauren perching herself on my desk. Her eyes flit over my face, and there's concern written all over hers.

"Have you even slept?"

"Not really."

"She's okay." If her words are meant to make me feel better, they really miss the mark. How could she possibly be okay after everything?

"She's pregnant." I don't mean to say the words aloud, but they seem to just fall from my lips.

"I know," Lauren whispers. Reaching out, she places her hand on my shoulder. "How are you holding up?"

"I miss her. I just...I don't really know, to be honest."

"You've fallen in love with her, haven't you?"

My heart thunders in my chest as I realise that it's true. "Yeah, I think I have."

I didn't expect any of this. I thought I'd leave Sarah and embark on a new life as a single man. I never even considered that I'd find love again, especially not so soon, but it's not like I can do anything about it. Erica has completely stolen my heart. If only she'd give me the opportunity to win hers.

"Have you told her?"

"What do you think?" I ask with a sigh.

"I know I probably sound like a broken record, but you need to fight for her. Prove to her how you feel and don't give her the opportunity to forget you." The thought of Erica forgetting about what we had has a sharp pain shooting through my chest. Surely it's not possible?

"She won't listen to me. She won't even see me."

"You need to make her. I've heard from a very reliable source that you aren't one to lie back and take it. So get out there and figure out a way to get back into her life...into your *baby's* life."

"Fuck. I'm gonna be a dad again." Lauren smiles down at me warmly.

"You didn't hear it from me, but she's moved back home."

Lauren pushes away from the desk, leaving me to wonder what I'm meant to do with that information. Erica made it very clear that she'll contact me when she's ready. As much as I want to demand that she spends time with me so I can prove myself, I also respect her wish for time. That means I need to keep myself in her thoughts even when not there—although after everything and her pregnancy revelation, I can't imagine she's had much chance to forget me.

Pulling up the website I ordered her flowers from last time, I find the most expensive bunch they have to offer and quickly pay, this time sending them to her actual flat. I also organise for a tub of the ice cream she loved so much to be delivered. I've no idea how she feels about her pregnancy, so I hold back from sending anything maternity related. For all I know, she isn't going to keep it. My stomach twists painfully at the thought, and my mouth waters like I'm about to puke. No, if she's even considered not going through with it, she'd have told me, right? She wouldn't have been unknowingly placing her hand on her belly like she was already protecting the little one growing in there.

Unsure of what else I can do right now, I try to focus on what I *should* be doing, but every few minutes, my mind wanders. I think back to when Sarah was pregnant and the things she said made her life a little easier. Grabbing a Post-it note, I scribble a few things down, intending on buying them for Erica when I get a chance.

Once I've emailed off the price I'm working on, I give up and head out of the office with my laptop tucked under my arm, intending to do some more from home. At least in my flat I don't have to stare at her empty desk. *No, but you'll know she's beneath you,* a little voice says. I push it away and climb into my car.

I SPOT Joe's van pulling into our building's car park as I get out of my car and pull the couple of bags of shopping I stopped off for on the way home.

"Hard day?" I ask when he steps from his van with a large sigh.

"Yeah, you could say that. The job I'm on is a nightmare, fucking asbestos everywhere."

"You fancy going for a drink?"

He pauses at the front door and looks up, I assume considering his roommate who's hiding out upstairs. "Uh..."

"I know she's back, and I promise to do as she asks and stay away, for now. I could just really do with—" Thankfully, he cuts me off from having to admit that I need someone to talk to who knows her.

"Yeah, no worries. Let me shower and I'll come up to you when I'm ready."

It's almost an hour later when there's a knock at my door. I was starting to wonder if he'd stood me up.

"Sorry, Erica got chatting. Shit, I'm sorry." I tried to hide my reaction at hearing her name and knowing she's just downstairs, but I think I failed.

"It's fine. Let me grab my coat and we can go. The less time I'm in this building, the better."

"You moving?" Joe asks from behind me, looking down at the houses I'd printed out as potentials.

"I've no idea what the fuck I'm doing right now. I rented this place as a temporary thing until I figured out what to do with my life."

He nods, but I sense he wants to ask more as he backs out of my flat, allowing me to lock up.

"Is the pub around the corner okay, or did you want to go somewhere more..."

"Somewhere more..." I prompt.

"Fancy?" he asks with a wince.

"You think I'm pretentious?"

"I don't really know you. I'm just going by the fancy suits and the expensive car. I don't really picture you in a London boozer."

I chuckle. "You're something else, you know that?"

"So I've been told," he says sadly. I'd ask more if it weren't for the closed-off expression on his face.

The pub is pretty packed, but I manage to find a table at the back while Joe heads to the bar for a couple of pints.

"So those houses you're looking at. They family homes?" he asks with a raised eyebrow, dropping into the seat beside me.

"Of course. I only printed them yesterday."

When he looks back up at me, his eyes have softened. "You're really serious about her, aren't you?"

"Yeah, I am."

"Baby an' all?"

"I'll take her however she'll allow me to have her." I cringe— the words sounded better in my head.

"She needs you to fight for her," he blurts out but quickly snaps his lips shut. "Shit, I promised her I wouldn't give you advice."

"I'm trying to honour her wishes and give her some space. She said she'd contact me, and I'm trying really fucking hard to allow her that."

"That must be fun." The smug smile on his face shows me how much he's enjoying my torment after hurting her. It's clear how strongly he feels for her and that he only wants the best for her.

"Listen, she'll kill me if she finds out I told you this, but..." He glances around as if he expects her to jump up and shout at him for even suggesting getting involved. "She'd never admit it, but she really wants a white knight to sweep her off her feet and rescue her from herself. She's telling you she needs space, but really, what she needs is you. Get in her face, show her that you can't live without her. Prove to her how important she is to you, how much you need her."

"So you're suggesting I break your door down and demand she listens?"

"Ambush her."

"What?"

"Catch her off-guard. She won't have her walls so high as she would if she's expecting you."

"Okaaay. So..." I'm not asking for suggestions by trailing off; I'm more trying to scheme up a way to do what he suggests, but he helpfully gives me the answer.

"Her sister's wedding is this weekend. It's at St.—"

"Margaret's Church followed by The Ivy. I know, I saw the invite last week."

"So..."

"So what?"

"Get one of your fancy arse suits out and surprise the shit out of her."

His words are on repeat in my mind the whole time we're in the pub and long after I fall asleep that night.

CHAPTER SEVEN

I'm awake long before the sun rises on the morning of Samantha's wedding. I've been battling with what to do for the best ever since Joe brought it up.

Knowing Erica the way I do, I know that today is going to be a big deal for her. Her sister and her have a special kind of bond, and I'd hate to get in the middle of what should be a memorable day for both of them, but, in the end, my need for her gets too much. When I climb out of bed, I find my feet taking me towards my wardrobe to pull out a suit suitable for a wedding.

Erica told me little bits about today, so I know it's only an intimate ceremony with close friends and family. I already know my appearance will stand out like a sore thumb.

I'm ready hours before the ceremony is due to start, but I'm too much of a nervous wreck to sit about waiting and allowing a million possibilities of what today might hold run around my head. Instead, I grab my car keys and head out.

I drive around the city before stopping at the end of Oxford Street so I can run into Selfridges to grab a wedding gift. If I'm gate crashing this thing, I can't exactly go empty-handed. I've no bloody clue what Samantha and her new husband might want, so I settle on a nice set of wine glasses. They're always a winner...right?

By the time I arrive at the church, the small congregation is already seated and awaiting the bridal party's arrival. I slip in at the back, totally unseen, and find myself a seat in the shadows. I might want to surprise Erica but I also don't want to freak her out at the most important part of today.

Everyone's chatter increases as the bride's arrival gets closer, and the groom, who's standing at the altar with his best man, becomes more and more nervous to the point that I start to wonder if he's going to puke on the stone floor.

When the music changes to announce their arrival, everyone around me turns to look at the doors while my heart jumps into my throat. It's been almost a week since I saw her and over two since she was in my arms. I'm more desperate than ever to get my hands on her.

Time seems to stand still as I wait for her to appear. Everyone's faces light up, so I know they're right there in the doorway.

I close my eyes and suck in a deep breath. When I look back up, there she is, standing beside her sister and looking more gorgeous than I've ever seen.

My heart hammers in my chest and my temperature soars just from looking at her profile. I can only imagine how she'll affect me when she turns her green eyes on me.

It only takes me a second to realise what's different about her: the fiery red hair I'm used to has gone, replaced by a more natural brown. It's almost all up in an intricate hairdo, leaving just a few loose bits hanging down her neck. She's wearing a copper strapless dress that fits her like a second skin, and my fingers twitch for the opportunity to peel it from her body.

Sam moves toward her soon-to-be husband, Erica takes a step, but something makes her turn her head. It's like she somehow knows I'm here. Her eyes immediately find mine. They widen in shock, and her skin pales as our connection holds.

Sam moves again but soon realises that her sister's frozen to the spot. Her eyes burn into my skin before her smile catches my eye and she nods in approval, giving Erica a firmer tug and almost dragging her up the aisle.

I pay no attention as the ceremony begins. The sounds of people sniffing and quiet sobs of happiness fill my ears, but at no point do I take my eyes from Erica.

She knows I'm watching her, because every few minutes she flicks her eyes my way just to make sure I'm still looking—although I'm sure she doesn't need to. She must be able to feel my heated stare.

Her chest heaves, and even with the distance I can see her swollen breasts threatening to escape from her dress. I drop my eyes over the smooth curve of her waist and hips as I start to wonder what she might have beneath. A tiny lace set of lingerie? A sexy corset maybe? I tell myself there and then that I'm not leaving this wedding until I've discovered the answer.

The service goes on forever. Every minute that passes, my need to get up and drag her out of the church becomes more and more intense. Watching her every movement from back here is torture.

I breathe a sigh of relief when the vicar announces that they're husband and wife, forgetting about the damn signing of the register.

Every muscle in my body is pulled so tight I swear the fucking things are going to snap by the time the wedding party heads back down the aisle and we're all able to stand and follow them out.

My intention is to make a beeline for Erica and pull her aside.

I've no clue if that's to tell her how I feel once again and how I'm not letting her go, or to beg forgiveness for turning up here in the first place. I guess only time will tell, but when I get outside, I find her surrounded by people and I realise I've got no chance. Dragging her away from them is a sure way to piss her off...if I haven't already.

I stand off to the side and, thankfully, no one comes up to talk to me. They must just think I'm some lonely old guy who either needed some company or has a weird love of weddings. A few guests glance over at me, but that's about it.

Just when I think I'm going to get my chance, the photographer announces that he'd like the bridal party to line up in front of the church so he can get some shots.

I'm on the verge of losing my shit after watching the guy take photo after photo of the same fucking thing when he calls that he only wants the bride and groom.

It's now or never.

I make my way through the guests who, like me, weren't invited to be part of the photos, and I wrap my hand around Erica's wrist just as she's about to move away from me.

"We need to talk."

She's silent as she trails behind me and around the side of the church so we have some privacy.

Pulling her so she has no choice but to stand in front of me, I stare down at her. Her make-up is flawless, but it doesn't quite hide the dark circles under her eyes or the redness tinting the edges. She's been sleeping just as badly as me. It's also a reminder of the morning sickness she must be suffering.

"How are you feeling?"

"Fine," she whispers, refusing to meet my eyes. It's the first time I've seen this shy side to her, and although it's not really her, it's endearing. I find myself stepping a little closer, desperate to feel her lips against mine. "You shouldn't be here. You weren't invited." Her anger starts to get the better of her, and her eyes find mine.

My breath catches as I stare down into their depths. "I know, but I couldn't wait any longer."

"This isn't the time nor the place, Trey. It's my sister's wedding. The last thing I need is you ruining it for me."

"That's not my intention. I just..." I let out a sigh, not wanting to ignite her anger because she's right, this isn't the time. "I need you."

"Yeah well, you should have thought about that before lying to me."

"Erica, please." I've no idea what I'm asking for, but just the sound of my begging voice pisses me off.

"Trey," Sam sings, walking over with her giant dress pulled up around her ankles so it doesn't get muddy. "It's so nice to see you."

"Is it?" Erica mutters, and I can't help but smirk. I'm glad my little firecracker is still in there somewhere.

"I'm sorry I gatecrashed. I just needed to see this one."

Sam glances between the two of us like she's trying to decide what to do for the best. Erica's eyes narrow in warning, but Sam seems to ignore her.

"It's fine. I'd actually really love it if you'd stay. Our mum wasn't well enough to attend today, so we've got a spare place. What do you say?"

"What the hell are you doing?" Erica spits. "He can't stay."

"Of course he can. Plus, it'll give you both a little time together."

Erica fumes while Sam turns to me and winks. I know she far from approves of what I did, but it's good to know she's rooting for us.

"Thank you so much, I'd love to. And congratulations, by the way."

"Thank you. We're heading to The Ivy for our reception. We've arranged transport for everyone, but I'm assuming you drove. Erica," she says turning to her angry little sister, "why don't you go with him?"

"Don't you need me?" she asks through gritted teeth.

"Nope. I'll be fine. You should go with Trey."

I can feel the anger coming from Erica in waves as Sam smiles sweetly at both of us and walks back toward her waiting husband.

"Traitor," Erica calls out, making her shoulders shake with a laugh.

"Shall we?" I ask, holding my hand out to her. She looks down at it like it might burn her before she turns and storms off in the direction of the car park.

With a chuckle, I follow behind her, watching her arse sway in her fitted dress.

She doesn't say anything the whole way to the hotel. Instead, she stares out the window, her shoulders tense and her back twisted towards me. It's not exactly what I was hoping for, but at least she's in the same car as me.

I must be breaking her down, because, when I pull the car to a stop in the hotel's car park, she doesn't immediately throw the door open and run.

She lets out a huge sigh, and I can't fight back my words any longer.

"I miss you, sweetheart."

Sitting back, she glances over at me through her lashes. Tears fill her eyes, threatening to drop, but she fights them.

"Not good enough, Trey. I didn't want to trust you, but you didn't give me a choice. You made me promises, and, like an idiot, I believed them. I should have followed my gut. I should have learnt by now that no man can be trusted."

Scrubbing my hand over my face, I try to come up with something new to say. There are only so many times I can apologise. "It was my past, Erica. I was trying to focus on my—on *our*—future. I wasn't intentionally hiding it from you."

"But you didn't tell me. You had so many opportunities, but you just ignored it and allowed me to be ambushed."

"I know, I know. It's something that I'll regret forever. I never meant to hurt you, Erica, but I also can't live without you."

She sniffles, and my heart aches. I so badly want to pull her into my arms and make it all better.

"I need more, Trey. I can't keep being hurt like this." I open my mouth to respond, to tell her how I really feel, but she's too fast and I'm forced to watch her walk away and join the rest of the wedding party.

I debate whether I should just turn around and leave, but I figure that would be the easy way out. She said she needs more, so I turn the engine off.

I'm ready to give her everything.

CHAPTER EIGHT

Skimming my hand across the small of her back, my fingers wrap around her hip, pulling her into my body slightly. "Dance with me, sweetheart."

She stiffens, but, when she looks over her shoulder, her face is softer than I've seen it all day. Maybe it's the old romantic within that she fights like hell to keep buried, or maybe she's just fed up of fighting me—I've no idea, but when she steps away slightly and slips her hand into mine, everything in my world is suddenly right again.

I follow her lead and join the other couples who are already on the dance floor. Most of the night has consisted of fast-paced songs that have had Sam, Erica and their friends up on the dance floor. As fun as it's been to sit back in the shadows and watch as she wiggled her hips in time with the music and laughed like she had no cares in the world, we both knew that wasn't true. It's nice that's she's able to pretend, even if just for a few hours, but now the DJ has slowed the pace down a little and the silly dance moves and laugher has given way to a more romantic feel as couples of all ages sway and smile lovingly at each other.

I expected her to refuse my offer, so I make the most of pulling her body into mine once she comes to a stop on the edge of the dance floor. My hands come to rest on her lower back, teasingly close to her full arse. I press her tightly against me, reveling in the feeling of her soft curves against my hard planes. Her eyes flutter closed as our bodies move together.

She remembers.

Her hands slide up the lapels of my jacket and goosebumps prick my skin, wishing the fabric wasn't between us. As if she can't help herself once her arms are over my shoulders, her fingers start to tease the short hair at the nape of my neck. The sensation alone is enough to have my cock threatening to go half-mast. Having her this close, her sweet scent filling my nose, is a temptation I'm not sure I can resist.

"Have you had a good day telling everyone that you're my boyfriend?" she asks, her eyebrow lifting in amusement.

I shrug, a smile twitching my lips as I remember the first person who came up and introduced themselves to me today. I greeted them like I had a fucking clue who they were and, when they asked who I was, I couldn't resist.

"You're mine. It's about time everyone knows it."

"Trey," she sighs, and my heart constricts, waiting for her to dismiss what's between us once again.

Dropping my head, I brush my lips against her ear. "I need you, and I know you need me too. Please allow me to make it up to you."

The longer I talk, the more her breathing increases. I know I'm getting to her.

"You can't tell me that you don't want me to take you to your hotel room right now and show you just how much I've missed you. You can feel that, right?" I thrust my hips, ensuring my now fully erect cock presses into her stomach.

A groan is her only response, but it's enough.

"You're remembering how good we are, aren't you? Remembering just how hard I make you come, how much you love following my demands. I can give you that right now, you've just got to ask, sweetheart."

She pulls back, her hungry, dark green eyes finding mine. She searches for a few seconds before they drop to my lips. It's all I need to know she's on board.

Reaching up, I pull her arms from around my shoulders and take one of her hands in mine, leading her from the dancefloor.

She's silent behind me for a few seconds.

Stopping at the table where I know she dropped her bag, I pull her into me once again and stare deep into her eyes. "If you don't want this, you need to tell me now, because once I'm alone in a room with you, I can't promise I'll be able to stop."

Her neck ripples as she swallows and considers her next move, but much to my delight, she reaches out, grabs her bag and takes a step towards the exit.

"What are you waiting for?" she asks over her shoulder, and I rush to catch up with her.

We join another couple waiting for the lift. Thankfully, it arrives only seconds later and we all step inside.

"Four, please," Erica says politely when the lady asks what floor we need.

I move to stand behind her, wrap my arm around her waist and pull her back into me. With her high heels on, her arse lines up perfectly with my cock.

Brushing the tip of my nose against the sensitive skin of her neck, I smile as her body trembles in my arms.

"Do you reckon I could get you off before the doors open?"

Turning to look at me over her shoulder, she doesn't give me a verbal answer. Instead, she licks her bottom lip before completely turning in my arms and pressing her lips to mine.

It's been two weeks since I've had her like this. Electricity shoots through my body the second our tongues tangle together, making my knees a little weak.

I lose all track of time as I focus on her kiss, and it's not until the couple occupying the enclosed space with us clear their throats that I look up and find the doors open on level four.

I nod at them appreciatively as I regretfully remove Erica from my lips and guide her from the lift.

"Have a good night," the guy calls as the sound of the woman's giggles filter down the hallway to us.

As much as I want to confirm that I intend to do just that, I keep my mouth shut and follow Erica as she makes her way to her room. I'm too focused on her and what's to come to worry about anyone else.

Her hand trembles as she lifts the key card to unlock the door. I wrap my own around her delicate one and hold it steady. Together, we swipe the card through the lock. Reaching around her, I push on the handle and open the door.

She hesitates at the threshold, and I fear she's about to change her mind. Taking matters into my own hands, I place one arm behind her back and sweep her legs out from beneath her. "Shit," she gasps as she leaves the floor.

Stepping into the room and shutting the door behind me, my heart hammers in my chest. But the second I look down at her, everything inside me settles.

I'm home.

"I'm not the one who needs carrying over the threshold tonight."

"Maybe not tonight, but one day." I've not considered what happens after I win her back. It wasn't my immediate concern, but now she's in my arms, I know without a doubt that one day in the near future I'm going to ask her to be mine officially.

Her chin drops as my words register in her head. "Trey, I—"

"Stop. Stop worrying about tomorrow. Next week. Next month. This is about us and tonight. Let me show you how things should be." Just in case she intends to argue, I drop her feet back to the ground and back her up against the wall.

"How. It. Should. Be."

My lips find hers, my tongue sweeping across her bottom one, encouraging her to open up for me. She hesitates for the briefest moment before she allows me entry, and my tongue immediately twists with hers. Her unique taste mixes with the lemonade she's been drinking all night, and my mouth waters.

Her hands grip the edges of my jacket so she can pull me tighter against her.

"Trey." Her breathy moan has my cock swelling and pressing against the zip of my trousers. "Give me your all."

Taking a step back, I pull her hands from me and her face drops. She just told me that she wants my all, so that's what she's going to fucking get. It took me years to be able to act on the dominant urges that have bubbled beneath my skin.

Sarah and I had a decent sex life in the beginning of our relationship, but we were just kids. I tried to push the limits a little as the years went on, but she was never really interested in the kinky stuff I wanted to experiment with. But now...now I've got Erica, who seems to be all for my kinky side, and if she wants me like our first night when I thought she was a stranger I'd never see again, then she'll damn well get it.

"Trey, what are you doing?" The panic in her voice makes me

smile. She clearly doesn't understand how much she means to me if she's questioning whether this is going to happen or not. Nothing, and I mean nothing, could stop me from having her right now.

"Stand at the end of the bed, facing the pillows."

Her mouth drops open, defiance filling her face like she's about to tell me to go to hell. But then a small smile twitches at the corner of her mouth as she realises I'm just fulfilling her previous wish.

She drops her bag on the dresser as she passes and does exactly as she's told. My heart pounds in my chest as a million and one things I could do to her run through my head.

Slipping my jacket from my shoulders, I take my time in walking over and dropping it over the chair. Erica's heavy breathing is the only sound in the room. Knowing how much the anticipation is affecting her has me moving even slower.

I pop my cufflinks out, dropping them to the countertop. They bounce, and I delight in watching Erica flinch. She's so aware of her surroundings and my every action.

Tugging at my tie, I pull it through my collar and step up behind Erica. Sliding the silky fabric through my fingers, I lift my arms and place the slim teal fabric over her eyes.

She gasps but otherwise doesn't move as I secure it in place.

"This way, the sensation of every touch I give you will be increased." My lips gently brush over the smooth curve of her neck, and she shudders, her skin covered in goosebumps. She moans as I continue kissing down over her shoulder blade. The temptation to forget everything and just sink deep inside her is strong, but I'm stronger. It'll be worth it in the end.

"No," she complains when I step back once again, leaving her trembling.

"I'm not ready for you yet." It's a bare-faced lie, and she probably knows it. "I'll be back, don't move."

I imagine she thinks I'm joking, so I picture the look of horror on her face when the sound of the door opening and then slamming behind me sounds out around her.

Deciding to take the stairs, I jog down to the bar and place my order.

CHAPTER NINE

In less than ten minutes, I'm back and slipping Erica's key into the lock. Much to my delight, she's exactly where I left her.

"Good girl."

She growls in response. Perfect, she's gagging for it, just the way I like her.

Placing the tray in my hand down on the side, I make quick work of unbuttoning my shirt, pulling it from my arms and dropping it to the floor before toeing off my shoes and removing my socks. I leave my trousers in place, for now.

Grabbing the strawberry at the top of the giant pile I was given, I run it across Erica's full bottom lip. She gasps but is quick to follow instructions when I tell her to open up.

"Bite." She does, and the juice from the strawberry runs down her chin. Stepping forward, I lick it up before continuing along the line of her jaw.

"Trey, please," she moans.

"What is it you need, sweetheart?"

"You."

"Hmmm." Reaching back, I grab another strawberry. "Open." She follows orders again, but this time I let the juice run down onto her chest before I clean her up.

Her dress was hardly containing her swollen tits earlier, but now they're fighting to be released.

"As much as I love this dress, I think it needs to go."

Kissing over her shoulder, I start the complicated task of undoing the lacing at her back.

"Fuck," I grunt when I allow the fabric to drop to her feet and find I've unwrapped a really fucking impressive present.

Her corset and thong are the exact shade of the dress and something dreams are made of.

"Your sister plan what you were wearing beneath this dress?"

She shakes her head.

"So you were expecting to spend the night with someone who'd appreciate it?" The thought of her spending tonight with someone who's not me has anger and jealousy swirling around uncomfortably in my stomach.

"No. I just wanted something nice. I didn't...I wouldn't..."

"Good answer."

Dropping down to my haunches, I tap her ankle and she lifts her foot, allowing me to move the dress. I do the same with the other side and push the fabric away. Placing her foot back to the floor, my fingertips slowly trail up the side of her leg as I stand. Her arse wiggles in my face as she tries to relieve the pressure building between her legs.

"No," I bark, sinking my teeth into the plump skin.

"Shit," she gasps in shock before bringing her hand around to rub the sting.

"Don't even think about giving yourself pleasure. That's for me and me only."

My fingers continue their journey up, dancing over the intricate patterns of her lace corset. If it wasn't so beautiful, I might rip it from her body, but it'd be a shame to waste something I could stare at her in every fucking day.

"You need more of these." Walking around so I can get a good look at the front of her, I understand why her breasts looked like they were about to pop out of her dress.

"Fuck me." A smug little smile appears on her red painted lips.

"Good, right?" Lifting her hand, she trails one of her perfectly manicured fingertips along the fullness of her breasts. I allow her to continue for a few seconds just because the sight's too good to miss, but soon enough I'm batting her hand away.

"Enough," I bark, standing between her and the bed, forcing her to take a step back. Dropping my head, I lick across the edge of the corset and down into her cleavage. If it's possible I swear they swell even more.

"Jesus, Trey. I need...I need more. I need everything."

Lifting my hands, I unhook the first clasp on her corset. I'm just as desperate as she is to get her out of it and get my hands on what lies beneath.

"Yess," she hisses as the restrictive fabric starts to loosen around her body.

The second it's undone, I throw the fabric to the floor, take both her breasts in my palms and lift them to my lips. I suck one peaked nipple deep into my mouth making Erica moan and writhe under my touch.

They're more sensitve than I remember. I lick, suck and bite across both of them until she's almost at the point of no return. My name is a plea on her lips, but as much as I'd love to watch her come undone from this alone, there's no way in hell I'm letting her come until my cock's buried as deep inside her tight little pussy as physically possible.

"Fucking hell, Trey," she whines, reaching for me.

"You're forgetting who's in charge here, sweetheart."

Resting back on my palms, I take my time in running my eyes from the top of her head, over the silk fabric of my tie around her eyes, over her full, needy breasts and the soft curve of her waist before taking in her hips and mound that are still covered in copper lace.

"Take them off. I want to see all of you."

Tucking her thumbs into the fabric, she does exactly as she's told. Bending over, she puts on a show of pushing the scrap of fabric down and wiggling her hips to keep it moving.

Unable to hold back any longer, I reach out, wrap my hands around her tiny waist and lift her onto my lap.

I bring her close so her center rubs over my steel length and her breasts press against my chest. My fingers find their way into her intricate hairdo and force her lips to mine. Her mouth opens for me immediately, and she moans the second my tongue starts dancing with hers.

My fingers dig into the flesh at her hips as she tries to grind on me to find her release.

"Trey, please," she begs, "I'm gonna explode."

"Too fucking right you are. Lift up." She does as she's told and I push her upwards and lie back so the only thing I can see is her glistening pussy right above my face.

Pulling on her hips, I bring her down to meet my tongue. Her body shudders in my hands as I circle her clit again and again, driving her crazy. Sparks shoot through my body as her fingers twist in my hair and pull harshly in her attempt to get me closer, to get more of what she needs.

I chuckle against her and she moans in pleasure as the vibrations push her that little bit closer.

Lifting my head, I give her want she wants and suck her clit into my mouth. She cries my name and my chest swells. There have been times over the past two weeks that I really didn't think I'd be here again. I know we've still got a lot to work through, but surely this is a sign that she's going to forgive me and see where this thing between us goes.

Her body starts to tense above me, and I know she's nearing the end. Lifting her, I manage to maneuver us both so she's on her back and I'm standing at the edge of the bed, staring down at her as she squirms, her chest heaving and her tits rising and falling.

"If you don't let me come soon, you might not leave this room alive," she warns.

"Is that right?"

"Yeah. I really—" Her words are cut off as my hands go to my waistband seconds before my trousers and boxers drop to the floor. I kick them from my feet and crawl between her legs.

"You were saying?" Taking my length in my hand, I rub it though her juices, coating myself ready to slide into her.

"That I...That I need...*that*." She nods down to where I'm holding myself and bucks her hips to offer her entrance.

Lining myself up, I reach out my spare hand and entwine my fingers with hers, lifting her arms above her head.

"Ready?" A smirk pulls at my lips.

"Like you wouldn't fucking believe."

She barely gets the last word out because I thrust forward, ensuring that I fill her to the hilt in one smooth motion.

"Yes, Trey. Yes," she cries out, her hips shifting a little as she tries to adjust to my sudden invasion.

When I don't move again, she soon stops. "What? What's wrong?"

"Nothing." Letting go of her hand, I reach up to the tie around her head and slip it off. Her eyelids flutter as the light hits her, but her eyes soon find mine. "I need to see you. I want to watch your eyes as you fall apart."

"Please." Her hips grind, and I'm powerless to resist picking up the pace.

With her hands back in mine and my other on her hip to keep her in place, I thrust my hips forward again and again. Her tight walls ripple around me, and I soon find myself gritting my teeth in order to hold off my imminent release. All that teasing might have brought her right to the edge, but I was right along for the ride as well.

"Fuck, Trey. Fuck," she cries, her eyes not leaving mine for even a second.

"Come, Erica. Come all over my fucking cock," I grunt, holding back until she's found her own release.

On demand, her screams fill the room before her body locks up tight and she twitches and convulses beneath me. She loses her fight, and eventually the pleasure becomes too much, her eyes fluttering closed. I watch her ride out every second, committing the sight to memory before I allow my own release to consume me. I roar my long-awaited orgasm into the room as I fill her with everything I have.

I WAKE up a couple of times in the night and pull Erica closer to me. Everything seems right when her body's pressed up against mine, but just when I think everything's beginning to sort itself out, she throws me for a loop once again.

Coming to, I reach out to find her but her side of the bed is empty and cold. Pulling myself up so I'm sitting, I glance around the room. Seeing her dress still pooled on the floor where I left it, I relax, knowing that she can't have gone very far. Then I hear her.

She's in the bathroom, throwing up. Rushing from the bed, I crack the door open and peer in. The sight of her kneeling in front of the toilet with her head in the bowl damn near has me on my knees. I know it's morning sickness and that she's not really ill, but still, I hate it.

Rushing in, I place my hand on her back to do anything I can to help her, but she flinches at my touch.

"Don't."

The harshness in her voice has me standing and backing away.

"What's wrong?"

"Can you just leave, please." The sadness in her voice breaks my heart.

"Okay, I'll wait outside."

"No. I meant leave the hotel."

"But—"

She looks up at me with tears pooled in her eyes, and my words vanish.

"Last night was a mistake. It shouldn't have happened. I don't care what you say, I can't trust you. One night of hot sex certainly won't change that. So please, just leave."

She heaves again, and I hesitate, but her hard, angry eyes hold mine, and I'm powerless.

"This isn't over, Erica. Not by a long shot."

CHAPTER TEN

It's been two weeks since I walked out of that hotel and away from her. Two weeks since I heard her voice, since I touched her soft skin, since I looked into her vulnerable eyes and tried to prove to her that she can trust me.

Two weeks of pure hell.

I know she's okay, because Lauren gives me little updates every day, but I have no more information other than that she's alive. Every time I ask about Erica's pregnancy, Lauren's face gets all soft and sympathetic, and she just repeats that everything's fine. Fire burns through my veins every time I hear that damn word. 'Okay' could be a huge variety of things.

Every day after work, I knock on her door. Almost every day it goes unanswered, unless I'm late and Joe's already home. He neither confirms nor denies that she's inside, and every time he repeats that sentence, my fists clench at my sides. I have no desire to physically force my way in, but I'm bordering on desperate.

I find myself working more and more, or begging Sarah to

spend more time with my girls. I need a distraction from the fact that Erica could be downstairs, pregnant with my baby.

One night when my desperation gets the better of me, I drive to Sam's house. I know they're away on honeymoon, and I wonder if Erica's staying there, but, just like her flat downstairs, no one answers the door.

I'm starting to give up hope that she'll ever allow me to see her again, let alone touch her, when a knock on my front door has my heart leaping into my chest. No one ever comes here—hell, most people from my life have no clue where I live since moving out of my old family home.

Putting my knife and fork down, I head over to the door and pull it open. I knew something was wrong the second the knock came, but the look on Joe's face as he stands on the other side is enough to have my stomach twisting in dread.

"What's wrong? Where's Erica? Is she okay?"

Refusing to meet my eyes, Joe asks if he can come in.

I rush to stand aside and, with his shoulders slumped in defeat, he walks in and falls down onto my sofa.

"Joe, you're scaring the shit out of me. What's happened?"

"I shouldn't be here," he mumbles, his elbows on his knees and his head hanging low. "She'll kill me."

"Joe," I bark, fed up of his cryptic statements.

"Her mum's died."

"Shit. But she's okay?"

"I don't fucking know. I don't know what to do. She's locked herself in her room. She won't come out, she won't talk to me. I'm so fucking worried about her."

Looking up, the worry lines on his face are even more prominent, and the circles under his eyes seem darker.

"She's not eating, drinking...I don't know what the fuck she's thinking but—"

I don't need to hear any more. Pulling the front door open so wide it crashes back against the dresser behind, I run down the stairs as fast as my legs will carry me.

"Trey, what are you...*fuck*," Joe calls out behind me before he follows.

Our footsteps thunder down the stairs as we head towards their flat.

"Open the fucking door, or I'll break it down," I shout as Joe rounds the corner a few seconds behind me.

He's as quick as he can be, sliding the key in the lock, but even that's too fucking slow.

"Get out of the fucking way." I shoulder barge him away from the door.

Pushing the key into the lock with a little more precision, I fling the door open in seconds and race towards her bedroom door.

"Erica?" I call. I wait for a beat just in case she responds, although from what Joe's just said I'm not expecting her to.

"She stopped talking to me a few days ago."

Fucking hell, Erica. What are you playing at?

"Erica, open the door or I'm going to break it down. I'm not letting you do this."

Silence greets us but, after a second, I hear the most blissful sound. Even though it's rough and full of emotion, it still makes my heart beat that little bit faster.

"Go away."

"Not going to happen, sweetheart. We're worried about you. Please let us in so we can look after you."

"I don't need you. I don't fucking need anyone."

"I know, I know." Agreeing with her pains me but she's right, she doesn't need anyone. She's strong and stubbornly independent, only, she's falling apart right now and can't do this alone. "We know, but we want to help.

"You've already done enough." A sob sounds out through the gap under the door, and my patience snaps.

I take two huge steps back before charging forward. My shoulder slams into the door, the wood splinters, and it swings open on twisted hinges.

"Fuck," I cry when I find Erica curled up in the center of her bed, sobbing into her pillow.

Racing towards her, I scoop her up into my arms and carry her from the room, much to Joe's horror.

"What the hell are you doing?" he fumes.

"What I should have been doing this whole time. Taking care of my woman."

He opens his mouth to argue but soon closes it again when he gets a look at the serious expression on my face.

"Shout if you need anything," he calls as I carry her out of their flat.

I know she's aware of what's going on. How could she not be, seeing as I've just lifted her from her own bed, but she doesn't move or make a noise aside from her subsiding sobs as I make my way back up to my flat.

Walking through the still wide open door, I come to a stop at the sofa and gently lower her.

"Don't move," I warn before heading to my bedroom to find her a blanket.

She's exactly where I left her when I reappear and wrap the soft fabric around her.

Dropping down to my haunches in front of her, I take her cold hands in mine. "What do you need, Erica? Tell me how to make this better and I'll do it. Please."

It takes a couple of seconds, but eventually her head lifts and her eyes find me. My breath catches and my heart aches looking back at her, so broken and tormented.

"Fuck, Erica." Releasing one hand, I reach out and take her face in my palm. The moment she leans into my touch, I know she's accepting my help. She doesn't need to say the words; I've always been able to know exactly what she needs without saying anything out loud.

"Don't move."

Standing, I stare down at her for a few seconds to make sure she doesn't need me to stay before heading into the kitchen. Thankfully, this flat is open plan, so as I get to work preparing her some food, I'm able to keep an eye on her. She has a tendency to run when things get hard, so I don't want to give her the opportunity to slip away from me now I've got her here.

My culinary skills aren't that great. Most of my life, I've had someone else to cook for me. My mum is incredible in the kitchen, and I moved out of my parents' house into mine and Sarah's first place—she was at home taking charge of what we'd be eating, so I never really had a chance to hone my limited skills. Living by myself the past few months has been a bit of a challenge. Thank fuck I live in London and can have just about everything I could desire delivered.

Pulling a tub of chicken soup from the fridge that I picked up from a deli down the street a few days ago, I pull the top off and pour the contents into a saucepan. I grab the packet of part-baked bread I have in the cupboard and pop it into the oven.

While I wait for everything to heat up, I make her a coffee and take it over.

"Here, this might help."

"I...I can't drink coffee."

"It's decaf." Turning, her tired eyes find mine and they narrow in question. "I bought it hoping you'd come around one day."

A small smile twitches at her lips before she reaches out and lifts the steaming mug to her lips. She takes a hesitant sip before her eyelids flutter in pleasure.

"I did some research to find out what brand was the best. Just because you can't have the caffeine, it doesn't mean it should taste like shit."

"Thank you," she whispers, the sadness of her voice almost ripping my heart in two.

"I'm sorry to hear about your mum. I can't imagine how you must be feeling."

"Empty."

I open my mouth to say something, but I soon realise I've no idea what to say to that. I'm lucky, I've still got both my parents.

"Please let me help. I'll do anything to make this easier on you."

She looks at me over the top of her mug. I can tell she's fighting what's on the tip of her tongue, but after a couple of seconds she says it anyway. "You already are."

Warmth spreads through my body, knowing that I'm a comfort to her right now, maybe even proving myself, who knows.

The timer dings on the oven, breaking our moment.

"I'll be right back." She grants me a small smile before I get up, confirming to me that I'm helping.

I make quick work of getting it dished up before returning with it laid out on a tray. "Chicken soup and warm bread," I say when she looks over inquisitively. "When was the last time you ate?"

"I had a packet of rich tea biscuits in my room."

"Well, that's okay then," I say lightly.

A humourless noise passes her lips as she sits up straighter so I can place the tray on her lap.

I allow her time to eat, although she only has a few spoonfuls of soup and a couple of chunks of bread before she places it onto the coffee table.

"I can only have little bits at a time or I'll throw up." Turning herself so she's sitting in the corner of the sofa, she looks up at me through her lashes.

"Talk to me, please, Erica."

She blows out a long breath, making me think she's going to ignore my demand, but eventually she looks away and starts explaining.

"I got the phone call from the care home in the middle of the night. She's been in that place for so long that I started to think she'd just be there forever and that my Sundays would always be taken up visiting her. It really threw me for a loop. My first instinct was to pick up the phone to call my sister, but there was a reason I was the first person they told."

"She's on honeymoon," I mutter, putting two and two together.

"Yeah. I had no idea what to do for the best. I didn't want to ruin their time away. Our parents have already managed to ruin most of our lives—this was one time in her life that I wanted Sam to just forget about everything and enjoy herself."

"Have you told her?"

"I rang a couple of days ago. I wanted to have organised everything before I told her so she wouldn't have any reason to come back early."

"You've organised everything?"

"Why is that such a surprise? I'm more than capable." Her face hardens and I panic, thinking that she's about to start shutting down on me.

"I know that, sweetheart. I was more thinking that you didn't have to deal with everything alone."

"No one else needs to be dragged into my bullshit. Anyway, I didn't have a lot to do. It's not like I have any relatives to notify or invite to the funeral, and there's not any hidden millions for Sam and I to argue over."

"When is the funeral?"

"Tomorrow."

"What time? I'll go with you."

"I'm not going." Clearly not wanting to argue about it, she turns away from me.

"Erica. I really think—"

"No. You don't get to think anything. You've no idea about my childhood and my mother. There's no way you could understand how I feel now she's gone. You had the perfect upbringing with doting parents; it's a million miles away from how I lived."

"You're right. I'll never understand, but I want to support you, and I think no matter what's happened in the past, she's still your mother, and one day you'll regret not going. You'll only get one chance at tomorrow—whether that's to say goodbye or just to start a new chapter in your life, I think it's important."

She lets out a huge sigh. "I'll think about it."

"You can just admit that I'm right, you know?"

"No chance." Her lips curl up, and I find just a little bit of the Erica I know and love hiding behind all the betrayal and heartache.

Silence stretches out between us as I think about the fact that I caused most of said heartache.

"Erica?" I ask, feeling the sudden need to confess how I really feel.

When she doesn't respond, I look over, finding her fast asleep.

I get up as quietly as I can and tidy up what's left from dinner before sliding my hands under her and carrying her down to my bedroom. She's dressed in a pair of leggings and an oversized t-shirt. As much as I might want to strip her down so I can feel her skin against mine, I know it's not what she'll want. So I just pull the covers back and place her down gently.

"Thank you," falls from her lips as she curls up, her breathing instantly slowing as she falls back to sleep.

I might want to crawl in next to her, but I know it's too early for me to be able to fall asleep.

Grabbing my laptop, I fall into the chair at the other side of the room and continue scrolling through the same website I was searching through before leaving for work this morning, looking for the perfect family house.

CHAPTER ELEVEN

I wake up much like I did the morning in the hotel after Sam's wedding: alone in a cold bed with the sound of her throwing up filtering through from the en suite.

Hoping that might be where the similarities end, I quickly make my way to her. I don't say anything as I enter, assuming that the squeaky door is enough to announce my entrance.

Dropping down beside her, I take her hair in one hand and rub her back with the other. She tenses for a second, but, unlike last time, she relaxes before heaving once again.

I sit silently beside her, hoping that I might be helping but feeling completely useless. I wish I could take it all away from her.

<hr>

"I CAN'T WAIT for this stage to be over," she says, dropping my toothbrush back into the glass and finding my horrified eyes in the mirror. "What? What's that look for?" Shaking my head, I push aside the fact that she stole my toothbrush and focus on what's really important.

"Are you…" I hesitate, because I'm sure no pregnant woman wants to be asked the question I need the answer to. "Are you keeping it?"

"Are you fucking kidding me?" Erica runs from the room faster than I've ever seen her move before. "How can you even ask me that?"

Racing after her, I wrap my fingers around her wrist. She stops but keeps her back to me. "Because I don't know, Erica. I've no idea how you feel about this."

"Does it matter? You told me that you didn't want any more kids."

"No, I told you that I didn't *think* I did. But that was before any of this." Spinning her around, I place my hands on her cheeks so she's got no choice but to look into my eyes. "Finding out you were pregnant was the shock of my life, but," I continue when she looks like she's about to interrupt, "I want it all with you, Erica. I want the house, the babies, the forever. And do you know why?" She shakes her head as much as I'll allow with my hands cupping her face. "Because I love you, Erica Wilde. I love you so fucking much that it scares the shit out of me." The tears that were filling her eyes spill over and hit my thumbs.

Pulling her trembling body to mine, I wrap my arms around her as she sobs. Dropping my nose to her hair, I breathe her in and immediately relax. We stand there long after her sobs have passed, just holding each other.

Eventually, I take a few steps backwards and drop us both down to the edge of the bed.

Pulling her arms from my shoulders, I force her back a little so I can look into her eyes. I hate to end our embrace, but it's important.

"What time is the funeral?"

"Ten-thirty," she whispers. Glancing over the top of her head, I notice the time on the alarm clock next to my bed.

"Shit, we'd better get moving."

"Do I have to?"

"If you really don't want to, I'll respect that, but I really think—"

Placing her fingers over my lips, she stares into my eyes. "No, you're right. I'd regret it."

"We'd better get moving then." She lifts an eyebrow in question.

"Yeah, *we*. I'm not letting you do this alone."

I expect her to argue, but instead all she does is to drop her head back to my shoulder.

"As much as I'd love to spend the rest of the day with you in my arms, we've got something we need to do first."

"I don't want to."

"I know, sweetheart. I know."

Threading my fingers into her hair, I pull her face from my shoulder so I can find her lips. Her kiss is hesitant and gentle, and as much as my body urges me to push her into something more passionate, I know it's what she needs right now.

Nonetheless, my cock swells inside my boxers, and, when I lift her from my lap and place her back down on the bed, it's making a nice tent.

"Good morning, Mr. Bennett." Her eyes run down my naked chest until she finds my excitement. Her teeth sink into her bottom lip and her eyes darken.

"Stop getting ideas, we don't have time."

"We could do it instead."

"Nice try."

Turning my back to her, I pull my wardrobe open and find my

black suit. I grab a clean pair of boxers before dropping the pair I'm wearing to the sounds of Erica's frustrated groan.

She says nothing, but when I glance back at her, I know she's scheming up her revenge.

"Okay, let's go downstairs so you can get ready," I say once I've made two coffees—one decaf—and put them into travel mugs ready for the journey.

"Morning," Joe says, racing towards the front door when Erica unlocks it.

"What are you doing here?"

"I've got the day off to accompany you. Not that it looks like you need it now."

Stepping away from me, she walks up to Joe and throws her arms around him. "I'm so sorry."

"It's okay, sweets."

"Did you still get to go out last night?"

"Yeah, I knew you were in safe hands."

"I'll be as quick as I can." After releasing him, Erica races down to her bedroom. I'm desperate to follow, but with Joe's eyes boring into me like he wants to talk, I stay put.

"Go anywhere nice last night?" I didn't pay any attention at the time, my concern solely on Erica, but the memory of him standing at my door dressed in a white shirt with braces and thick-rimmed glasses fills my mind. It's not a look I've seen on him before.

"Oh...uh...just meeting a friend?"

I quirk my eyebrow at him, not believing a word of it, but he quickly changes the subject. "So, how's she doing?"

"Well, I've convinced her to go today, so I take that as a win."

"Has she told you about her childhood? Her parents?"

"Snippets but I think there's probably a lot more to it."

Nodding, he stares off into the distance. "Did you know them?"

"Who?"

"Her parents."

"Oh, no. We've only known each other for about five years. I can just sympathise, having my own fucked up parents." He shakes his head. "But that's a story for another day. It's Erica we need to be focusing on right now."

I couldn't agree more, but I'm now even more intrigued than ever about Joe. He seems to have mastered the skill of keeping everyone around him at arm's length, and it frustrates the hell out of me.

When Erica reappears, all my thoughts about Joe vanish. She looks incredible in her simple black dress that hugs her slightly more curvaceous body. But it's the look on her face that captivates me. Her pain and grief shine in her eyes, but her face is twisted, showing her lack of confidence as she stands there under our stares. It's unnerving to see it, because she's always been so confident and sure of herself.

Pushing myself from the sofa, I walk up to her and take her hands in mine.

"What's wrong?"

"My dress doesn't fit," she whispers sadly.

"Weird, because it looks fucking awesome to me."

"I feel huge already."

"You look beautiful." Standing back, I allow my eyes to drop, and I take my time running them over every one of her curves. I need her to understand just how much she captivates me. Yes, her curves are sexy, but hell, she could hide them under a black bag and I'd still be drawn to her. "If we didn't have to go out right now, I'd show you just how good you look. But for now, just know how much you affect me." Stepping back towards her, I place her hand against my thick length. "I just want you, Erica. Baby bump, stretch marks and all. I promise you that nothing will put me off."

Hope shines in her eyes, but as soon as she blinks it's gone. She doesn't want to believe it, just like she doesn't want to believe how I feel about her or how she really feels about me. It's not lost on me that I told her I loved her earlier and she didn't say it back. But I feel it. I feel it every time she looks at me, with every touch of our bodies. She just believes that living in denial will make it all easier. Sadly for her, I'm not going to allow that.

I wasn't really sure what I was expecting from today, but it certainly wasn't the very small welcoming party we had waiting for us at the local crematorium. I recognise every single person standing by the entrance as I drive towards the car park with Erica to my left and Joe practically filling the entire back seat of my car. The second we're spotted, Sam starts running and Erica begins fumbling with the seat belt. The moment I park, I help her out and press the button allowing her to jump from the car and into her sister's arms.

They stand and cry together as Joe and I get out and come to stand beside them. Cliff, Sam's new husband, comes over to join us, along with Lauren and Ben. Ben shakes my hand, his over-the-top protectiveness on full display in his eyes.

"How's she doing?" he whispers when he tugs me towards him.

"Surviving. Just be glad she's here."

"She wasn't going to?"

I shake my head, but I swallow down the words I was going to say when Erica snuggles into my side, her cheeks damp with tears and eyes rimmed red.

"Thank you for coming," she says to Lauren and Ben.

"Shut up. As if we'd be anywhere else."

"I really appreciate it."

"You being nice to him?" Lauren asks, flicking her eyes up at me.

"As nice as he deserves."

"Good luck, Trey. This one knows how to hold a grudge."

"I do not," Erica sulks.

"Are you kidding? You didn't talk to me for about a week not long after we met because you didn't get your own way."

"He's totally lying. It was like thirty minutes," she says, looking up at me with a smile on her face.

Silence falls over our small group as people start to leave the crematorium from the previous funeral.

"You ready for this, kid?" Sam asks, once again wrapping her arm around Erica's shoulders.

"So ready." It's an odd thing to say. I can't imagine it would be my reaction to a parent's funeral, but then I've had a very different upbringing to them both, so I keep my mouth shut and follow their lead.

"I can't believe you did all of this yourself, you nutcase."

"It was time I took control for once and allowed you to enjoy yourself."

"I love you, kid. You know that, right?" Sam ruffles Erica's hair, much to her disgust.

The seven of us walk in and take seats at the front. A few others eventually join us, but when Erica points out that they're carers from the home, my heart aches for everything she must have been through, not having anyone but her sister to support her. The more and more I learn about her, the more I understand why she shields her heart quite so fiercely.

The ceremony is...quick. Erica said that she didn't think her mum deserved too much fuss and, from the length of the service and the lack of anyone standing up to say any words, it's clear that she really meant it. It's so sad that a mother can have both her children at her funeral and neither are willing to stand up and say anything about who she was. It makes me want to go and find my girls and hold them that little bit tighter so they know that, although I may no longer be at home with them, I've by no means stopped caring. I make a note to text them both when I get a moment.

"What's next?"

"I just booked a table for the four of us. Seemed pointless planning an actual wake." I can't really argue with that, so after we've said goodbye to the others, I follow Sam and Cliff to the restaurant Erica chose.

"Were you expecting that kind of turn out?" I ask as we drive away from the crematorium.

"Less, actually. I had no idea Lauren and Ben we're coming or the carers. I just thought it would be Sam and Cliff." She sighs and looks out the window.

"Our child will never experience anything you did, and you're going to be an incredible mum." She sniffs, and I know my words are getting to her. "If your own experiences have taught you anything, it's how not to do it."

"Something good's got to come from it," she agrees, a humourless laugh falling from her.

THE RESTAURANT'S a quaint little place on the outskirts of the city.

"Why here?"

"I just wanted to get away for a bit. Leave it all behind."

"Me?"

"Huh?"

"You wanted to leave me behind?"

Her eyes soften as she blows out a breath. "No, I—"

"It's okay. This isn't the time for this conversation. Let's go and have an incredible meal, and then I've got a surprise for you."

"What is it?"

"It's a surprise, so it should be obvious that I can't tell you."

"It better be bloody good," she mutters as she gets out and joins Sam and Cliff.

"A word?" Sam says, her small hand holding my forearm to stop me and to allow Erica and Cliff to walk off ahead.

"She's been hurt time and time again, but this time it was different. This time it really hurt, and that's because it's real. I see the connection between you—it's why I didn't send you on your way on our wedding day. I can see how much you love her, more than anyone in her past. She's going to try to ruin this whichever way she can because she thinks being heart-broken and alone is what she deserves for some fucked up reason I'm yet to fully understand. If you want her, you're going to need to fight like hell. She might forgive you this time, but she'll find another reason to push you away. Maybe not tomorrow, or next week or month, but she will, and you're going to have to cling on for dear life as she tries to self-destruct. Are you ready for that? And more importantly, can you continue holding on? Because if the answer is no, you need to let go now before you get in too deep."

"I'm not going anywhere, Sam. You can trust me."

"I know that, but I'm not the important one."

"I've got her...I've got them."

"That's what I thought."

"What's going on?" Erica asks when we get to where she's holding the door open, waiting for us to join them.

"Sam was just giving me her big sister speech."

"Please tell me you weren't," she begs Sam.

"What?" she asks innocently. "I don't care how old or ugly he is, I need to look out for my kid sister."

"I don't need looking out for."

"No, but I want to, and you're stuck with me, so suck it up, sista."

They both laugh as they walk through the entrance to the restaurant arm-in-arm. It's nowhere near what anyone would expect on the day they said goodbye to their mother, but after everything they've been through, it's good to see the smiles on their faces. It'll take a hell of a lot more than today to break them.

"Are you going to tell me what it is yet?" Erica asks once she's woken up from her nap. We'd only been in the car a few minutes before her head dropped back and she was gone.

The meal was probably the longest of my life as Erica picked at her bland food in an attempt to not spend the entire time we were there in the toilets. It worked because, as far as I'm aware, she's not thrown up since first thing this morning.

"Mornin'," I say with a chuckle.

"Laugh away, but this whole growing a person thing is exhausting. I can only imagine what it'll be like when I'm the size of a whale."

"You won't be the size of a whale."

"You wanna bet? I saw pictures of Mum when she was pregnant with both me and Sam, and she was colossal."

"Doesn't mean you will be. Anyway, it doesn't matter if you are, you'll still be gorgeous."

"Hmm...we'll see."

"Does that mean you're keeping me around long enough to see you that pregnant?"

"This is your baby too, Trey. Regardless of what happens between the two of us, I'd never take him from you."

"Him?" I ask, trying to push aside the emotion her words drag up my throat.

"Yeah, I just feel like it might be a boy."

A wide smile finds its way onto my lips. I can't deny that I wouldn't love to have a son, especially already knowing what dealing with teenage daughters is like.

"Would you be willing to meet my girls?"

Her head snaps around to me, the shock of my question clear on her face. I know it might be a bit much, but I fully intend on having Erica in my life for a long time to come, so it's important that she meets my girls sooner rather than later. Ella already knows about Erica and is rightly concerned after what she's overheard her mother talking about. I want them to meet her so they can fall in love with her, just like I have.

"One day," she agrees, and that's good enough for me. She's got a lot to process right now; I don't want to put more on her. "Are we visiting someone?" she asks when she looks back out the window and realises that we're driving down a residential street filled with well-maintained terraced Victorian houses.

"No, I want to show you something."

"Here?"

"Here. Come on."

A frown creases her brow as she accepts my hand and allows me to pull her from the seat to join me on the pavement.

"These houses are stunning. I bet they're seriously expensive."

"They're not cheap, that's for sure."

I bring her to a stop between two cars just up ahead and pull her across the road once it's clear.

"This is the one."

"Ooookay."

She follows me up to the front door and waits to discover what's about to happen when I knock.

It only takes a second or two for the door to open, and a young woman dressed in a suit greets us.

"Mr. Bennett, it's good to see you. And this must be Miss Wilde?"

"Yeah, hi."

"Hello, I'm Leanne. Come on in."

Leanne's aware that this is a surprise, which is why she doesn't explain who she is. "I'll leave you guys to it. If you need me, I'll be outside. Please take your time."

Erica's silent as Leanne walks out the front door, leaving us in the house alone.

"Trey, what the hell is going on?"

"Come on, let's look around."

"Why?" It's like she nails her feet to the floor, because when I move she point-blank refuses.

"Trey?"

"Humour me?"

Blowing out a frustrated breath, she agrees and follows me towards a room that turns out to be the kitchen. Surely she's figured out where this is going, but I want her to look around before we get into an argument about the future.

"Wow," she breathes, expressing my exact thoughts when I saw it online this morning. The kitchen is an extension from the back of the house. Its back wall consists of huge sliding doors which allow so much light in—combine that with the sky lights, and it's almost like being in an outside kitchen.

Each room gets better and better as we walk around, but it's not until we're in the smallest of the four bedrooms that I take Erica's hand and pull her into my body.

"So what do you think?"

"I think it's stunning, how could I not? It's for sale, isn't it?"

"It is. We're the first, and depending on what you're about to say, the only people to view it."

"Trey, this is crazy. There's no way I can afford to live somewhere like this. My flat is a serious stretch every month. I have no savings. I can't even dream—"

"Stop, please," I beg, cupping her chin with my fingers. "I'm not asking about your financial situation. I'm asking if you want to live here. Can you picture yourself in his house...in this room, nursing our baby?"

Stepping away from me, she pulls out the office chair that's neatly tucked under the desk in here and lets out a sigh, her hand protectively falling on her belly. She's probably totally unaware of the move, and it's one of the reasons I know she's going to be an incredible mum.

"This is crazy, Trey."

"I couldn't agree more. But—" I fall down at her feet. I take her free hand in mine and place my other hand next to hers on her belly. "I'm in love with you, Erica. You're mine, both you and the little peanut in here. If we're doing this, I refuse to do it in a little flat with a lift that works some of the time. I've always given my kids everything they could possibly need, and this little one is no different."

"But—"

"No more buts. We both know them all. Stop worrying about what might happen and focus on what you want. Drop those walls a little and start listening to your heart, not your head. How do you picture your future, Erica? Is it with me and our baby?"

Slowly, she starts nodding. "Of course I want to be with you and our baby. And this house is incredible—it's more than I could ever dream of. I'm just scared."

"I know you are. Trust me, I am too. The idea of having a newborn again scares the shit out of me, but I know we can do it... just like I know we can as a couple. We're meant to be, sweetheart. Take the chance with me, please?"

"I don't have time to really think about this, do I?"

"You can have as much time as you need, but you might have to picture a different house when you do it. This place will be snapped up by the end of the day, either by us or by someone. Trust me when I say there aren't many like this around."

"You've been looking for a house for us?"

"I've been looking for a place before I even moved out, but I hadn't been able to find the right one. When I discovered your pregnancy, my priorities changed from bachelor pad to family home."

"You're really serious about this, aren't you?"

"Yeah. If you want this house, it's yours, sweetheart."

"I don't want you to buy me a house."

"Okay, well, we can put yours on the market and you can put whatever you get into this place if it makes you feel better. I'll be truly ours then."

She chews on her bottom lip as she mulls over my suggestion. Just that one simple move has me hard as fuck and ready to christen every single room in this house.

"How much is this place even up for?"

"We'll discuss that once you decide. The price doesn't matter."

She narrows her eyes at me, clearly unhappy with the amount I'm willing to spend.

"And you have the money to buy this place, just like that?"

"We'll probably need a small mortgage. I'm not that rich."

"The fact that you're even searching for houses like this suggests you're pretty loaded." Her mouth drops to a frown, and she turns away from me.

"What's wrong?"

"You're here suggesting we buy this insane house, yet I don't know the most basic of things about you. I know most of it is probably not all that important, but I want to know it all."

"It does matter. I want to know it all too. But our relationship was never going to be conventional, so while others might learn all that stuff while they're dating, we can do it while we're here, together."

"*If* I were to agree to this. How long until we move in?"

I can't help the smile that twitches at my lips at the knowledge that she's already considering moving in. I know she's holding back, because the sensible side of her brain is telling her to protect herself, but her heart is all in.

"We can move in whenever you like. If you want to wait, maybe date for a little while, then we can."

My words seem to perk her back up. She jumps from the chair and walks from the room. She's halfway up the stairs to the converted loft room when I catch up with her.

"Wow, this room is gorgeous."

"When I found it online, I thought it might be a nice room for Ella and Sofia for when they come to stay, but now I'm seeing it, I'm not sure I'd want to give it up."

Erica's deep in thought as she wanders around the room and pokes her head into the walk-in wardrobe.

"If I agree to meet your daughters, can we keep this room?" I can see the trepidation in her eyes when she talks about them. I know she's having a hard time trying to accept me having a past before her, I understand that. But I think she's making it out to be worse in her head and that things will seem better once they've met and she realises they're not all that scary.

"You can have whatever you want."

"Hmmm."

The walk back down to the ground floor is in silence. I've no idea what she's really thinking, but my heart races as I glance into each room we pass, seeing her in them with our baby in her arms. I picture her in the kitchen at a high chair feeding, curled up on the sofa with a baby on her chest as they nap together. I can hear the laughter and joy of a family that used to make me feel so complete before everything started to derail.

I'm still lost in my thoughts as I follow Erica through the front door to find Leanne, the estate agent, on her phone at the front of the house.

"Oh," she says quickly stuffing it into her pocket. "What did you think? It's a beautiful house, right? It'll be snapped right up."

"We'll have it," Erica interrupts, shocking both Leanne and myself.

"We will?" I ask, sliding my arm around her waist and pulling her to me. She stares up at me, a slight frown between her brows. I run my eyes over every inch of her beautiful face while my heart races so fast I think it might just explode.

"Just make me one more promise?"

"Anything."

"Don't make me regret it."

"Never." Lowering my lips to her, I pepper kisses across them, but she soon gets greedy and opens for me. As I sweep my tongue past her lips, her taste explodes in my mouth, making my cock ache for her. Everything surrounding me vanishes, and it just becomes the two of us embarking on the rest of our lives together.

Leanne clears her throat, and I regretfully pull away.

Still staring down at Erica once I've put some space between us, I say "Yes, we'll have it. Full asking price. Let's get it moving."

"Sure thing, Mr Bennett, Miss Wilde. You've got a hell of a house here. I'll be in touch with details ASAP."

CHAPTER THIRTEEN

"Is it wrong that I don't want to leave?" Erica asks with a laugh.

Leanne left us to it ages ago, promising to confirm our offer as soon as she contacted the seller, leaving me to get in touch with my financial advisor to sort out the financial side.

"No, I think that's a really good sign. I'd move in right now if I could."

"Are you sure you don't think this is too fast?"

"I wasn't aware there were rules to this kind of thing. I'm just going by what I want and what I think is best for our new family." Placing my hands on her flat belly, I stare down at her in amazement. "You're growing our baby. How incredible is that?"

"Do you still think so, even though you've been through it twice before?"

"Is that something you're worried about? That this isn't my first time?"

"Yeah." She tries to cast her eyes away, but I capture her cheek and force them back to me. "I've no clue what I'm doing, and I'd kind of like it if you were equally as clueless."

She frowns when I laugh, but I can't help it. "Don't worry, I feel totally clueless. Having my girls feels like a lifetime ago. Plus, I wasn't really around much in the early days, so it will feel like it's the first time."

"Why weren't you around?"

"I worked too much," I say regretfully. "Sarah's dad had a small building firm. I'd worked there my entire life until I made the decision to leave her. That day, I waked away from my wife, my kids, my house, and my job. He told me I could stay, but I needed a fresh start. Still working there would keep me tied to the family more. I'd bump into Sarah regularly, and I didn't want to make it harder on any of us. I'd been there since he offered me an apprenticeship at sixteen. It was all I'd ever known, but it was the right thing to do. So when I heard about the job at Johnson & Sons, I knew I couldn't turn it down. A small family firm that was in need of rescuing was right up my street. You've no fucking idea how happy I am that I took the job."

"It's a pretty great place to work."

"Does that mean you'll come back?"

"I...uh..."

"Don't stop doing something you love because you want to punish me. You'd told me before how much you need it. I know Ben and Lauren are desperate to have you back."

"I'll speak to them about it."

"Is that a yes?"

Her lips twitch with excitement and her green eyes sparkle in a way I've missed so fucking much. "It's a maybe."

"Whatever you say." I chuckle. "Come on, I've got more planned for today."

"Where now?"

"Wait and see."

We drive for a few minutes before pulling up into a retail park. Erica sits nervously beside me as she stares at the huge baby shop in front of us.

"Are you okay? You look like you're about to puke."

"Uh...I think I might."

"Why?"

"Just looking at that place makes it all seem so real. I'm not sure I'm ready. I can barely look after myself."

"Bullshit," I snap, a little too harshly if her flinching is anything to go by. "Sorry. It's just that you've been looking after yourself pretty much your whole life, from what you've told me. This will be a walk in the park for you."

"I've never even held a baby," she whispers, her cheeks brightening with the confession.

"Neither had I before Ella came along." Slipping my hand into hers, I squeeze in support. "You'll be the best mum, Erica, I have no doubt. You're so caring and supportive. Our little one will be lucky to have you."

She sniffles and fights the tears pooling in her eyes, but there's a smile on her face. "Damn you. I'm pretty sure I've cried more in the last few weeks than I have in my life."

"I think that's pretty standard. It's the hormones."

"That should have clued me in on what was going on, really. I was an emotional mess."

"How did you find out?"

"It was Ben. He said something about me being emotional like a pregnant woman, and I freaked out. With everything I'd been experiencing, it made total sense."

"That was the day you went home sick." I think back to how

she must have felt. "Why didn't you tell me that night?" I don't mean for it to come out as an accusation, but it does nonetheless.

"I was terrified, Trey. I'd done the bloody test in a Starbuck's toilet because I couldn't wait to get home to find out the truth. I had no idea what you'd think. If you'd think I'd done it on purpose or something. We barely knew—we barely *know* each other. Hell, I didn't know how to react."

"It's okay. I understand that you needed time to process it."

"I was going to tell you that night at the restaurant. I'd spent all day practicing my speech but then—" She lets out a sigh.

"I ruined it."

"Something like that," she says sadly. "You should have just told me about her at the beginning. I wouldn't have cared."

"I know. I just didn't expect...well, any of this. I didn't think I'd see you again after that night, and then when I did I just got swept away. You were everything I'd ever wanted, and I knew I was going to ruin it."

"Wasn't Sarah everything you ever wanted?" I open my mouth to respond, but she beats me to it. "I'm sorry, I'm just trying to understand."

"I thought she was, but we were so young. When she had the girls, our lives became about them. We never took the time to think about us, aside from a date night every few weeks where we mostly let out a deep breath, just glad to have a few hours of peace. We'd grown apart over the years, like I said before. We'd been travelling down different paths. I wanted more and she wanted to stay the same."

Her face twists in uncertainty.

"What is it? I'll tell you anything."

"Were you...when you were..." she blows out a breath and decides to just get to the point. "Was your sex life like ours is?"

"Wow. Erica Wilde, seductress extraordinaire, is shy about asking a sex question," I say with a laugh.

"Trey," she groans.

"No, sweetheart. It was nothing like us." That seems to settle whatever she was worried about. "You ready to do this?" I nod towards the shop.

"No, I'm really not."

"That's a shame, because we're going in."

She's still in the car when I get around to her side, pulling the door open, I reach into take her hand. "I promise it won't be as scary as you're making it out to be in your head. We're just going to look. Just think how cute that little room will be full of nursery furniture."

"I guess," she mutters, allowing me to pull her out.

She's silent as we walk through the sliding doors. I watch as she looks at the pushchairs directly in front of us before she glances around the shop.

The colour drains from her face before she pulls her hand from mine. "I can't do this. It's too much. I don't even know where to start."

"We start with the maternity clothes. You're going to need some, right? Have you bought new bras yet?"

"New bras?" she asks, the movement of her chest starting to increase with her panic.

"Come on, we're just clothes shopping."

We do three laps of the maternity clothes. Erica selects a couple of items before she comes to stop in front of a display of newborn baby clothes.

I stand aside slightly as she reaches out and runs her fingertips across the front of the soft fabric. She glances down at her belly and then back to the babygrow, biting her bottom lip.

"Is he really going to be this small?" she asks when I come to stand beside her and pull her into my arms.

"He might even be smaller."

"Smaller! How is that even possible?"

"Why, did you want to push a bigger one out?"

Her lips press into a flat line as she considers my question. "Christ, what have I got myself into?"

"Come on, let's have a look at the nursery furniture."

"How are we meant to choose? It's all so cute."

"Do you want to find out the sex?"

"Um...I don't know. Do you?"

"I don't mind. It just might help with picking."

"But what if we have another?"

"Do you want more?"

"I've no idea. I'm not sure I'm going to know how to deal with this one. Let's see if I can do that before discussing the possibility."

"Okay, let's stick with neutral then, just in case."

"Jesus. I can't believe I'm doing this with a man I don't even live with."

"That can be fixed." *And soon, hopefully.* "What about this one? I like the oak."

"Yeah, me too."

For someone who I thought was going to refuse to walk any farther than the door, she didn't seem to want to leave after what was probably our fourth lap of the place. We left with a stack of new clothes for her, along with a couple of bras and a *What to expect when you're expecting* book in the hope it'll give her some confidence about what's to come and to prove that she's more than well-equipped to be a mother.

"You hungry?"

"Yeah, as long as the food's bland."

"Uh...McDonalds?"

"Perfect."

Erica orders a kids meal, explaining that she thinks a full meal would be too much, but then proceeds to polish off two McFlurry's like they're going out of fashion.

"What's so funny?"

"Nothing, sweetheart."

"You think I'm a pig, don't you?"

"Not at all. You can have anything that makes you feel better."

CHAPTER FOURTEEN

We're halfway home when the sound of my phone ringing fills the car. Glancing down at the screen, I see my ex-wife's name staring back at me.

I look over to Erica, who's also staring at it, wondering what to do.

"It's okay. You can get it. I'll be quiet."

"I'll be quick, I promise."

She nods, then turns to look out the window.

Hitting accept, I wait for her voice to fill my ears. It might be familiar, but it doesn't affect me in any way. It hasn't for a very long time.

"Trey, I need your help. Ella and I have had a...disagreement. She's refusing to come out of her room and demanding to see you."

"Uh...what do you want me to do?"

"Come and talk to her. Tell her that she's too young to be going out with boys."

"She's fourteen, Sarah. Isn't that what kids do?"

"Not my kid, and not with the boy she wants to go out with."

"But—"

"No buts. I need you to back me up on this one and trust that I'm right."

"You know that stopping her will only make her more determined to do it."

"I don't care. I'm not letting her spend time with that...tyrant."

Letting out a frustrated breath, I glance over at Erica, whose shoulders are pulled tight with tension. "Give me an hour, and I'll be there."

"An hour? This has already been going on long enough. Can't you be here any sooner? I need to go out."

"So just go out. She'll be fine sulking."

"Or sneaking out."

"Do you mind if we go over?" I whisper to Erica.

"Is that her?" Sarah snaps.

"Enough. Do you want my help or not?"

"Fine."

"Give me a minute, I'll call you back."

Sarah complains, but she hangs up nonetheless.

"I can drop you off if you don't want to come."

Erica is silent for a few seconds before she turns back to look at me, her face set with determination.

"No, if we're really doing this...us, then I'm coming with you." Her eyes narrow, and I can't help but feel like she's testing me somehow.

"It might not be pleasant. Sarah's not exactly your biggest fan."

"I'm sure I've dealt with worse."

The reminder of her past twists my stomach like it always does. I wish I could go back and erase it all for her.

"Okay then. Let's do this." My voice comes out sounding much more confident than I feel. Erica is wrong if she thinks I want to hide her. I'm more than happy for anyone to see us together. I'm more concerned about her and my daughters than I am about Sarah's opinion of our new relationship.

Redialing her number from my steering wheel, she picks up on the first ring. "We'll be there in twenty."

"We?"

"We." Hanging up, I blow out a calming breath, trying to imagine what kind of mother-daughter war I'm about to walk into. It's not the first. Ella and Sarah clash on the best of days, and I'm sure it won't be the last.

"You sure you want to do this now? Today's already been pretty stressful."

"Yes, I'm sure."

"Okay, well...let's do this then."

Climbing from the car, Erica joins me and, hand in hand, we walk towards my old front door and I ring the bell. The time has long past that I felt able to just walk in. My name might still be on the deeds for this place, but it's by no means my home anymore. Home is where the heart is, and that's wherever Erica is.

It's only a few seconds before the sounds of footsteps running down the stairs rings out and the door's pulled open.

Sarah doesn't even bother looking at me. Her eyes zero straight in on Erica.

"Christ, Trey, she looks even younger than I remember."

I go to say something, but Erica beats me to it. My chest swells with pride that she's confident enough in us to stand up to my ex-wife.

"Hi, I'm Erica, but I'm sure you remember that from when you gatecrashed our date. My age isn't really any business of yours, and neither is what your *ex*-husband gets up to, but just for your knowledge, I'm almost twenty-six so fully legal and capable of making my own decisions, thank you."

My eyes flick between the two of them, waiting to see how

Sarah responds. She's never really been one for confrontation, one of the reasons I never expected her to surprise Erica in the way she did. I guess it's true: women really do do crazy things for love.

"What the hell's going on?" I say, barging into the living room and making my way to the kitchen.

"Dad!" Sofia squeals, jumping from her seat and rushing over to wrap her arms around my waist.

"Hey, baby. I've got someone I'd like you to meet. This is Erica, my—"

"I know who she is. Mum's told us all about her. She's the reason you left."

Sarah retreats slightly into the corner of the room while Erica pales.

"That's not true in any way, Sof. I don't expect you to accept this straight away. I know it's hard. But Erica's a permanent part of my life now, and I think you'll really like her once you get to know her."

I glance back to Erica and hold my arm out for her. She steps up to me, but not before she swallows down her insecurities.

"Hi, Sofia. It's so nice to meet you at last."

Sarah doesn't give Sofia a chance to respond, because she steps forward.

"I'm sorry to ruin this little family bonding time, but the issue we've got right now is our daughter who's locked herself in her room, not your little plaything."

Fire burns through my veins that she has the audacity to speak about Erica that way when she's in the same fucking room.

"That's enough. Whether you like it or not, my life is with Erica now. This isn't a fling or a midlife crisis or whatever else it is you want to call us. This is serious. We're serious."

"Bloody hell, Trey. The next thing I know, you'll be telling me she's pregnant and you're marrying her."

My anger fades slightly at her words, while Erica's hand squeezes mine.

"Oh my fucking god. She is, isn't she? You got her fucking pregnant?"

The sound of wooden chair legs scraping across the tiled floor makes the three of us wince as Sofia runs from the room.

Christ, could this get any worse?

"Well done."

"What? How was I supposed to know it was true?"

"Let me just talk to Ella, and then we'll get out of here."

"Oh great. Just storm in, cause an even bigger mess than you already have, and then run away *again*."

"We're only here because you demanded I come and sort your problem out."

"Yeah, you...not *her*."

"Enough. Sarah, I don't expect you to like it, or even accept it, but I love her, okay. And yes, we're having a baby. No, it wasn't planned or expected, but sometimes life is a little unpredictable. So can we please go and sort our daughter out so you can go out and we can leave?"

"Fine," Sarah sulks, blinking away the tears that are filling her eyes.

With one final look at Erica, who's glancing between the two of us with concern twisting her features, I follow Sarah out of the room and up the stairs.

"Ella, baby. Can you let me in please?"

"Is she still there?"

Assuming she means Sarah, I say, "Uh yeah, your mum's here."

"Ella, this is ridiculous. Just come out," Sarah snaps, clearly losing patience with our oldest daughter.

"You said you were going out. Why don't you do that?"

"I'm not leaving her here to sneak out."

"She won't. I'll make sure of it."

Sarah stares at me, I guess trying to decide if she can trust me or not, before huffing out her frustration and storming back down the stairs. I don't hear any words from downstairs, so I can only hope she ignored Erica before slamming the front door so hard the house shakes.

A few seconds after the rumble of her engine roars on the drive, there's a click in front of me and the door opens.

Ella stands there with tears running down her face, and her chin trembles.

"Come here, baby." She slams into my chest with such force I have to take a step back.

"Thank you," she mumbles into my chest through her tears.

Guiding her over to her bed, I sit us both on the edge as she begins to calm down.

"What's going on with your mum, then?" For as long as I can remember, Ella and Sarah have clashed. Even as a baby, Ella was constantly testing her patience. It always made me wonder why she wanted another when the first one caused her so much stress.

"She's always treating me like a baby. I'm almost fifteen. I just want to do what all my friends are doing."

"And what is that exactly?"

"Loads of stuff. Going to parties, having days in town shopping, going to concerts without parents tailing along. She just makes me feel like I'm eight years old still."

"She's just being protective. You're her baby. She's finding it hard to let go." I know Sarah; at times in my life I've known her better than I've known myself, and I know exactly what she's doing here, but holding Ella back isn't going to help. She really needs to embrace that her baby is growing, and that she's responsible enough to be doing most of the things she just mentioned. If I've learnt anything from Erica, it's that you've got to try to trust people, my daughters included.

"It's so stifling, Dad. And I miss you so much. I hate this house without you in it." My heart aches, knowing that I'm playing a part in her pain right now.

"I'm so sorry. Ella...your mum said something about a boy?" I ask through gritted teeth, because as much as I think Sarah is being a little too controlling, I also hate the idea of her dating. She'll forever be too young to be spending time with boys, but I know it's something I have to accept.

Blowing out a long breath, she pulls away from me and stares at the wall. "Josh," she whispers. "He's Jade's older brother."

"I see." My insides twist. The boy my ex-wife was referring to is actually two years older than Ella. No wonder she was having a hard time with it.

"He's so sweet, Dad. He really makes me laugh and looks after me. We only wanted to go to the cinema and for some food. Nothing else was going to happen. I'm not stupid, I know what Mum's worrying about, but she needs to trust me."

"Yeah, I'm suddenly understanding why she's so worried."

"Dad," she complains. "Not you too."

I'm silent as I think about the right thing to say to her that doesn't totally undermine her mother. We were all young once and know how important things like this seemed at the time. But also, I was once a teenage boy and know exactly what my intentions were at that age when it came to girls.

"Does Jade know about you spending time with her brother?" I ask, deciding to take a different spin on it.

Ella's cheeks flush pink, giving me the answer before she says anything. "No. She hates him and his friends, she thinks they're idiots. She's right some of the time, but he's different with me. He's...sweet."

Every muscle in my body tenses. *Of course he's fucking sweet to her.* I want to stand firm and forbid her to see him but I know that won't do either of us any good. She's fast turning into a young adult and sadly, she needs to make her own mistakes and trust her own judgement.

"Ella," I say on a sigh. "I so badly want to point blank refuse to this because you're my baby and all I want to do is protect you. But I also trust you, and if you say he's sweet, I have no reason not to believe you." Her face brightens as she looks up at me with hope shining in her grey eyes. "But," her groan of frustration makes me laugh, "I also agree with your mum. You're young, and he's a teenage boy. I know you don't want to imagine it, but I was one once, and I know exactly what's going on in his head."

"Dad, it's not like—"

"I'm going to have to talk to your mum about this, but how about we set up some rules and compromise a little? Just until we get to know him."

Her teeth grind as she thinks about my offer, but I know she knows she's not going to win with me if she tries throwing another tantrum. "What does that mean exactly?"

"It means, cancel tonight. Tell him that you've got a family thing or something. Then we'll come up with a plan to do something tomorrow and you can meet him. I don't want to be that annoying, overprotective dad, but I need to meet this boy you seem so taken with."

She really doesn't want to agree, but eventually she nods. "Thanks, Dad."

"If you're up for it, there's someone I'd like you to meet downstairs."

Her face pales once again, but after a few seconds she agrees, showing me just how mature she really is despite the arguments with Sarah.

My concerns about Sofia finding out about Erica being pregnant like she did haven't left me, but as we descend the stairs, I soon realise there wasn't any need to worry.

Joyful female voices and laughter filter up to us.

"Sofia seems to like her," Ella says with a smile.

"You will too, baby. She's pretty awesome. But before we go in, I need to tell you something. Sofia already knows because you mother dropped it on her when we first arrived, but—"

"She's pregnant."

"How'd you—"

"I was eavesdropping at the top of the stairs."

"Oh, okay...well..." I stutter, not really expecting that.

"I'm really happy for you, Dad. Just like all that stuff you just said to me upstairs, I just want you to be happy too."

A ball of emotion climbs its way into my throat, blocking any words, so instead I reach out and pull my eldest daughter into my chest and hold her tight.

Things with Sarah and me might have gone south over the years, but, no matter what happens, I'll always remember she gave me two incredible daughters.

Once I feel able, I release her and look down into eyes that are so similar to mine it's almost scary. "Ready?"

"As I'll ever be."

"Well this is surreal," Erica whispers in my ear as she looks at my daughters eating their way through pizza as if they've not eaten for a week.

After a quick call to Sarah, she agreed to let us take the girls for the night. I've no idea where she'd gone, but she was a little too happy about the prospect of a child-free night so I was assuming it was a date. Fair play to her if it was—it's good to know she's trying to move on as well and stop dwelling on the fantasy that I'll return.

"Are you feeling okay?" I ask, watching her pick at her margarita pizza.

"I'm good. You're daughters are awesome. You should be so proud of them."

My chest swells that she sees exactly what I do every time I look at them.

When Ella and I rounded the corner into the living room, we found Erica and Sofia sitting on the sofa taking selfies using ridiculous Snapchat filters. Seeing them laughing together was everything to me, and the emotion that I'd just about swallowed down from Ella's words crawled its way back up.

"I am, but I'm sorry they kind of derailed our evening."

"Don't be silly. I'm enjoying myself."

"Me too, but it isn't the kind of fun I had in mind."

"Shush, they'll hear you."

"Hear what?" Sofia pipes up, making Erica's cheeks heat.

"Nothing, baby. Doesn't your mum feed you?"

"Of course."

"Leave them alone," Erica says, swatting my shoulder to stop me teasing them.

ALTHOUGH OUR EVENING WAS NICE, my girls were much quieter than they usually would be. I'm so unbelievably grateful that they seem to have accepted Erica, but I know it'll take time for it all to feel normal. Just like Sarah, they both had hopes we'd work things out eventually.

Dragging their giant bags from the boot of the car, Erica reaches in and pulls her shopping out before we head into the building.

Going for the stairs, seeing as the lift's still got an 'out of order' sign taped to the front, I'm expecting to head all the way to the top.

"What are you doing?" I ask when Erica comes to a stop on her floor.

"I'm going to leave you guys to spend some time together. I'm exhausted. Today's been...emotional, to say the least."

The girls loiter on the steps, waiting for me to follow them. "Here, you two take the keys and let yourselves in. I'll just be a few minutes." Ella takes the keys from my outstretched hand and the two of them disappear.

As soon as I'm confident they're out of view, I step forward, crowding Erica against her door. "There were so many things I wanted to do to you tonight."

She groans in frustration, her chest rising and falling at a rapid rate.

"Your girls need you. It's fine."

I hear her voice, but the words don't register in my brain as I watch her full lips moving. Fuck, I want them on my body.

My cock swells as memories of how they feel wrapped around it fill my mind.

"Fuck," I grunt, closing the space between us and pressing her into the wood at her back. Our bodies line up perfectly. Taking her face in my hands, I nudge my nose against hers. "Have I told you how fucking beautiful you are?"

"Trey," she whimpers, her desire for me getting the better of her. I love that she's so open about what she needs when we're together. She's never been shy of telling me exactly what to do.

"You are. So fucking beautiful. Thank you for tonight, I know it wasn't how you wanted it to go, but it means so much to me, you accepting my girls."

"They're you're daughters, Trey. I wouldn't have it any other way."

"Fuck, I love you."

My lips find hers, my tongue sliding past her lips so it can tangle with hers. The last two weeks without her have felt like a lifetime. Now she's here, beneath my hands, and I want everything she has to give, but I can't...although that doesn't mean I can't leave her wanting me just as much I as do her.

Dropping one hand from her face, I skim it down her body, circling her hard nipple when I find it pressing against the fabric of her black dress. Continuing down over her stomach, I teasingly rub between her legs over the material. She gasps, her desire making me need more.

I make quick work of finding the hem of her dress and pushing it up around her waist, exposing her tiny lace—soaked—underwear.

"Trey, please. I need you," she breathes when I pull my lips from hers, brushing them across her jaw.

Pushing the wet fabric aside, I run my fingers through her silky folds. She's dripping for me. The temptation to fuck her right here for anyone on this floor to see is high, but picturing the two girls upstairs waiting for me, I know I can't.

"Oh god, Trey." Her head falls back against the door with a bang as I plunge two fingers deep inside her, bending them to hit the spot that has her racing towards release.

"Yes, yes, yes," she chants but, right before she falls, I pull my fingers from her body and stand back.

The sight of her heaving for breath against the door with her dress hitched up around her waist is almost my undoing.

Her dark, hungry eyes narrow on me as if she's about to kill me. "You fucking—argh," she screams, and I rush forward as the door's pulled open and she starts falling.

Thankfully, Joe's the other side and just about manages to catch her as she stumbles back into him.

"What the fuck's going—oh," he says with a laugh when he takes in the state of Erica's dress. "I thought someone was knocking, but please continue."

Stepping up to Erica, I pull her dress down, putting a stop to his roaming eyes.

"Seen it all before, mate. No need to hide it."

Fire like I've never experienced before roars in my belly and radiates out through my veins.

"You what?"

Looking between the two of us, her eyes wide in panic, Erica steps up to me, placing her palms on my chest.

"Ancient history. Put the caveman away, please." She stares into my eyes, begging me not to make a big deal about this, but the idea of any man putting their hands on what's mine makes me feel murderous. "Go inside please, Joe." Not even a second after the words leave her lips does he retreat back into their flat.

Her thumbs rub over the scruff on my cheeks as she continues looking at me. "Me and you, Trey. Me, you, those two upstairs, and this one growing in here." Dropping one hand, she takes one of mine and presses it against her stomach. "No one else matters. Not Sarah, not Joe, or anyone else from our pasts. Me and you," she repeats again just to drill the point home.

"Me and you." I nod. "You sure you don't want to come up?"

"No. I'm going straight to bed. I'll come up in the morning before we go out."

"I'll miss you."

"I'll miss you too."

With one last kiss, I take two giant steps back, forcing myself to walk away from the woman who owns me. "I love you, Erica."

She nods slightly and smiles, but she still fights saying it back. Thankfully, I can see exactly how she feels in her eyes, and it's everything I need.

By the time I get upstairs, the girls are curled up under a blanket on the sofa in their pyjamas. They've made themselves mugs of hot chocolate and have found some awful looking chick flick on Netflix. Looks like I'm in for a good night.

THE GIRLS WENT to bed over two hours ago, leaving me to thankfully turn the TV over—not that there's much I'm interested in watching. My mind is still focused on the woman beneath my feet and wondering what she might be wearing right now.

Turning the TV off, I take the glasses to the kitchen and start flicking the lights off as I head towards my bedroom when a light knock sounds out from the front door.

My heart lurches.

Turning on my heels, I reach for the door, hoping like hell that it's her. Cracking the door open, I know immediately that it is because the scent of her perfume fills my nose.

My mouth waters as I pull the door wider, getting a look at her.

"Hey, I thought you were going straight to bed."

"I did, I even fell asleep for a bit, but then I had this dream, only when I woke up, I realised it wasn't really a dream and the throbbing between my legs was very, very real."

I swallow the desire to pull her into my arms right this second in favour of hearing what else she's got to say.

"Are the girls asleep?"

"Y-yes," I stutter as she steps into the flat wearing what looks like just a long coat.

"Good." She pulls the fabric open, and my chin drops.

"Fuck me."

"That was the idea."

She's standing in my doorway in the most incredibly small set of black lace lingerie, garter belt, stockings, the whole shebang. Her bra is cupless, and the sight of her pert nipples has my knees weakening to drop to the floor and suck them into my mouth. My eyes run down over her curves and take in what I suspect is also crotchless knickers to complete the set.

"Get in here right this fucking second."

Reaching out, I grab her hand and pull her inside, making quick work of shutting and locking the door behind her.

When I turn around, she's already halfway towards my bedroom. Fuck, this woman's going to be the death of me.

I follow behind her, powerless to resist temptation and quietly close the door. I fight to drag in a breath as I stare at her standing at the end of the bed, waiting for me.

"You were saying…" I encourage, wanting to hear more about the state I left her in.

"There's this guy I know. He did this thing to me earlier."

"Oh yeah, what was that?" I ask, playing along.

"He put his hands on me. Drove me crazy. Then he walked away." Images of having her backed up against her door fill my mind, and my cock strains against the fabric of my trousers.

"Arsehole."

"My thoughts exactly."

"Hmmm…I considered using my little battery operated friend. I even thought about filming it. But, in the end, I decided it just wouldn't do."

"Why?"

"Because only one man could relieve the ache."

"Right answer, sweetheart."

Standing behind her, I take the fabric of her coat in my hands and pull it from her shoulders and down her arms.

"And what is it you need him to do exactly?"

"I need him to make me come. With his fingers, his mouth and his cock. Not necessarily in that order."

I smile, pressing my lips to the nape of her neck and kissing down the length of her spine until I hit the fabric of her thong. She's not wrong, her arousal is so strong I can smell it and my mouth waters for a taste.

"I think I'll forego the first option. Bend over, palms on the bed."

She does as I say without any hesitation or argument. The

sight that greets me is fucking incredible and proves I was right about her thong being crotchless. Nudging her legs wider with my shoulders, I settle between her legs. Parting both the lace fabric and her swollen lips, I lean forward and run the tip of my tongue over the length of her. Her hips buck as she groans in frustration.

"Silence." I'd fuck her right now no matter what, but not waking the girls would be preferred. I've already put them through enough; they really don't need to listen to me making Erica scream.

Focusing my attention on her clit, I circle it until her legs are trembling and she's moaning into the duvet. Lifting my hand, I tease her entrance.

"Fucking hell," she screams into the fabric.

"Silence," I repeat, and she immediately stops. I fucking love the power she gives me like this. It's exactly what I've been craving for years.

I continue my actions, bringing her right to the edge of release before stopping and allowing the feeling to subside.

She should know by now that I won't allow her to come until I'm buried deep inside her. I'm not giving up the feeling of her squeezing down on me for fucking anything.

Sucking her clit into my mouth, I pull my fingers from inside her and lift one fingertip to her puckered arsehole. Sitting back, I watch as I circle it, my finger glistening with her arousal.

"I'm taking all of you tonight." She shudders under my touch, and I take that as her approval as she says nothing to make me think otherwise. "Stand."

She does as I say, and I sit back on my haunches and watch as she stretches her back out.

"Lie on your back."

Once again she follows orders.

"You own any more sets like this?" I ask, feasting on her lace-covered body.

"A couple. Make the most of them, because they won't fit soon."

"Oh sweetheart, you'll only look better when you're swollen with my baby." Her thighs rub together, and I growl my disapproval. She immediately opens them, gifting me a shot of her centre.

Pulling my t-shirt over my head, I drop it to the floor with her coat, then make quick work of adding my trousers and boxers in the same pile.

Once I'm naked, my desperate cock bobbing in front of my body, I crawl onto the bed between her legs.

Leaning over her, I pull one nipple into her mouth. Her hips leave the bed as she desperately tries to find some friction to help push her over the edge, but I stay just out of reach.

Biting down on her peak, a gasp leaves her lips as she thrashes her head about.

I give the other side the same attention before licking and sucking my way up to her neck and then her ear.

"I'm going to fuck your pussy until you're begging for release. Then I'm going to finish deep in your arse."

"Yes, Trey. Now," she breathes.

"My kinky little bitch," I mutter, taking myself in my hand and rubbing the tip through her wetness, coating me in her juices ready to plunge inside her.

"Trey," she moans again.

Lifting my hand, I press my fingers to her lips to silence her.

Her eyelids flicker as I push the head of my cock inside. Her pussy ripples, trying to suck me in deeper, but I hold back, wanting her so desperate for me that the only thing she can think of is what I'm going to do next. Right now, nothing outside this bedroom exists. There's no ex-wife, no dead parents and no bullshit. It's just us.

"Just you and me," I promise as I push into her as far as she'll allow.

"Trey, fuck," she complains when I move painfully slowly, keeping her orgasm right on the edge. One wrong move and she'll crash over before I'm ready for her to.

Pulling out of her, I lean over and pull the drawer of my bedside table open. Her eyes follow me and they lock on to the little bottle of lube I pull out.

Her lips form an O as she watches me pop the top open and squeeze a generous blob onto my fingers.

"Say no if you're not up for it."

'Do it,' she mouths, finally learning her lesson about being quiet. It took fucking long enough.

Rubbing the lube around her opening, I slip one digit inside. She tenses for a second but soon relaxes once again. Pressing my thumb down on her clit, I slowly start moving my finger inside her.

"Oh shit," she groans. "Shit."

A smile twitches the edges of my lips as I watch her try to ride me. Once she's building up to orgasm again, I slip another finger in, making her purr like a fucking kitten.

"Fuck me, Trey, fuck me."

"You sure?" I ask, not wanting to push inside her until she's good and ready.

"I'm fucking sure. I need you inside me now."

Pulling my fingers from her tight hole, I squeeze more lube on my cock and press it against her entrance.

"Oh, oh, oh," she chants as I push, trying to get past the muscle that wants to keep me out.

"Relax," I say, once again circling her clit.

She does as I say, and I push inside. Biting down on the inside of my cheeks, I fight the loud growl that wants to crawl its way up my throat. This women beneath me is so fucking incredible and so fucking mine.

Pushing in deeper, my balls almost immediately draw up, her tightness igniting my own release.

Hitting the point of no return, I press down harder on her clit. "Come," I demand, although my voice is barely a groan as I try to hold off as long as possible.

At the first clench of her orgasm hitting, I lose all fight of my own. My cock twitches violently as I fill her with everything I have.

Dropping my face to the crook of her neck, I roar out my release as she milks every last drop from me.

Collapsing on top of her, my eyelids begin to close as I enjoy the pleasure that's racing through my veins and continuing to make my muscles twitch.

"Trey?"

"Yeah?" I ask, just about managing the effort it takes to lift my head to look at her. Her eyes are tired but so soft and full of emotions.

"I love you too."

Tightening my hold on her, I place my lips to hers and kiss her as if it's the last thing I'll ever do while my heart threatens to explode in my chest.

CHAPTER SIXTEEN

I t seems to be becoming normal that when I wake up in the morning that I'm alone, the other side of the bed cold, almost as if her body lying beside mine was all a dream.

Sitting myself on the edge, I wipe my tired eyes and head towards the en suite, assuming it's where she'll be.

The small room is in darkness when I get there, and flicking on the light confirms what I suspect. Turning, I rush back into the room hoping to find her elsewhere in the flat but already guessing that she's escaped home. I can only hope that doesn't mean she's regretting everything that's happened between us in the last few days...or agreeing to the house. My mind flicks back to walking around the new house with her yesterday. Even from the moment we stepped through the front door, it felt like home.

I spot the note on the bed as soon as I step out of the en suite.

I've gone downstairs to get ready. Come and get me when you're ready to go out.

I love you.
E xx

Those three words make my heart pound violently in my chest, making me want to storm straight downstairs and claim her as mine once again. I'm not sure this all-consuming need for her is ever going to abate. No matter how many times I have her, it's never enough.

Giggling from outside my door is a sobering reminder that I can't do exactly what I want right now. I've got two other people to worry about first.

Pulling on some clothes, I head out to meet my girls.

"Morning, did you both sleep okay?"

"Yeah, thanks, Dad."

"Ella's been awake hours. She's excited," Sofia sings, much to Ella's mortification.

"No, I'm not. My body just knew I was somewhere different and woke me up earlier than usual."

"Whatever." Sofia rolls her eyes at her sister and turns to me. "What's for breakfast?"

"You know you're going to like a boy one day and I'm going to get my own back."

"Ugh, I doubt it. Boys are gross."

"That's what they all say," Ella says while staring into her phone, a smile appearing on her face.

I try not to think about what—or who—is making her so happy. I want her to have the same opinion about boys as Sofia. I'm not ready for this.

"Okay so, we've got...toast or cereal."

"Wow, exciting."

"I'd offer to take you out, but we're already going out for lunch so..."

"Toast is great, Dad. Thanks."

Knowing she's downstairs and waiting for us means every minute ticks by at a snail's pace.

"What time have you agreed to meet Josh?" I just about manage to get his name out through gritted teeth.

"Eleven-thirty outside Costa. Our film starts at midday."

"Okay. I'm going to shower and dress. Do either of you need anything?"

"No, we're good. I'm going to come and get ready too."

"I look over at my eldest daughter who's currently still wearing her pyjamas. "Ella?"

"Yeah?"

"Can you do me a favour?"

"Sure, what is it?"

"Make sure you're suitably covered up for this...this afternoon. I'm doing you a massive favour allowing it to happen, so it's for the best that you don't push your luck."

"I wasn't planning on going dressed like a hooker, don't worry."

I open my mouth to respond, but no words come out. Instead I just stand there, watching her skip off to the room she shared with her sister last night.

"She's growing up so fast," Sofia says, clearly watching our interaction.

"Smart arse," I mutter, heading off to my own bedroom and leaving her with her tablet to keep her entertained.

It takes Ella forever to get ready.

"I'm going to go and get her. She'll miss the whole thing if she doesn't hurry up."

She runs off down the hallway, leaving me with my own anticipation about today. I hate what I'm allowing Ella to do, but I know it's the right thing. I don't want to stop her growing up, no matter how much I might hate it. But I need to know she's going to be okay, and I want to meet Josh. Not to give him 'the dad speech' but just so I can look him in the eye and get a sense for the kind of boy he is. I just pray that he's someone I'm going to be able to trust. If he looks like a scumbag, I've no issue with dragging Ella back out the way we came and locking her inside her bedroom for the next ten years.

When she eventually emerges and I glance over, a lump forms in my throat. She's so beautiful and looks way older than her almost fifteen years. Her hair is hanging straight around her shoulders, she's got dark but minimal make-up around her eyes, and pinker than usual lips, but it's her outfit of choice that makes my heart swell. I expected her to attempt to get out of this house wearing the shortest skirt she could get away with, but in reality she's standing in front of me in a pair of grey skinny jeans and a black t-shirt sporting a band's name that I've never heard of.

"What? Why are you looking at me like that?"

"I'm just wondering how I helped make something so beautiful."

"Aw, you getting all soppy, old man?"

"Enough of that, please."

"You're right, we should stop referencing your age just in case Erica realises her mistake and dumps you."

"You cheeky little—"

I reach for her to pull her in for a hug, but she side steps me and goes for her jacket and then the door instead.

"Come on, we're going to be late."

"And whose fault would that be?" I call after her with a laugh. Sofia and I both grab our own coats before following her out of the flat to go and get Erica.

Ella's waiting beside the door when we both step onto her

floor. "You said you met her at work. How come she lives in the same building?"

"Total coincidence." Her brows draw together. "I'm serious. I had no idea for weeks."

"That's weird but hilarious."

Shaking my head at my daughter, I lift my hand to knock. The door opens almost immediately, but instead of Erica appearing, it's Joe.

"Hey, is she ready?" The moment my eyes land on him, I'm reminded of the comment he made yesterday about being intimate with Erica, and the fire it started in my belly reignites.

"She's in the toilet. I just wanted to apologise for last night. What I said was thoughtless, and you were right to be pis—angry," he corrects when he spots my girls behind me. "It was a long time ago and..." he pauses, his face twisting in uncertainty. "Anyway, what have you got planned for Thursday?" His voice is barely a whisper, forcing me to lean in a little to hear him.

"What's Thursday?"

Rolling his eyes, he tuts. "Erica's birthday of course," he says as if it should be obvious.

My stomach drops. "Shit, I had no idea."

"There's still time to pull it out of the bag, but with the number of times she throws up every morning, I'd suggest you do something seriously special."

"What are you two whispering about?" Erica asks as she walks our way.

"Just naughty things we don't want the kids to hear."

"Jesus, Joe. Do you ever stop talking about S-E-X?"

"We can spell," Ella calls with a laugh.

"Fuck."

"We know what that means too."

Joe snorts out a laugh while Erica looks like she's waiting for the ground to swallow her up.

"You still sure about me being a mother?"

"Most definitely. Just ignore them, they're too smart for their own good."

I don't need to turn around to know they're probably sticking their tongues out at me or something equally as stupid. Erica's amusement gives them away.

"Are you ready to go?"

"Yes. Let me grab my bag and we'll get this date on the road."

"Don't remind me."

Ella is silent as we drive towards the shopping centre where we're meeting Josh. I've agreed to allow them to go to the cinema and then to get some food after while Erica, Sofia and I have lunch ourselves and do some shopping. I feel better knowing we'll at least be close should she need me, which I know she won't.

"It's sweet how nervous she is," Erica whispers as we follow the girls towards the shops. "I remember being that excited. Young love is so sweet."

"I don't know. Old love is pretty awesome too."

"Old! Speak for yourself. I've got a few years until I can be considered old yet, thank you very much."

As we round the corner, heading towards Costa, there's a floppy-haired teenage boy loitering outside. Glancing over at Ella, I notice her shoulders are pulled tight as she fiddles nervously with a lock of her hair.

"Is that him?" I whisper in her ear.

"Yeah. Dad, please don't embarrass me."

"I promise. I just want to meet him."

Erica, Sofia and I hang back as she walks up to him. The second he sees her, the widest smile spreads across his face and his eyes go all soft. It's everything I needed to see.

His smile turns goofy as she steps up to him and they greet each other.

"Oh my god, they are so cute," Erica coos beside me. "I think he might be a good one."

"I hate to admit it, but me too."

Ella hesitantly turns to us, and I step forward. "This is my dad and his...girlfriend." She hesitates to introduce Erica that way, and I understand why.

"Josh, nice to meet you," I greet with a curt nod of my head. I might have had good first impressions, but I'm not allowing him to see that I might approve of him spending time with my baby.

"Mr. Bennett, it's so nice to meet you. Ella always talks about you."

"Really?" I ask, looking at my daughter, who's trying to hide behind him in embarrassment. "And it's Trey. Mr. Bennett makes me sound old." Erica stifles a laugh behind me that ensures she's in for a long night once we drop the girls back at home.

"So...now that's all out of the way, we're gonna go," Ella points over her shoulder. "We'll meet you back here at four, yeah?"

"Yeah just—"

"Keep my phone on just in case. Yeah, I know. We're good, right?" She glances at Josh who just looks between the two of us with slight panic in his eyes.

"Yeah. It was nice to meet you. I promise to get her back on time."

"I should hope so. Be good." Ella fumes at my words and turns to storm off.

"Did you have to do that?" Erica chastises.

"Couldn't help myself. He needs to know who he's going to answer to if he fucks this up."

"Just give him a chance. He could be your future son-in-law."

"Fucking hell," I mutter, stepping forward into the crowds. "Where to first?"

I spend most of the day following Erica and Sofia around the shops. They do a good job of trying to keep me distracted, but I can't help worrying about Ella and wondering what she's doing and if Josh is behaving.

We walk towards Costa a few minutes before four o'clock. I'm expecting to have to wait for them but, to my shock, both Ella and Josh are standing outside with a takeaway cup in hand.

"Wow, I'm impressed." Ella blushes while Josh looks pleased with himself. "Okay, well...we'll just wait over here while you say goodbye. No tongues though, please. I'm not sure my heart could cope with that."

IF THE SILENCE in the car as we drive towards my old house tells me anything, it's that everyone feels the same about going back there. There's a high chance that Ella and Sarah will probably end up in another argument; I could tell by her tone on the phone when I told her what I was going to do that she wasn't happy about it, and Sofia will be left to listen to them shouting at each other.

I know they both love Sarah—she's their mum and she's good at it—but I still hate dropping them off every time I get to spend decent time with them. I miss them so much.

Erica and I say our goodbyes and see them both into the house from the car. I've no intention of getting an ear-bashing from my ex-wife for what we did today. I'll stand by my decision to allow Ella and Josh to spend time together, once she's really thought about it she'll know I was right.

"You'll see them again next weekend, right?"

"I guess. It's just not the same as seeing them every day."

"I can't imagine how that must feel. I've only known about this one a few weeks, but already I feel weirdly attached. I can't imagine going any amount of time without him—sorry," she says with a wince when she sees the pain on my face. "What can I do to distract you?"

"I've got a few ideas. I might even let you scream tonight."

"Good to know. Take me home then."

The drive is tense and hurried. Both of us know what's going to happen the second we're behind closed doors, and both of us are desperate for it to begin.

I pull the car to a stop haphazardly in my parking space, not giving two shits as to whether it's within the lines or not, and jump out. Erica's already halfway out when I get around to her. Not wanting to wait for her, I grab her around the waist and lift her over my shoulder.

"Trey, put me down," she squeals but soon stops when I slap her arse.

With her securely in place, I jog up the stairs to her flat.

"Keys," I demand and take her bag from her when she offers it to me. Stuffing my hand all the way to the bottom, I eventually wrap my fingers around her giant fluffy keyring and tug.

I've got the door open in mere seconds and we're pushing our way in. I'm intending on walking straight down to her room, but the moment I look up towards her door, my body freezes finding someone—or two people—in our way.

"Trey, what the hell?"

It's only when Erica's voice fills the room that the bodies in front of us still before looking our way, total horror covering their faces.

"What's going o—oooh!" Erica giggles as I lower her feet to the floor and her eyes also land on a half-naked Joe with his hips pinning a petite dark, haired-woman to the wall. Although her dress is hitched up around her waist, it just about covers her dignity, but it's pretty obvious what's going on right now.

"Fuck. I thought you said it would be safe."

"I didn't think...fuck. Some privacy?"

"Yeah, shit. Sorry. Let's go to your place."

Both of us back up. I turn to head towards the door, but Erica keeps her eyes on Joe, some kind of silent conversation passing between them before she eventually turns her back on them and we both head up to my flat.

"Who was that?"

"I've no idea, but I'd put fucking money on the fact she has something to do with whatever he does every Thursday night."

"Oh?" I ask, intrigued as to what Joe's up to.

"I've no idea what he's doing. He's been really evasive about it, and I don't like it. He's made some really fucked up decisions in the past, so I wish he'd talk about whatever this one is."

"I'm sure he will when he's ready," I say, shutting the door behind me and nuzzling my nose into her neck, breathing in her scent.

"I guess."

"Now, stop worrying about him and start worrying about your boyfriend."

"Boyfriend?" Her eyebrows rise in delight where as my stomach drops slightly at just being her boyfriend. That's not enough for me. She's carrying my baby, and we're about to buy our first house together. I want more.

CHAPTER SEVENTEEN

As desperate as I was to do something totally over-the-top for Erica's birthday, I knew she wouldn't thank me for it. She's not that kind of girl. So in the end I went with something a little more low key that I knew she'd love.

She won't admit it, but I know she's feeling a little lost since losing her mother. They may not have had a relationship aside from Sunday morning visits where her mum was only usually present in body but still, losing a parent is huge, even if they weren't really there in the first place.

Her pregnancy might have been a total shock, but looking at it now, I think it's the best thing that could have happened. It's given her something to focus on. Her mum's gone and Sam's busy embarking on married life. It's time to show her that what she might be lacking in actual family she makes up for with others in her life.

It took some serious string pulling and sweet talking, but I manage to book a table at my favourite restaurant for tonight. I thought the vein in Mark's temple was going to explode when I turned up demanding a setting for eight at four days' notice in a restaurant that's booked out months in advance. Thankfully, knowing the chef and spending countless amounts of money here in the past meant I secured the table.

Erica has no idea what the plan was for tonight. It wasn't easy seeing as she returned to work on Monday and started nagging Lauren for answers about what I was planning, but thankfully, Lauren kept her lips sealed. The only thing she knew was that a taxi would be waiting for her about twenty minutes ago and that she was to just go with the flow—not something I'm expecting her to be all that happy about. She might tell me now that she trusts me, but I'm fully aware that in reality she probably never fully will, and that's okay. She's had her trust smashed by people time and time again. The fact that she trusts me as much as she does after what I did to her is a blessing. She would have been well within her rights to never talk to me again. I guess I once again need to thank that surprise little person growing in her belly. I've no idea what would have happened if he wasn't there.

"Is she here yet?" Lauren asks, rubbing her palms on her thighs nervously.

"Don't think so. Why are you nervous? It's not like we're going to turn the lights out and scare the crap out of her."

"I know. I'm just excited for her to see what you've done. She probably expects to just find you waiting for her."

"I haven't really done anything. It's just a meal with friends and a few balloons."

"It's more than that and you know it. You've brought her family together when she needs it most. Don't think I can't see exactly what your plan was, Trey. And also don't think that I don't see she's struggling. I failed her once before by not noticing what was going on with her, I made her a promise it wouldn't happen again."

"I know, and so does she. It's exactly why you're here right now."

"Where the hell's Joe?"

"It's a Thursday night, who knows."

"He still hasn't said anything?"

"Nope, just that he'd be here as soon as he could."

"I need to have words with that boy," Lauren warns, clearly as concerned as Erica is about what he's up to. "Oh, oh there she is."

Lifting my eyes to Mark at the maître de stand, I find her immediately, wearing a loose-fitting shift dress that shows off her incredibly shapely legs.

"Don't even think about getting your hands up there in this fancy restaurant, Mr. Bennett," Lauren growls quietly, reminding me what happened on our last group outing.

"I'll do my best, but at times they have a mind of their own."

"Don't I know it," she mutters before falling silent when Erica looks directly at me. I don't think she even sees the others surrounding me.

To begin with, concern fills her eyes. I'm not surprised: this is the exact place where her world exploded in front of her, but as far as I'm concerned, it still has the best food in the city and I want her to experience it and hopefully to overwrite her previous memory of the place.

Eventually, she takes a step towards me. Pushing out the chair behind me, I stand and hold my hand out for her.

"I have to say, I'm glad you're here first this time."

"We wanted to surprise you."

"We?" It's only then when she looks down to her right and finds everyone looking up at her. "Oh my god." Her eyes land on everyone around the table. Lauren, Ben, their friend Danni—which I've discovered was where Erica was hiding after her first visit here—Ella and Sofia, then finally an empty chair.

"Joe said he'd be here as soon as he could."

Shaking her head, she plasters on a smile, trying to hide her concern. "I can't believe you did this. Thank you so much."

"Happy birthday, sweetheart."

We both take our seats before I pick up the small square box I placed on the table when we first arrived. I hand it to Erica.

"What's this?"

"Your birthday present. What does it look like?" No one else knows what's in the box and all of their eyes soon zero in on it as Erica removes the wrapping. I know exactly what they're all thinking, and I hope they're not too disappointed. They don't know her like I do, and as much as I want it to be what they're hoping for, I know she's not ready. Lauren's eyes bore into me; I can practically hear her screaming that I should be on one knee.

Her hands tremble as she flips the lid open, and I hope that's a sign that I did the right thing. She gasps. "Oh, they're gorgeous. Thank you so much."

"You're more than welcome." Reaching out, I wrap my hand around the back of her neck and pull her lips to mine. Our kiss is much more reserved than I want to give her, but knowing everyone around the table is watching, including my daughters, stops me from shoving my tongue deep in her mouth.

"I love you, sweetheart. Happy birthday."

"I love you too. Thank you."

The waiter interrupts our moment to take our drinks orders. When Erica's distracted, Lauren leans over.

"What the hell? Where's the ring?" she hisses. The day my solicitor rang to tell me that Sarah had at last signed the papers, I took Lauren out on a little shopping trip to help me find the right one. She begged the entire day to find out what I was planning, but I refused to say anything.

"It's coming. Have a little patience." Her lips purse in frustration, but she sits back nonetheless.

Sitting back, I silently take in Erica chatting with her friends and trying to drag Ella and Sofia into whatever it is they're talking about, and I wonder how I ended up here. There was a time not so long ago that I thought I was destined to be stuck in a life I wasn't happy with, but then just when I needed her most, there she was, like a guardian fucking angel. She has no idea, but she saved me. She saw the man I was desperate to become and she allowed me to be myself. I'll never forget everything she's given me.

EPILOGUE

Erica

When I held that little black box in my hand the night of my birthday, I'd have put money on it being an engagement ring. I thought I would have been scared—terrified actually—but in reality it just felt right. Things hadn't been easy since meeting Trey, but even with everything, I wouldn't want anyone else beside me for the journey we're about to embark on.

When I opened the box, I found a stunning set of diamond earrings staring back at me. They were gorgeous, don't get me wrong, but my heart dropped a little. Neither of us had talked about marriage; we were too tied up with my surprise pregnancy and the house. I had no idea if Trey even wanted to get married again but, without realising it, I'd been hoping for it. From the disappointment on everyone's faces around me, I'm pretty sure they were expecting it too.

I've never been one to dream about my wedding, my dress and what the colour scheme might be. I was too focused on getting through life without meeting another arsehole who was intent on ruining it. But the second that non-engagement box was placed in my hands, it was suddenly all I could think about. I took that as a very good sign. It was telling me that he was the one and that I was ready to jump in with both feet. From that moment, everything seemed a little less scary. My worry about being a mother waned a little, although that was never going to disappear entirely. I stopped second-guessing the house and just tried to enjoy our second chance.

Knowing how happy he makes me, I can't help feeling stupid for running away when I discovered his secret, but if I've learnt anything about life, it's that living in the past is pointless. It's always better to focus on right now and the future, the things you can change and make better.

And that's exactly why, every time something big comes like Christmas and then New Year, I expect that little box to appear.

But it never does.

We spent Christmas with Ben and Lauren. They'd booked a huge, gorgeous house in the Cotswolds for the entire holiday. It was probably one of my best Christmases, surrounded by people I love. The only people who were missing were Sam, who spent the festive season with Cliff's family, and Ella and Sofia, but they came to us for New Year.

I'd never expressed my desire to feel the weight of Trey's ring on my finger, but every time Lauren looked at me, I knew she could feel it. I waved her off every time. If Trey wasn't asking, he had a very good reason, and I had to trust him. I also made a point not to ask, afraid of coming off like I was demanding to tie him down because really, I wasn't.

I just wanted everything and to have the same surname as our baby.

"Are you ready?"

"Nearly. You know the appointment isn't until eleven, right?" I ask, glancing at the clock, seeing that it's not even nine."

"I don't want to be late. There might be traffic."

Chuckling at his excitement, I grab my coat and head out into the kitchen of my flat to find him. After we discovered Joe and his mystery woman in the hallway, it was agreed by all that maybe it was time to rethink our living arrangements, so Trey moved down here with me and Joe moved up to his flat. It was the perfect solution as it allowed us to live as a couple and gave Joe his freedom to do his own thing without worrying about getting caught. I still remember the horror on his girl's face that night.

"What the hell are you going to be like as my due date approaches?" I ask after Trey pulls me in for a kiss.

"Ready. I'll be ready."

"I guess it could be worse," I mutter lightly.

"Come on, I want to see our boy."

"You know it might not actually be a boy, right?"

"Of course."

Hand in hand, we head out of the flat to find his car, avoiding the boxes littering the hallway. We're meant to get the keys to our new house on Friday. I thought I'd be sad to leave this place, but knowing that house with all its space is waiting for me, I'm a little less concerned about the whole thing.

Trey's knee bounces the entire time we're sitting in the waiting room. I know I found out about my pregnancy a little later than most women probably do, but now I'm sitting here waiting to see my baby for the first time, it feels like the weeks have just flown by, which is a little odd seeing as almost everything about my life has changed in that time.

"Miss Wilde, please."

My heart jumps up into my throat knowing that it's my turn. Trey reaches out and takes my trembling hand as he leads me towards the sonographer.

"You okay?"

"Yeah, I'm excited."

"Me too, sweetheart." Leaning over, he places a sweet kiss to my temple and my eyelids shutter closed for a second.

I hop up on the bed and do everything I'm told while my heart threatens to pound out of my chest. Adrenaline is buzzing around my body so much that I don't even flinch when the gel is squirted on my body like I always see on TV.

"Okay, are you both ready?"

"Yes."

With that, the sonographer presses a white wand thing into my belly and stares at the screen. She wiggles it about a little while her focus stays on whatever is in front of her. Tears burn my eyes that I can't see my baby and she can, but only a couple of seconds later, she turns the screen.

I gasp, my hand coming up to cover my mouth as Trey squeezes my other. There on the screen is a perfect black and white picture of a baby. He must be lying just right, because I can make out every bit of his body.

"Oh my god," I sob.

"I need to take a couple more measurements, but everything's looking good. Would you like me to print pictures?"

"Y-yes please."

Her words barely register as I continue to stare at the screen through tear-filled eyes.

"That's our baby," I whisper in total amazement.

"It is." The sound of Trey's choked voice is just about enough to drag my eyes away from the screen, and I'm so bloody glad I do because the look of awe and amazement on his face as he stares at our little person is the most incredible sight I think I've ever seen.

"That's our baby," he confirms, turning his equally damp eyes on mine. "I love you so much."

"I love you too."

The rest of the time with the sonographer rubbing the wand across my belly is a total daze. Before I know it, we're done and Trey is paying for our photos and we're left alone with the images of our baby so I can clean up.

"That was incredible," I say as I swing my legs from the bed, dropping the goo covered tissue into the bin beside it.

Standing, I pull my leggings up and am just about to right my top when movement at the end of the bed catches my eye.

"Trey, what are you—uh," I gasp once again when he slowly drops to one knee.

"I can't wait any longer." He reaches out a hand for me, and I step forward, although my brain doesn't register the movement. "Erica, I've been holding off until I thought you were ready, but I'm done waiting. I want to make you mine officially. When I'm with you, I'm the man I've always wanted to be. You make me a better person, and I can't imagine the rest of my life without you in it. Erica Wilde, will you marry me?"

A sob erupts before I manage to form any words. The tears that were still in my eyes from seeing our baby spill over and drop to my cheeks. "Yes, Trey. Yes," I whisper. What I really want to do is scream it from the rooftops, but the emotion blocking my throat stops me.

Reaching into his coat pocket, he pulls out a familiar little black box.

"I hope there's no earrings inside that," I say with a laugh.

"Not this time, sweetheart."

He opens the box and my eyes almost pop out of my head. "It's huge."

His lips press into a thin line as he fights not to make a joke in what should be a serious situation. "Only the best for my fiancée."

He plucks the giant solitaire diamond from its cushioning and slides it up my trembling finger.

"I knew you were different the moment I saw you sitting at the bar that night. I never could have imagined how much you'd change my life."

Dragging my eyes up from admiring my new piece of jewellery, I drink in the love that's pouring from his eyes and I know without a doubt that the disasters of my past were only there so that one day it would lead me to Trey. Stepping forward, I reach up and press my lips to his. "I love you."

"I love you, too. And our little nugget," he says, placing his hands on my belly. "I can't wait for what's to come."

Are you ready for Joe's story? The Temptation Duet is NOW LIVE.
DOWNLOAD NOW!

ACKNOWLEDGMENTS

Erica and Trey orginially weren't going to have a book. I was intending on going in a totally different direction, but I'm glad they screamed so loud. I've loved writing this intense duet and experiencing them fall for each other not only in the first book but even harder for each other in this second. It's been a bit of a bumpy ride for them both, but they got there in the end.

And that baby...what do you think—boy or girl? I'm hoping we find out in the next duet in the series.

As always, I've got a huge list of people to thank for helping and supporting me with this book. Michelle, as always, for being an epic alpha reader and telling me exactly how it is. Deanna, Lindsay, Susanne and Tracy, for patiently waiting for the second installment of Erica and Trey's story and not sending me too much abuse for it. I was feeling the pressure after writing Ben, but you reassured me that Trey stood up...and maybe even overtook him at times.

Samantha, you've been a life saver with everything you've been doing. I'm not sure how I ever coped without you!

Evelyn, again, for putting up with me and my incredibly repetitive typos. One day I might spot them myself—we can only hope!

Paige, for proofreading and making this as perfect as possible.

And, last but never least, my long-suffering husband and daughter for putting up with my crazy arse. I love you x

ABOUT THE AUTHOR

Tracy Lorraine is a *USA Today* and *Wall Street Journal* bestselling new adult and contemporary romance author. Tracy has recently turned thirty and lives in a cute Cotswold village in England with her husband, baby girl and lovable but slightly crazy dog. Having always been a bookaholic with her head stuck in her Kindle, Tracy decided to try her hand at a story idea she dreamt up and hasn't looked back since.

Be the first to find out about new releases and offers. Sign up to my newsletter here.

If you want to know what I'm up to and see teasers and snippets of what I'm working on, then you need to be in my Facebook group. Join Tracy's Angels here.

Keep up to date with Tracy's books at
www.tracylorraine.com

ALSO BY TRACY LORRAINE

Falling Series

Falling for Ryan: Part One #1

Falling for Ryan: Part Two #2

Falling for Jax #3

Falling for Daniel (A Falling Series Novella)

Falling for Ruben #4

Falling for Fin #5

Falling for Lucas #6

Falling for Caleb #7

Falling for Declan #8

Falling For Liam #9

Forbidden Series

Falling for the Forbidden #1

Losing the Forbidden #2

Fighting for the Forbidden #3

Craving Redemption #4

Demanding Redemption #5

Avoiding Temptation #6

Chasing Temptation #7

Rebel Ink Series

Hate You #1

<u>Trick You</u> #2

<u>Defy You</u> #3

<u>Play You</u> #4

Inked (A Rebel Ink/Driven Crossover)

Rosewood High Series

<u>Thorn</u> #1

<u>Paine</u> #2

<u>Savage</u> #3

Fierce #4

<u>Hunter</u> #5

Faze (#6 Prequel)

<u>Fury</u> #6

Legend #7

Maddison Kings University Series

<u>TMYM: Prequel</u>

<u>TRYS</u> #1

<u>TDYW</u> #2

<u>TBYS</u> #3

<u>TVYC</u> #4

<u>TDYD</u> #5

<u>TDYR</u> #6

<u>TRYD</u> #7

Knight's Ridge Empire Series

Wicked Summer Knight: Prequel (Stella & Seb)

Wicked Knight #1 (Stella & Seb)

Wicked Princess #2 (Stella & Seb)

Wicked Empire #3 (Stella & Seb)

Deviant Knight #4 (Emmie & Theo)

Deviant Princess #5 (Emmie & Theo

Deviant Reign #6 (Emmie & Theo)

One Reckless Knight (Jodie & Toby)

Reckless Knight #7 (Jodie & Toby)

Reckless Princess #8 (Jodie & Toby)

Reckless Dynasty #9 (Jodie & Toby)

Dark Halloween Knight (Calli & Batman)

Dark Knight #10 (Calli & Batman)

Dark Princess #11 (Calli & Batman)

Dark Legacy #12 (Calli & Batman)

Corrupt Valentine Knight (Nico & Siren)

Corrupt Knight #13 (Nico & Siren)

Corrupt Princess #14 (Nico & Siren)

Corrupt Union #15 (Nico & Siren)

Sinful Wild Knight (Alex & Vixen)

Sinful Stolen Knight: Prequel (Alex & Vixen)

Sinful Knight #16 (Alex & Vixen)

Sinful Princess #17 (Alex & Vixen)

Sinful Kingdom #18 (Alex & Vixen)

Knight's Ridge Destiny: Epilogue

Harrow Creek Hawks Series

Merciless #1

Relentless #2

Lawless #3

Fearless #4

Ruined Series

Ruined Plans #1

Ruined by Lies #2

Ruined Promises #3

Never Forget Series

Never Forget Him #1

Never Forget Us #2

Everywhere & Nowhere #3

Chasing Series

Chasing Logan

The Cocktail Girls

His Manhattan

Her Kensington

SNEAK PEEK

The Forbidden series is a spin off from my *Falling* series. If you've not read it then keep reading for a sneak peek at *Falling for Ryan,* my friends to lovers romance that kicks off the series.

FALLING FOR RYAN: PART ONE
CHAPTER ONE

Molly

Present

It's midnight, and I've been sat on Ryan's doorstep for nearly an hour. I've already started on one of the bottles of wine. Although it was a scorching summer's day, the heat has now worn off, the clouds have gathered, and it's lumping it down with rain. I'm trying to tuck myself into his little porch to stop from getting so wet, but with the wind direction, it's not doing much good. I'm soaked through. It was a silly idea to pick white t-shirts when I rebranded the coffee shop; thank God for padded bras!

By the time I'd cleaned and locked up, it was just gone ten. I love working at Cocoa's and have done so since I was sixteen. Hannah and Emma's parents own it. Susan started the business after she finished university. She came into some inheritance and, with the money, Cocoa's was born. The place was a huge part of my childhood. Hannah, Emma, and I would go there after school to do homework or just chat about boys, and it pretty much stayed that way until we finished university. We still have a booth in the back corner dedicated to us.

I will forever be grateful for Susan and her husband, Pete, whom she actually met as a customer in Cocoa's. It was love at first sight for them. Not only did they give me a job, but they took me under their wing when I was much younger.

Megan, who works in the evenings, had a phone call from her boyfriend at eight o'clock saying their little boy was really sick. I let her go home to be with him and finished up the rest of the night on my own.

Once I got in my car, all I could think about was having a nice hot bath and snuggling into bed in my tiny one-bed flat with my boyfriend, Max. We've been together on and off for the past three years, but when Hannah, whom I'd lived with above the coffee shop, decided eight months ago that she wanted her own boyfriend to move into the flat, I decided it was time I moved out and left them to it. Max had suggested I move in with him. I wasn't thrilled by the idea, to be honest, but at the time I didn't have the money to find anywhere decent to live. I hate being alone. I would have had to find someone who was renting out a room anyway, so it seemed like a sensible suggestion and a logical step in our relationship.

A week later, we all moved. Me into Max's flat, and Hannah's boyfriend into the one we'd shared for the past six years.

The ten-minute drive to our home seemed to take forever. I pulled up out the front; it was weird to be parking next to Max's car. He had worked nights the whole time I'd known him.

I dragged my body up the stairs to the third floor and let myself in. I shut the door behind me; the only light was coming from the bedroom. My heart dropped into my stomach when I heard voices and strange noises coming from down the hallway. As quietly as I could, I tiptoed towards them.

When I got to the door, I couldn't believe my eyes. Now, I knew Max was no angel, but I was under the impression that we had put the past behind us when we decided to live together and had become a monogamous couple. Yes, the past few months had been a strain, but still.

What was happening before my eyes on our bed showed me how wrong I was.

I numbly slipped back down the hallway and grabbed a couple of pairs of knickers that, luckily for me, were drying on the radiator, and left.

I tried to keep myself together as I made a pit stop at the shop on my way to Ryan's house. I didn't want to be one of those emotional women sobbing in the alcohol aisle, trying to decide which bottle would make me forget.

Once I'd paid for two bottles of my favourite wine and a crate of lager for Ryan, I made my way over to his new house. He'd only moved in two weeks ago, although it was months ago that he made the decision to buy the three-story townhouse in the new development on the outskirts of the city. It was basically a pile of bricks when he took me with him to see it for the first time, but I could see why he'd fallen in love with it. It was modern and spacious, with amazing views across fields from the back. From the front, you could see all the lights from the city in the distance. Because it was yet to be finished, it meant Ryan could choose a lot of the interior to suit his taste, and he didn't have to spend his whole summer re-decorating.

Grabbing my phone, I open up my messages to re-read the conversation I'd had with him earlier. He said he was going out tonight to celebrate the end of the school year but that he wasn't expecting to be home late. I guess that didn't really go as planned

—not that he'd be expecting me to be sitting here waiting for him.

I'm starting to think I should have gone somewhere else. It's not that I don't have any other options, but out of all my friends and family, Ryan knows me the best.

What we've been through this year has made us close. I think I can safely say he's turned into my best friend somewhere in the last six months.

As I wait, images of what was happening on my bed flash though my head. I guess I should have seen it coming, really. A leopard never changes it spots, right?

Eventually, the tears come flooding out. To add to my misery, I now have black mascara streaks running down my cheeks and red puffy eyes.

Finally, I see headlights coming my way and Ryan's white Honda Civic pulling into his drive. At first, he looks shocked to see me. That changes to anger as he strides towards me.

Ryan

AS I COME TO A STOP, I can see that there's a very wet Molly huddled in my porch. She looks dreadful. I come to a very quick conclusion that it's because of her dickhead of a boyfriend. I knew it was coming; it was just a matter of when.

"Ryan," Molly sobs as I lift her tiny frame off the ground and into a hug. She shakes from both the cold and the sobs wracking her body.

Tucking her into my side, I grab her bags and let us in. On the ground floor, my townhouse has a large room with French doors looking out to the courtyard garden, and a bathroom. I thought it would make an excellent gym. The middle floor is an open-plan kitchen, living, and dining room with a small cloakroom, and the top floor has three bedrooms, one being the master with ensuite and the other a large family bathroom.

I love it.

From the moment I looked at the plans, I just knew it was going to be my little piece of heaven, and I'm still in awe that I was able to buy this place. I'll be forever grateful for the generous gift from Susan and Pete. Nothing will ever make up for what we all lost, but thanks to them, I've been able to attempt to move on with my life.

Currently, there are boxes everywhere. I haven't had much time to unpack with everything I had to do at school to end the year, but my first holiday job is to get this place sorted and looking like a home.

Anger fills my veins as I lead us up to the living room. "It's going to be okay. Let's get you warm and dry and you can tell me what the fucker did." My fists clench. I want to beat the shit out of him for treating her so badly for so long.

"How do you know he's done anything?" Molly asks in a quiet voice.

"I can read you like a book, Molly Carter. Plus, he's a massive dickhead. I think I've mentioned that before. Only Max can make you feel this bad about yourself."

"Why was I so fucking stupid? I had my doubts, everyone had their doubts, but he convinced me that it was what he wanted. I'm not really surprised, but what does shock me is how much it *hurts*."

"Come on, get your arse upstairs and in the shower. I'll find you a t-shirt to wear."

AS I ROOT through a suitcase in one of the spare bedrooms, the door to my ensuite shuts. I pull out my Oxford Brookes polo and leave it on my bed. I hope my choice will make her smile, remembering happier times.

I knock lightly on the door. "Have you got everything you need?"

There's silence for a few seconds, and I can imagine her checking out all the products in the shower, realising they're all for men. Eventually, I hear a quiet "Yes" from the other side of the door.

"Okay, I'll see you downstairs when you're done. Take your time."

I gather up her wet clothes and take them with me. They may be soaked, but I can still smell her vanilla scent on them. It makes me feel oddly warm inside. She's been my rock for the past six months. I don't know what I would have done without her.

As I put everything in the washing machine, I spot her bra poking out of the pile. "What the fuck do I do with this?" I mutter to myself. Something in me wonders if it needs some kind of special cycle in the machine, but fuck if I know. I decide to shove it all in and just put it on a cool, quick wash.

That shouldn't do it much damage, right?

DOWNLOAD NOW to continue reading